The NEBADOR series:

NEBADOR

Book Two
Journey

an epic young-adult science fiction adventure

by

J. Z. Colby

Nebador Archives

Cover art by Rachael Hedges
Illustrations by J. Z. Colby, Amanda Herman, and Mireille Xioulan Powers

For other print editions, ebooks, dramatic audiobooks, previews, samples, biographies, comments, questions, artwork, writing contests, Ask Kibi advice, deep learning notes, Nebador citizens, and more, please see:

www.nebador.com

Nebador Archives
Kelso, Washington, USA

Library of Congress Control Number: 2010903894
Manufactured in the USA

ISBN: 978-1-936253-09-8
NEBADOR2PBG: paperback, 6" x 9", 195 pages, global edition
(10-point Georgia type)

Greetings, young people of planet Earth,

In *NEBADOR Book One: The Test*, we met a young ship's captain, Ilika from Satamia in Nebador. After arriving in a medieval kingdom, he revealed that his final test, as a new captain, was to find and train his own crew. He looked for them in many places, but finally discovered they could only be found among the young and spirited slaves (with one exception) who had lived through more than their share of misfortune and hardship.

To identify his potential crew members, he had to figure out how to test many illiterate slaves and one innkeeper's daughter. The group then had to find a way out of the medieval walled city with political, psychological, and physical dangers on their heels. The "test," therefore, took place on many levels.

The author trusts that those who hate learning and growing quit somewhere in the middle of *Book One*, just as Kodi quit, and have not bothered to get this book. That leaves more books and more adventures for the rest of us.

Although they walk the same roads, the "journey" in *Book Two* is different for each of the characters, just as it is different for each reader. But something about a journey, of one kind or another, seems to be necessary for people to make leaps forward in their growth.

Even though we don't yet know much about Ilika's ship, it is obviously no place for children. The young adults who will become Ilika's crew are leaving childhood far behind. The Muse keeps whispering to the author that many young readers will soon be forced by events in the world to do the same, sometimes long before they might like.

J. Z. Colby
2010

Acknowledgements

Wonderful people throughout the author's life provided unique and irreplaceable lessons and inspirations:

Juniper Russell
Vicky Ball
Linda Dezzutti
Jennifer Carolyn Gates
Rachael Bleich
Paula Wells
Sarah Satterthwaite
Ashley Riddle

Esther Smith
Dottie Frisbie
Martha Higgins
Susanne Koller
Charleen Cox
Meredith Herzog
Patricia Sharp
Antonya Pickard

Valuable readers gave the author feedback after digging through early drafts of the book:

Ardith Libby
Cecelia Harper
Holly Chalcraft
Karen Pihlak
Shelley Johnson
Brendan Aragorn
Katie Norris

Dan Clark
Karen Oster
Toni Corkran
Cherish Broker
Jimmy Johnson
Deborah Meier
Aurora WindDancer

Excellent critiquers commented on thousands of passages, then provided reactions during in-depth interviews:

Sidney Oster, 8
Sarah Bray, 10
Mitchell Bendis, 10
Catherine "Cat" Harper, 10
Aditya Srinivasan, 11
Madison Frasier, 12
Jasper W. Romero, 12
Katheryn Brunswick, 13
Hannah Li Powers, 14
Alex Chalcraft, 15
Kathryn C., 16
Abby Powers, 17
Elwin Aragorn, 17
Winn Barrientos
Beth Littlewolf

Dylan Oster, 10
Joshua Clark, 10
Jessica Johnson, 10
River Lyons, 11
Courtney Snyder, 11
Thurston Coatney, 12
Mariah Bruns, 13
Kristen Voie, 14
Margaret Brunswick, 15
Patrick Murray, 16
Stephanie Louie, 16
Brie Polette, 17
Rachael Hedges
Elizabeth Renguso

Careful publishing assistants and proofreaders brought the final manuscript as close to perfection as possible:

Sarah Bray, 11
Joshua Utter, 14
Amanda Herman, 17
Deborah Meier

Mariah Bruns, 14
Alex Chalcraft, 16
Rachael Hedges

Contents

Chapter 1: The Shack in the Wilderness

A horn sounded from the tower over the Traveler's Gate, causing wagons and carts to quickly scramble off the roads. Four horsemen of the City Guard poured through the stone gateway as morning light gathered just below the eastern horizon.

Without hesitation, they turned onto the westward road to Port Town and spurred their horses to a trot. They had only gone about a mile when the lead horseman raised his hand and all four quickly came to a halt beside a huge old oak tree.

"You there in the woods!" he yelled. "Show yourself and give good account!"

A few seconds later, a large and stocky brown-haired lad of about fourteen years came out, yawning and stretching. "Sorry, Sir, just catching some sleep before market opens."

"Why should I not think you a run-away slave?" the guard challenged.

Boro swallowed. "Um ... would a slave have a money pouch ... with copper and silver pieces?"

The guard frowned. "Show me your silver."

With shaking hands, Boro pulled the pouch from his cloak pocket and fished inside. He felt the great gold piece, but avoided it as he pulled out an assortment of small coins for the guard to see.

"I'm ... supposed to buy supplies, but ... um ... one of my silvers is yours for ... guarding the kingdom well." He picked out a shiny coin and offered it up to the guard.

The lead horseman nodded to one of the others, who snatched the coin. "Don't be caught lurking around in the trees again."

"Yes, Sir."

All four guards set spurs to their horses' flanks and were gone as quickly as they had come.

✳

Boro stood beside the road trying to master the trembling in his legs as Ilika and the other eight students, still in sopping wet clothes, gathered around him.

Shaggy black-haired Kibi squeezed his shoulder. "Good thinking!"

"You were great!" young but stocky Sata said with admiration, wrapping her strong arms around him for a moment.

Miko, holding hands with Neti, looked at Boro with intense dark eyes and mumbled words of appreciation. Neti, pretty even in wet, muddy travel clothes, sensed a hint of jealousy in her beloved.

Toli, with clumsy words and fidgeting hands, and fourteen-year-old Buna, with her twisted grin, added their thanks while standing as far apart as possible.

Slender, quiet Rini just smiled at his friend and continued shivering.

Last to arrive, thirteen-year-old Mati leaned on her crutch. "I think it was actually me they saw," she said with a guilty tone through chattering teeth.

"It doesn't matter," their teacher Ilika said, his fair hair catching the morning light. "We're on this journey together, and a problem for any of us is a problem for all."

"That's what I was thinking," Boro said. "We just got out of those wet, slimy tunnels under the walls. We don't need to go to the dungeon or — worse — back to the slave market."

Everyone chuckled and nodded.

"That wouldn't have happened," Ilika said with a reassuring voice and a slight smile, his right hand touching the wide metal bracelet on his left arm.

✳

As the guards were long gone and the road remained empty, Ilika and his nine students looked up at the giant oak tree once more.

"You were right, Mati," Ilika said in a calm voice. "It does look strong and ... almost wise. A tree that size is hundreds of years old."

Mati shivered. "Really? That's older than people live!"

"Yes. And I've heard there's a tortoise in warmer parts of the world that lives four or five hundred years."

"What's a ... tor ... toise?" Boro asked, fumbling with the strange word.

"A turtle about four feet long. You can ride them ... if they let you."

Sata's eyes grew wide with wonder. "That's huge! Could we get *them*, instead of horses?"

Ilika laughed. "I'm afraid you'd die of old-age trying to get somewhere on a tortoise. I've seen worms that can go faster."

While the others talked, sixteen-year-old Miko and slightly-younger Neti began looking for the trail. The healer had promised it would be near the old oak tree. Finally enough light gathered in the morning sky. "Shack's this way!" Miko announced.

The rest gladly followed. A faint trail wound through the trees and underbrush, giving the impression it went nowhere and was not worth exploring. After a few minutes of walking, the group entered a clearing with an old, partly ruined cottage, and a little wooden corral, both green with moss. The two-tone call of a donkey greeted them.

Mati immediately smiled and hobbled toward the old corral, stopping just inches from the shaggy gray head that stretched through the rails. The donkey drew deep breaths to take in Mati's scent.

Miko went toward the old wooden shack to see what he could find. Shutters dangled at odd angles, one wall was completely missing, and the rock chimney had crumbled long ago. He was soon back outside. "The roof only covers about half the floor, but it's enough for our bedrolls. There's a saddle and other stuff for the donkey, and a few old dishes."

Just then Neti and Sata pranced back into the clearing. "The stream's just a little way down the trail, and the water tastes good," Neti said, a drop still lingering on her chin.

As Ilika looked around and listened to their reports, he took on a serious expression. "Remember, this is the wilderness, in some ways safer than the city, in some ways more dangerous. Everyone take at least one friend if you leave the clearing."

"I'll choose wilderness any day!" Kibi assured him with a grin, then danced away toward an old stone campfire circle covered with years of dead leaves and fallen branches.

Just then the sun rose over the eastern hills in a cloudless sky. All their faces glowed in the orange light, and everyone began removing wet cloaks and boots, or opening bedrolls.

At the old fire circle, Kibi cleared off a log and began slicing fruitcake and cheese. "Okay, here's breakfast, and I'll be asleep in the sunshine very soon."

Sata took some food over to Mati where she sat on a stump near the corral, talking to the donkey. Soon the pair of friends were yawning and stretching out on blankets near each other.

With an effort, Ilika shook off his weariness, picked up the rope Toli had dropped, and selected several trees that would stay in the sun most of the day.

A few minutes later, Boro turned over to try and get more comfortable on his bedroll, and saw Ilika unpacking saddlebags and hanging wet clothes over the rope. He hopped up and spoke in a friendly but scolding tone. "You're not supposed to be working while we're sleeping! You're the captain!"

"What do you think a captain is, Boro? You led us through those tunnels. Does a leader avoid tasks that need to be done?"

"Um . . . no, I guess not."

"A captain is a servant, Boro. He serves his ship, his passengers, and his crew. You did more than your share today, and you saved my life. Go, sleep, and I promise I will be doing the same very soon."

Boro returned to his bedroll. Though he wore a thoughtful expression for a few minutes, he was soon fast asleep.

✳ ✳ ✳

Chapter 2: A Bit of Paradise

When Ilika awoke in the late afternoon, most of the clearing was in shade and someone had put a dry blanket over him. He sat up and looked around. Mati was by the corral, pulling grass and handing it to the donkey. A fire burned in the ring of stones near the shack, and Miko was arriving with an armload of wood. Sata waddled up from the stream with an old bucket, sloshing with water, and slid it under the corral fence.

As Ilika shook out his blanket, Kibi returned to the clearing with a large pile of mushrooms on an old board, and Neti followed, an assortment of fresh greens in her hat. Rini and Buna had bowls full of berries.

Ilika smiled as he wandered over to the fire. An old iron cooking pot held simmering water to which Kibi added mushrooms after scraping off the dirt.

"Ilika, we need to get some salt," she said after greeting him with sparkling eyes and a smile.

He stood behind her and touched her hair. "And something we can take with us for a cooking pot. That thing looks too heavy."

"It is. Did you find onions, Neti?"

"A few. We borrowed your knife to start the fire, Ilika."

Ilika looked puzzled. "I'd like to learn that trick."

"Miko can teach you," Neti said with a proud smile.

"And since you guys can find food," Ilika began, "we won't have to leave here so soon."

"We really need at least one more day to get everything dry," Kibi said thoughtfully. "And Mati has to figure out how to ride Tera."

"Tera?"

"That's the donkey's name. It's a jenny."

Ilika frowned, remembering the kingdom's rigid naming customs. "I know a priest who would wet his pants if he found out we were using a four letter name for a donkey. He'd probably try to have Mati arrested."

All those around the fire burst out laughing.

"We reminded her about that," Neti said, still snickering, "and she promised to use 'Ter' when we're around other people. But Mati insists the donkey's name really is Tera."

Miko and Boro arrived with another sitting log, so Ilika moved out of the way and wandered toward the ruined cottage. Inside he found all the coin pouches open, slowly drying, each still containing a great gold piece. Seeing the tube of gold coins he had entrusted to Kibi, beside her comb and bottle of lice potion, made him smile. Most of the blankets and clothes were already dry and folded.

As Ilika wandered out toward the corral, he could hear laughter coming from his students at the fire circle and down by the stream. Mati was sitting on a stump talking to the donkey, so he approached.

". . . and I'm going to brush you every day . . . who's coming, Tera?" Mati turned her head. "Hi, Ilika! Tera, this is Ilika, our teacher and the captain of a ship."

Ilika scratched the shaggy head that stretched through the rails. "Hello, Tera. You sure are a beautiful donkey. I bet you and Mati are going to have fun together."

Mati grinned at Ilika's acceptance of the donkey's name.

"Do you know what she thinks of the saddle yet?" Ilika asked.

"No. Rini's going in with me tomorrow to brush her, then see if we can put on the saddle and bridle."

Ilika cleared his throat. "A bridle controls an animal by inflicting discomfort, even pain . . ."

Mati suddenly looked tormented. "I don't want to do that! Tera's my friend!"

"In that case, you could ride her with just a halter and reins, but it will take more time and effort to develop a good working relationship."

"I'll do whatever it takes. I was a slave, and I'm not going to make my new friend into one."

Ilika smiled. "Always remember, Tera is about a hundred times as strong as you."

Mati chuckled. "Boro and Miko have worked around donkeys. They said never stand behind one if you value your life."

"Sounds like wisdom to me. I think dinner is almost ready — hot mushroom soup."

"Yum!"

*

When the sunlight left the clearing for the day, those who were not busy cooking brought in all the boots and saddlebags, then gathered around the fire. Working with two chipped ceramic mugs from the shack, they took turns with cups of soup, or munched on pieces of cheese and edible greens.

"We're all wide awake. What are we going to learn tonight?" Buna asked cheerfully.

"I was just wondering that," Ilika said. "Something we can study just sitting around the fire and talking."

"How to ride a donkey . . ." Mati suggested, gazing into the flames.

"Sorry. You guys know more about that than I do. I had never seen a donkey until I entered your city. I can't help with wild foods either. But I think I should teach you basic chemistry."

"Oh! That's like healer stuff!" Toli said excitedly.

"Healers work mostly with bio-chemicals, but don't know the underlying chemistry."

Ilika took a minute to consider his approach to the subject. "It all starts with energy, the smallest and simplest particles that have any effect on our world. We studied this back at Doko's Inn, just before . . ."

"Radio!" Toli said with a proud look.

"Infrared," Boro added calmly.

Neti's hand shot up. "Light!"

"Ultra . . . violet," Sata added, struggling to remember the words. "That's why we use sun hats."

"Very good. But energy isn't always flying around like the radiation we've studied. Sometimes it settles down, organizes itself into families, little groups called atoms. One or more particles get together in the center. About the same number of a different kind whirl around the outside."

"Like girls and boys?" Neti suggested.

"Roughly like that. The two different kinds are attracted to each other, but have different jobs to do. As soon as those energy particles get together to form an atom, matter is born."

"Can you show us some?" Toli asked.

Ilika laughed. "There's no way I could keep you from seeing it! Everything around you is made of matter, lots and lots of little, tiny atoms. Rocks, water, even something you can't see like the air."

Everyone looked thoughtful, almost disbelieving.

"Are they really little, like a speck of dust?" Sata asked.

"Much smaller. A speck of dust is maybe a million atoms. Each different kind of atom, because of the different number of particles, has different qualities. The one with six protons in the middle is carbon, the black charcoal in the fire."

Ilika paused to drink from the mug of soup he was handed. Several students found a piece of cold charcoal to play with while saying the name.

"The element with seven protons is very different. It's an invisible gas, called nitrogen, that makes up most of the air. Element eight, oxygen, is the other gas in the air."

They tried to grab some air in their hands, without much success.

"Why can't we see it?" Kibi asked.

"It's just one of its qualities that light goes right through, just like gamma rays through our bodies. There's one more I see right here. Much heavier, with twenty-six protons . . . iron."

"The cooking pot!" Mati said proudly.

"Yes. Also black, but very different from carbon."

The group sat in silence for a few minutes, some eating, some just gazing into the fire. Kibi passed around the bowls of berries.

"Would you tell us about your magic bracelet?" Buna asked, changing the subject.

"I don't know very much about it myself."

"Where did you get it?"

"It comes with the ship."

"Is your whole ship magic?"

Ilika thought about her question for a moment. "What is magic but something you don't understand yet? To me, making a fire with a knife is magic . . ."

Miko grinned.

". . . and finding food in the wild."

Several of the girls snickered.

"To me," he continued, "it will be magic when Mati rides her donkey tomorrow, because it's something I've never done, and don't know how."

Mati smiled, but also wore a slight frown.

"Does your bracelet do other things?" Buna asked.

"Yes, but I can't tell you about them . . . unless it becomes necessary."

*

Midnight was at hand when they finally let the fire die down and crept into the ruined cottage to make their beds. Buna gladly accepted Kibi's invitation to sleep near her. When they were all settled, they discovered they could look up at the stars through the missing part of the roof.

"What are stars, Ilika?" Rini asked.

"Everyone knows what stars are!" Toli blurted out. "Even slaves know that!"

"Aren't they holes in the sky?" Neti asked, repeating what she had heard all her life.

"Of course!" Toli answered with complete certainty.

Ilika remained silent.

"Are you still awake, Ilika?" Kibi asked softly.

"Yes. I'm just wondering if this is a good time for astronomy."

"Don't you mean astrology?" Sata inquired.

"No. The two are different, even though they're both about the stars. I think it's too big a subject for tonight. I promise to do it next time we can look up at the stars."

"Thanks," Rini said.

"They're holes in the sky. Everyone knows that," Toli asserted before finally drifting off to sleep.

*　*　*

Chapter 3: Tera

Sometime in the dark hours, Sata had to get up for a few minutes. When she returned to her bedroll, she noticed that Mati's blankets had somehow disappeared, and the slender girl was lying on nothing but her bedroll cover, shivering.

Sata had no idea where Mati's blankets had gone, but moved close and pulled her blankets over the two of them.

Mati made a whimpering sound of gratitude, and was soon asleep.

When Mati awoke to find the sun peeking over the eastern hills, she noticed that Sata and Boro were already sitting by the fire, so she hobbled out to the corral. Rini, after stretching his arms to the sky, joined her. Tera stood by the fence, her hooves squarely planted on two muddy wool blankets.

Ilika wandered over and took in the situation, but said nothing.

As the three of them contemplated the scene, Buna appeared. "Whose blankets are *those*?"

"Mine," Mati said with a pout.

"Did you . . . sleep in the corral?"

"No. I thought Tera was cold, and she was lying right by the fence, so I put my blankets on her."

Rini entered the corral, but let the donkey come to him. Tera was happy to leave the blankets behind to get her neck scratched. "Good morning, Tera. You know, Mati, she still has her winter coat. It's a lot thicker than your blankets."

"I feel pretty foolish," Mati admitted, her face turning red.

"Learn anything?" Ilika asked, pulling the muddy blankets through the rails.

Mati sighed. "Yeah. Donkeys have their own blankets, and won't keep people blankets on. I'll . . . go wash my blankets."

"I'll help," Rini offered, carrying the blankets so Mati could concentrate on her crutch.

✻

A large group, including Ilika, took bowls and mugs down along the stream to pick berries to add to their breakfast.

Ilika shared his concern that he was going to accidentally pick poisonous berries, so Kibi picked two different berries and placed them in his hand.

"Eat one at a time. If it's terrible, spit it out. If it's good, start picking!"

Ilika chose one. The moment his teeth broke its skin, he started spitting violently.

"He learns pretty quickly," Neti said with a big grin. "Maybe we can let him be on our crew!"

Everyone else laughed while Ilika continued to rid his mouth of the terrible taste.

"Just so you know," Kibi said, "you can't use that method to find good mushrooms. You either know them, or you leave them alone."

Ilika promised to leave the mushroom gathering to them. Then he spat several more times.

✻

Well nourished on fruitcake and berries, blankets drying in the sun, Mati approached the corral with Rini at her side carrying the brush, halter, and lead rope.

Tera immediately walked to the far side of the corral and looked askance at the pair of humans.

Rini opened the gate so Mati could enter, then they approached the donkey with nothing but the brush.

Tera met them half-way and happily presented her neck.

"Tera, you are such a beautiful jenny," Mati said, "and I'm going to learn to ride you today."

The donkey's ears twitched, but she stayed right where she was, clearly enjoying the brushing.

Rini got the halter from the fence, and the donkey immediately walked to the far corner of the corral, leaving Mati leaning on her crutch.

Mati tried approaching with just the lead rope, with the same result.

Rini tried approaching with the saddle. Tera led the slender boy around in circles.

Ilika and some of the others started watching from a patch of sunny grass just close enough to see, but not interfere.

The drama continued. For the rest of the morning, Tera walked away from any attempt to approach her with halter, lead rope, or saddle. She looked with suspicion at the saddle blanket, but stood still while it was placed on her back. A moment later Mati found out why. Tera easily shook it off the moment Rini was no longer holding it in place.

Boro and Miko returned to the clearing with the iron pot full of edible roots. Neti and Kibi came in a little later with more mushrooms and greens, and set to work making a mid-day meal.

"This is boring," Toli said from where he sat near Ilika. "I wish we could do some lessons."

Ilika took a breath before speaking. "We won't have other important tasks very often. But getting a mount under Mati is very important today . . . unless you want to carry her."

"No thanks," Toli said, then went to sit by the fire that Sata was building.

Ilika joined Boro for some wood collecting trips, but kept an eye on Mati's progress. Buna arrived with more berries, then sat down to help Kibi prepare the roots. Soon, a hearty stew was simmering.

As mid-day passed, Mati and Rini closed the corral for the last time and plopped down on logs near the fire. Mati looked like she wanted to cry.

"I think I've spotted your problem," Ilika said.

"Me too," Boro said.

"What!" Mati snapped, still nursing hurt feelings.

After a moment, Ilika responded. "Let's get some lunch in our stomachs, then we'll talk about it. Other people might be able to explain it better than I can."

They shared the berries as an appetizer so the bowls would be free for stew.

"These roots aren't potatoes, but they're good," Ilika said.

"They're called turning-to-the-sun. You can even eat them raw," Kibi said.

When everyone had eaten, Ilika led the group out to a dry patch of grass near the corral. "What did you see, Boro?"

"They're treating the donkey like a person. They're saying 'please' and 'thank you' like they would to a person, but I don't think that will work with a donkey."

"But Tera *is* a . . ."

Ilika put his finger to his lips. "This is a time for you to listen to others, Mati. What do you think, Miko?"

"Horses and donkeys are pretty smart, but they're also very stubborn. They'll get away with anything they can, and you have to . . . *make* them work with you."

"I don't want to be a master with Tera my slave!" Mati burst out.

"I understand your feelings about a relationship like that," Ilika said in a calming voice.

Suddenly a look of understanding flashed onto Neti's face. "I think I see it."

"Go ahead, Neti."

"I don't think Tera is capable of working with you by her own choice, no matter how much grass you pull for her, no matter how much you brush her. I think she's more like . . . a three or four-year-old child, and you are her mother. Mothers must be firm with their children, sometimes make them do what needs to be done, sometimes even punish them."

"I think Neti is right," Ilika said. "Slavery is forced-labor of people who could be free and independent. Children can't be. I think the same is true for Tera."

"Isn't . . . Tera free to walk away, just like we are?" Buna asked.

Ilika thought for a moment. "Tera was born into human society, and probably doesn't know how to protect herself from the predators of the wild. She's had a fence around her and people nearby all her life. If she was set free, she would probably be killed by a wild animal very soon."

"Not a very good kind of freedom," Boro commented.

There was a long silence as everyone thought about the issues.

"I had a master who weighed no more than me," Toli said, "but who could make a big horse do anything he wanted, and the horse weighed . . . maybe . . . five times as much."

"But he didn't use physical force, right?" Ilika asked.

"No. That would be impossible with something so big and strong. He used words, and tone of voice, and sometimes signs with his hands."

"Good thoughts and observations, everyone. Are you starting to get some new ideas, Mati?"

Her face was twisted with deep thought.

Everyone wandered away, some to move boots and saddlebags that were no longer in the sun, some to look for wild edibles.

Mati and Rini wandered down to the stream to talk.

✳   ✳   ✳

Chapter 4: A New Team Member

About an hour after the discussion, Mati entered the corral, halter in hand.

Rini closed the gate behind her.

"TERA!" she said, looking straight at the donkey just a few yards away. "We are NOT playing games any more, and I AM going to put this halter on you, and you ARE going to let Rini saddle you, or we will LEAVE you here for the WOLVES!"

Tera lowered her head. This human girl had somehow learned that do-or-die tone of voice that Tera had heard many times before, always when she was about to be saddled or harnessed by as many strong hands and strong ropes as it took. And there was something else . . . the last sound the girl made . . . Tera remembered that sound being made by the humans long ago when sharp yellow teeth ended her mother's life.

Mati was trembling slightly, but wore a stern expression as she hobbled toward the donkey. Tera didn't budge as Mati leaned on her crutch and scratched the animal's shaggy neck. She spoke more softly, but no less firmly. "You and me are going to be a team, and I will *not* put up with silly games when we need to get things done. This is a halter. I'm sure you've had one on before. It goes over your nose like this, then over your ears, then I hook it and it's all done. You may not love it, but it's a lot better than having a knee that doesn't work, believe me, and a lot better than being eaten by wolves."

There was that human sound again, the one that would always make Tera shudder inside . . . and remember her mother.

Rini, looking through the fence, smiled at Mati's new-found confidence, born of necessity.

"Now we're going to walk over here so Rini can put a saddle on you," Mati said, moving around to Tera's left side. "Rini, Tera and I have come to an understanding, and she's ready for a saddle. I'll hold her while you put it on."

Tera didn't move for the saddle blanket, but when Rini approached with the saddle, she started to swivel around Mati.

"You STOP right there, you pesky donkey, or I will take the halter off and walk away and NOT LOOK BACK!"

Tera froze, sensing the seriousness in Mati's voice.

Luckily for Rini's slender arms, it was a light saddle made for a pony. After folding the stirrups on top, he was able to swing it up to the donkey's back.

"Good girl!" Mati said. "See how easy that was? Now Rini is going to cinch it, and you and me are going for a ride."

Rini secured the chest and belly straps, then checked to make sure the saddle wouldn't slide off. He got the lead rope from the fence and handed it to Mati.

"All I'm going to use is a rope hooked to both sides of your halter, so we're really going to have to work together. There, that was easy. Now I'm going to climb onto your back, and you are going to stand RIGHT here."

Mati put her left foot in the stirrup, grabbed the front of the saddle, and pulled with all her might. All her might wasn't quite enough, so Rini gave her a shove.

She landed in the saddle, but in the process her right foot caught behind the stirrup, forcing her knee to bend, and she cried out in pain.

Mati's cry spooked the donkey, who bolted forward, knocking Rini off balance.

Tera came to a stop when she reached the far side of the corral. Mati had somehow managed to hold on, but tears of pain filled her eyes. Using all her concentration, Mati finally straightened her right knee in front of the stirrup. The pain quickly passed.

Then Mati looked around while blinking tears out of her eyes. Rini was sitting on the ground watching her. "You okay?" she asked.

"Yeah. You?"

"I have to remember to keep my leg straight. It all happened so fast, I forgot!"

"I could feel it when you cried out."

Rini got up and walked over to the mount and rider. He spoke firmly to the animal while leading her this way and that, turning sharply right and left, stopping, even backing up. Mati focused on keeping her knee happy.

"Okay, Rini, Tera and I have to do this by ourselves now."

Rini left the corral and stuck his head back through the rails to watch.

Ilika and others watched from comfortable patches of grass as Mati developed a shared language with the donkey, a combination of firm words, tugs on the reins, and nudges with her one booted foot.

Whenever the communication did not go well, which was often during the first few hours, they heard, "NO, Tera, STOP!" Then Mati would try a slightly different combination of words and actions until she could finally say, "Good girl, Tera!"

*

The afternoon was waning toward evening, and some of the students were starting to prepare dinner, when Mati finally told Rini she was ready for the next step.

He opened the corral gate wide.

With a smile on her face, Mati guided her donkey to within a few yards of her teacher. "Tera, I would like you to meet Ilika, my teacher, and Sata and Toli, my friends."

They all gave Mati compliments and Tera kind words.

Mati then directed Tera to the fire circle. "Tera, these are my friends Kibi, Buna, and Boro."

Again they had kind words for mount and rider.

Finally, Mati guided the donkey down the trail toward the stream.

"Why don't we all pull a bunch of fresh grass for Tera so she knows we like her when she gets back?" Boro proposed.

Almost everyone nodded and hopped up to join in the effort. Toli rolled his eyes, but with everyone else involved, he didn't dare refuse. They quickly had a respectable pile of grass in the corral, and went back to preparing dinner.

*

When a quarter hour had passed and Mati had not returned, some of them started to look worried.

When the pair had been gone half an hour, Rini and Sata both began squirming. "Can we go look for her?" Sata asked.

Ilika thought about it. "You can look, but no yelling. And please stay together."

She and Rini agreed and headed down the trail at a fast walk.

*

Soon the sun left the clearing for the day, so Ilika drafted Toli to help him bring in boots and blankets.

After another quarter hour, with three of his students and the donkey well overdue, Ilika was the one looking anxious.

"Yes, you can go look for them," Kibi said with a smirk. "But no yelling!"

Ilika grinned back at her, and he and Boro headed down the trail. When they came to the stream, they could see both donkey tracks and boot prints in the mud on both sides. They continued across. The trail faded as it climbed the open, grassy hillside north of the stream.

When they came to the top of the first hill, they found Rini and Sata sitting in the grass looking across at the next hill.

Silhouetted against the glowing evening sky, donkey and rider walked or trotted back and forth, stopping on command, and turning with precision. In the stillness of the evening air they could faintly hear Mati's words of direction and praise every time Tera did what she wanted, which was now most of the time.

Ilika and Boro sat down.

"How can Mati take a friend on walks now?" Sata wondered out loud with a hint of sadness.

Ilika smiled slightly. "Tera will have to be that friend now."

* * *

Chapter 5: The Truth About Stars

When the twilight began to fade, Ilika finally stood up and waved to Mati, still practicing on the other hill. She walked her new mount down toward the stream. The four watchers carefully picked their way down the grassy hillside in the half-light, and found Tera, with Mati still mounted, drinking at the stream. Mati looked worn out, but had a gleam in her eyes as she nudged her donkey toward the corral.

*

"Every person, every creature," Ilika began, "has an environment in which they can live and be happy, and many, many other environments that would kill them . . . or at least make them unhappy."

Miko finished a bite of his stew. "You mean, if someone grew up in the desert, and then you stuck him in the snowy mountains?"

"Good example. Even if a creature can adapt to a new environment, it takes time to grow more fur, make new clothes, whatever. The smarter the creature, the more environments it can adapt to."

"Are people the smartest?" Kibi asked, nibbling on a slice of starchy root from her stew.

"In this kingdom, yes. But all of us, people and animals, learn most of our living skills when we're young. That's why it's very difficult, often impossible, to change environments when we get older. That's Tera's situation. She grew up in corrals and barns, and has probably never run from a wolf or a mountain lion in her entire life. So if she meets one, she may just freeze with fear."

"The wolf or mountain lion won't freeze," Buna pointed out with wide eyes.

"Very true. Tera might also panic and run in the wrong direction, like into a ravine and get trapped. So if that happens, Mati, both your lives may depend on YOU keeping your wits, keeping Tera under control, and selecting the best course of action . . . which might be running . . . and might be calling for help . . . and might even be attacking the predator."

Mati, with a bowl of stew in hand, looked very thoughtful.

"How do you think *we* are adapting to our new environment?" Neti asked.

"Very well. That was Kodi's problem. He wasn't ready for freedom. The rest of you figured out that your new environment of freedom and learning required complete trust and confidence among all of us, including when handling money. Kodi wasn't able to see that. Luckily, he was able to go back to his old environment."

"Slavery," Miko said grimly.

Ilika nodded, received a bowl of stew, and started eating.

✳

Mati checked on Tera several times during the evening, always talking sweetly and scratching her neck. Eventually all the students got comfortable in their beds and gazed up at the star-studded sky as the last flames of the fire died down.

"Are you ready to learn about the stars?" Ilika asked.

"You promised to teach us!" Buna reminded him.

"Even if some things you've heard are wrong?"

A moment of silence lingered before several voices found the courage to say, "Yes."

"The universe is far bigger and far stranger than anyone in this kingdom knows. The little stories you've heard are attempts to make the universe seem small and simple. We will go into much more detail in daytime lessons, but right now I'll just paint a picture with words so you can begin to glimpse the structure of the universe.

"We will start right here, where we are, and go outward. We are lying on the surface of a large ball of rock. You know about how far a mile is. This ball of rock, this world, is more than seven thousand miles across."

"What about the sea?" Sata said. "Isn't the sea made of water, not rock?"

"The oceans are just a few miles deep, like shallow puddles compared to the thickness of the rock."

"Oh . . ."

"The highest mountains in this kingdom stick up about two miles, and the tallest in the world are more than five miles high. The air we can breathe without much trouble goes up about two miles, then gets thinner and thinner and is very hard to breathe on the highest mountains."

"Do people live in the highest mountains?" Rini asked.

"No. There is nothing up there to eat, everything is constantly frozen, and the weather is terrible. No one, not even little animals, live higher than about three miles up.

"All the clouds and weather are in the bottom five miles of air. The blue color we call the sky is just what the air looks like when it is lit by the sun. The sky is not a solid shell, it's just air."

Toli squirmed in his bedroll, but said nothing.

"Above five miles, the air gets very, very thin, and slowly becomes nearly empty space. About ten miles up there is nothing to breathe, not even enough air to hold your body together."

"Spooky," Miko said with a wavering tone.

"I take it . . . that isn't an environment we could adapt to . . ." Boro said.

"Not with any amount of cloaks and gloves. Empty, airless space is most of what's out there, and all kinds of energy can zoom right through it without stopping.

"This ball of rock we're on, along with it's oceans and air, is called a planet. If we go out into space, the first thing we come to is another ball of rock called the moon. It's smaller, and has no oceans or air. You've probably all heard that our world is the center of the universe."

"No doubt that's bullshit too?" Boro proposed.

"Almost. We are the center of the universe to the moon, because it goes around us, but that's it. Everything else, including our planet itself, has a center somewhere else.

"There are between eight and twelve planets that go around the sun, depending on what you count as a planet. The ones closest to the sun are all balls of rock, about like this planet. Then there are some farther away from the sun that have grown huge with thick atmospheres. We call them gas giants."

Toli snickered. "Is that like a troll who ate too many beans?"

Everyone chuckled, and Mati startled awake. When the laughter died down and Mati was again still and silent, Ilika went on. "Tomorrow you can all tell Mati what she missed. Now we come to the stars. They are actually something much simpler than holes in the sky. You have all seen the sun during the day many times. The sun is just a nearby star. The stars are just far-away suns."

He paused to let them think about the concept.

"That *is* simple!" Rini said. "When I see a house a mile away, it looks just like a speck. When I see a huge eagle high in the air, it looks like a tiny fly."

"So . . . there's more than one sun?" Neti asked with disbelief.

"There are millions and millions and millions of them," Ilika said. "Almost every speck of light you see in the night sky is a sun."

After a moment of silence, Kibi frowned. "Almost?"

"A few of them are the other planets, much closer than the stars. But some are huge clusters of stars that are even farther away than the stars."

"Wow . . ." Rini breathed.

"Here's a final thought for tonight. Most of those suns up there also have planets around them, just like our sun. And some of those planets have life on them, just like our planet."

"And . . ." Kibi boldly continued the thought, "people could be up there, cozy under their blankets, looking at the sky, seeing our sun, and wondering what we are like . . ."

Ilika smiled. "Now you're beginning to glimpse what the universe is *really* like."

Ilika's students pelted him with questions about the mysterious universe he had just described, until one by one they drifted off to sleep.

Rini stayed awake the longest. "If the asteroids were once a planet that broke up, are there still buildings and trees on them?"

He never got an answer. Ilika was fast asleep.

They stayed at the ruined cottage and corral for two more days. Mati worked with her donkey each day, and Ilika used those days to improve their understanding of basic arithmetic. He also taught them more logic and continued their first chemistry lesson.

Of course, they wouldn't let him forget about their precious book. Godi and Tima were now grown and beginning their own adventures, but had not yet met each other. Several of the students noticed the parallel with their own lives.

Each night after crawling into their beds, they gazed up at the stars and asked Ilika questions about what they saw. He answered when he could, but when they tried to see animal shapes in the stars, he would just smile and join in the fun.

Finally, on the evening of their fourth day at the shack, Ilika announced he wanted to head out the following morning to replenish their supplies.

Everyone was happy with the idea, and Mati had a sparkle of excitement in her eyes that had never been there before.

Chapter 6: Farmer Keni

After putting on his boots, Rini looked down at Mati, still under her blankets, dead to the world. He went outside to pull some fresh grass for Tera.

Kibi had secretly saved half a fruitcake for their last morning at the shack, and when the rest learned of her surprise, she received more than her usual number of hugs and kisses. Half an hour later, when everyone else was making noise packing saddlebags and rolling up bedding, Mati finally came to life.

"I've never been so tired and sore in my whole life. I've had gentler beatings when I was a slave than what I went through learning to ride my donkey!"

"Your breakfast is at the fire circle," Rini said while chuckling. "I fed and brushed your cruel master . . . I mean your donkey."

Mati smiled.

"The weather is nice," Ilika commented, "and everyone else is anxious to leave. Today we have to put on your saddlebags before the saddle, and strap on your bedroll."

In spite of her soreness, Mati soon had her bags packed. She quickly ate breakfast, then hobbled out to the corral, Rini at her side.

Kibi and Neti conferred, and decided to take the two wooden bowls, but leave the heavy ceramic items.

After Mati mounted, Rini used a short length of rope to secure her bedroll behind the saddle, then put the crutch with his own gear.

When everyone was ready to go, they all fell silent and looked around with sad eyes. The clearing and its shack had been their home for four days, giving them everything they needed to go from the wet and cold of the old tunnels in the city walls, to the sunshine and freedom of the wild countryside in springtime.

Ilika sensed the mood. "Perhaps we'll be back someday."

After taking up their saddlebags, bedrolls, and other burdens, they crossed the stream for the last time and slowly climbed the hill beyond.

*

As they worked their way along the line of hills westward, Mati proudly rode at the front of the group. Kibi was at the back with Ilika.

"Do you have places in your country that are special to you?" she asked as they came to the top of a hill.

"Oh, yes. The most special are places like we just left, places that gave me shelter when I needed to rest, or ponder my life, or spend time with a friend."

Below them spread a small green valley, and they could see a farm about a mile away.

"How about you?" he asked.

Kibi was silent for a moment. "Just Doko's inn and the shack. I've never been anywhere else I could just . . . relax and think. Somehow, this kingdom doesn't feel like home. If I don't get onto your crew, I think I'll take that road I saw on the map that leads to the desert and see where my feet take me."

Ilika tried very hard not to smile.

*

As they came down off the hill and began to cross the grassy lowlands, they soon found themselves on a track that skirted the edge of the trees on the northern side of the valley. Mati would ride ahead a stone's throw, then come back to share what she had seen over the next rise or around the next bend. Boro kept a sharp eye on her, while Sata took turns with Rini carrying the crutch. Miko and Neti happily held hands in the middle of the group. Toli and Buna continued to keep their distance from each other, and still hadn't exchanged any unnecessary words since the pool under the city walls.

The track became a trail, with neatly stacked firewood here and there. The trail became a road, winding its way through an orchard. Neti squeezed a plum hanging low, but shook her head. The walkers rounded a bend to find Mati talking to a large man holding a pitch fork.

"Ilika, come meet Farmer Keni!"

He strode forward, trying not to let his nervousness show.

"Are you the leader of this troop?" the burley farmer asked as he looked them over carefully and saw no weapons of any kind. The little shovel and the crutch only made him smile.

"These are all traveling students, and I am their teacher. We hope to buy food and a few supplies. If that is not possible, we wish only to pass through peacefully . . ."

"If I have the wife kill a chicken and bake a pie, what color is your money?"

"There are ten of us, and we usually pay a silver for a good meal, perhaps a silver and three coppers if there's dessert."

The farmer's face lit up. "It shall be done!" Then his brow wrinkled slightly. "Il . . . ika? What kind of name is that?"

"One from a far-away land."

"No doubt. Come, Ilika, walk with me and tell me what supplies you might be needing."

"Kibi?"

She joined the two men. "Salt and whatever spices you have. A cooking pot that isn't too heavy. Wooden bowls or cups. A spoon."

"If it's no trouble," Ilika said, "we would take meals with you for a couple of days, and also buy bread and cheese, or whatever you have, for our journey onward."

"If your money is the color you say it is, you can stay as long as you like! I think the wife has a pot and a few other things she will part with. But alas, I only have one extra bed."

"All we need is a bit of barn or shed . . ."

"And I'd like to buy hay and grain for my donkey," Mati said. "Is a copper piece enough?"

"It certainly is, young maiden. For a copper, I'll even put molasses on it!"

"She'd like that! Her name is . . . Ter."

✳

The farmer's cottage and table could hold his family and a guest or two, but not ten, so they ate lunch in a grassy yard beside the kitchen garden, with an old stump for a table and overturned buckets or wooden boxes for chairs.

Farmer Keni's brown-haired daughter, about twelve, helped her mother constantly. His three younger sons, between four and ten, came and went on errands or play.

His wife, a large and serious woman, was quick to point out to her husband that they couldn't be feeding just any strangers who wandered by. He reassured her, and Ilika was happy to hand her a silver piece when he saw the bread, butter, cheese, greens, and fruits she supplied on short notice. She was completely content, and verified that there would indeed be chicken and pie at dinner.

The farmer showed them to the woodshed, just a roof supported by poles, nearly empty this time of year. They got comfortable on their bedrolls and Ilika brought out paper and pencils.

✳

Farmer Keni and his wife strode uphill toward the goat pasture.

"They're the ones those priests are looking for, aren't they?" she asked with a worried tone.

"I think so. The priest hinted they were criminals of some sort, but I see nothing in their eyes but innocence and kindness. Maybe too much of both for their own good. But the priest had fear in his eyes. You saw it."

"I did."

They came to the goat pasture and Keni counted his goats while his wife lifted their tails to look for problems. The farmer hoisted a young billy to his shoulders, rapidly getting too old to be safe around the nannies, and they headed back downhill.

"Do we welcome them," Keni asked, "or send them on their way?"

The woman was thoughtful for a moment. "We welcome them, as long as they pay for what they eat and use."

* * *

Chapter 7: Farmer Keni's Daughter

As Farmer Keni was tying up the goat near the house, he could hear the students and their teacher talking about addition and subtraction and other things about numbers that were pretty much a mystery to him, save what he could work out on his fingers.

His daughter came out of the cow shed with a heavy pail of milk. "Father, when I get my chores done, can I listen to the lessons?"

The farmer wrinkled his brow for a moment. "After all your chores, and only if your mother says it's okay."

"Thank you, father," she said with a happy smile and continued waddling toward the house with her pail.

Keni entered the cow shed, checked on all the cows, and slipped a lead rope on one. As he was passing the woodshed with the cow, all the students sat in a circle and one was opening a thick book. Just then his daughter dashed out of the house and approached the teacher timidly. "Can I listen?"

Keni continued on toward the lower pasture with the cow. He slipped the rope off as he opened the gate, and she trotted in, ready to work on the new grass that was sprouting everywhere.

An explosion of cackling came from the chicken house as Keni walked to the barn. He saw his wife emerge, dinner bird in hand. As he passed the woodshed, he could hear the students reading some fancy story about things that never really happened, and he could see his daughter intently looking over their shoulders. One of the boys, a tall one several years older, was stealing glances at her.

After the farmer spent half an hour carving the new axle for the cart, it looked about right. A thoughtful expression came to him, and he wandered out to the woodshed.

"Sorry to interrupt, but could I get a bit of help with something? My oldest son is way out in the orchard. Just one, perhaps this tall lad here . . ."

"Me?" Toli questioned.

"It won't take long."

Toli looked uncomfortable, but went with the farmer into the barn.

"I'll tap the axel through the hole on this side, and you line it up with the other side when it gets in far enough."

"Okay," Toli said.

Keni started tapping on the new axle. "My daughter Kora is a very pretty girl, and she's growing up quickly, but any boy who wants to court her has to, you know, stick around. We don't want her to rush into anything, or run off."

Toli turned red with embarrassment. "The axle is ... um ... getting close."

"I'll go slow," Keni said. "There's no harm in looking, of course. I did lots of looking before I found my wife."

"It's ... um ... lined up just right," Toli said nervously, "and looks like it'll fit."

Keni continued tapping, and the axle was soon in the right place. As he came around to the other hub to check it, he looked into the young man's eyes, and saw only youthful shyness and clumsiness. He tapped the axle back the other direction a bit, then declared it good.

"Thank you lad, all done."

"You're welcome," Toli said, "and ... thank you."

Keni nodded.

※

When Keni and Toli came out of the barn, the reading lesson was over, and the girl had gone into the house to help her mother make pies.

"Would someone review with Toli the new words we read while he was gone?" Ilika asked.

"I will!" Buna said excitedly. Then she swallowed her words and her face fell. "Oh ... but ... I guess he'd rather have ... someone else ..."

Toli looked at her, his expression changing several times during a long moment of silence. "Buna ... I'd like it ... if you'd teach me the new words."

She brightened.

Toli discovered that Buna was pretty when she smiled, and wondered why he hadn't noticed before.

※

After a break for stretching and discussing the paragraphs they had just read, Ilika got out a sheet of paper and wrote.

$$S \rightarrow U$$
$$U \rightarrow B$$
$$\therefore S \rightarrow B$$

"Sunshine implies Ultra-violet. Ultra-violet implies Burn. Therefore,

Sunshine implies Burn. See how the end of the first conditional is the beginning of the second one?"

"Yeah," Sata said, "so the two conditionals get linked together . . ."

"And the thing that links them disappears . . ." Rini added.

"And you just have the first cause . . ." Toli said.

"And the last effect, a royal sunburn!" Kibi said with a cheesy grin.

Ilika smiled. "Pretty easy, isn't it?"

"Yeah, but I want to see how we can get the hats into the logic," Buna asserted.

"Okay . . . we could just put them in with the sunshine, in the negative," Ilika said as he wrote.

$$(S \text{ and } \neg H) \to U$$

$$U \to B$$

$$\therefore (S \text{ and } \neg H) \to B$$

They looked at it and asked questions until they all understood, and agreed, with the logic.

"But what if we *do* have hats?" Mati asked.

"Okay, so we agree that the conclusion is valid. Now we apply it. If we do have hats, H is true, so 'not H' is false, right?"

"Um . . . yeah."

"So 'S and not H' is false, because both parts of the 'and' must be true for it to be true. Okay so far?"

"Yeah. Okay, so the result is false," Mati said. "So no burn!"

"Be careful! No burn from the sun, but don't sit too close to the fire! A false cause does not *guarantee* a false effect."

"Oh, yeah," Neti said with a shy grin. "We already made that mistake once before."

Farmer Keni sat on a log at the back of the shed pretending to sharpen his hatchet. A slight smile of understanding appeared on his face for a moment, but it quickly changed to embarrassment and he focused all his attention on finishing the task.

✳

It wasn't too long after the logic lesson that Keni's wife served dinner. The stew was rich with chicken, small pot herbs, dumplings, fresh spices, and, Kibi noticed, just the right amount of salt. Ilika was happy to place a silver and three coppers in the woman's hand. Even as they sat around the stump enjoying their meal, they could smell pies baking in the kitchen.

Keni built a fire in the pit near the garden and brought over extra logs for sitting. The group stayed up for hours reviewing astronomy concepts and practicing simple multiplication problems in their heads. Kora listened part of the time, but ran to do evening chores when her mother called from the cottage door.

※

Two more days passed joyfully at Keni's farm, with delicious food provided at every meal, a roof over their heads, and plenty of feed for Tera. Kibi purchased a small bronze pot from the farmer's wife, and the woman made them a cloth sack so the soot wouldn't get on everything. Sata arranged for pouches of salt, dried sage, and dried onions. Neti completed their cooking gear with three more bowls and a large wooden spoon.

Ilika introduced them to the fractional decimal places of tenths and hundredths, which the students found easier to understand than to say. They studied a hand-drawn chart of all the chemical elements, and had fun finding the elements they already knew, including the copper, silver, and gold in their pouches. Many others remained just mysterious names to them.

1 H																	2 He
3 Li	4 Be											5 B	6 C	7 N	8 O	9 F	10 Ne
11 Na	12 Mg											13 Al	14 Si	15 P	16 S	17 Cl	18 Ar
19 K	20 Ca	21 Sc	22 Ti	23 V	24 Cr	25 Mn	26 Fe	27 Co	28 Ni	29 Cu	30 Zn	31 Ga	32 Ge	33 As	34 Se	35 Br	36 Kr
37 Rb	38 Sr	39 Y	40 Zr	41 Nb	42 Mo	43 Tc	44 Ru	45 Rh	46 Pd	47 Ag	48 Cd	49 In	50 Sn	51 Sb	52 Te	53 I	54 Xe
55-82 heavy stable elements								79 Au	80 Hg			82 Pb					
83+ heavy unstable elements																	

H	hydrogen	water		Fe	iron
C	carbon	charcoal, soot		Ni	nickel
N	nitrogen	air		Cu	copper
O	oxygen	air, water		Zn	zinc
Na	sodium	salt		Ag	silver
Si	silicon	rock, glass		Sn	tin
S	sulfur	hot springs, rotten eggs		Au	gold
Cl	chlorine	salt		Hg	mercury
Ca	calcium	rock, bone		Pb	lead

Kora sat in on two or three lessons each day. She loved the reading and was interested in the chemistry, but seemed quite lost with the logic and math. Kibi, Neti, and Buna had great fun explaining things to her, as if they were masters of the subjects.

Toli still glanced at Kora occasionally, but also started taking longer looks in another direction.

※ ※ ※

Chapter 8: A New Student

On the group's last night at the farm, during dinner, Kora seemed to be bursting with some hidden secret.

"Father, are you going to ask him?" she begged in a loud voice.

"I suppose now is as good a time as any. Kora has gotten it into her head that she wants to read and write and do numbers and such. I told her you probably charge a lot of money to take on students, pay for their food and all, money we don't have. But I told her I'd ask, just so she could see for herself."

"Ilika doesn't charge us anything!" Buna blurted out. "We don't have any money, except what he gives us."

"Kora would be a really good student, I can tell," Neti pleaded. "Could we take her, to replace Kodi?"

Miko nodded. "We'd all help her catch up."

"Yeah, we all really like her," Mati said, glancing at Sata.

The other students nodded their agreement and willingness to take on one more student.

"Please, Father, can I learn to read and write and stuff? I really want to!"

"Now hold on a minute!" Keni said. "Just because he doesn't charge anything — and I can't say I understand that — it doesn't mean there aren't other good reasons to keep your head down here on the ground were it should be. You're part of a family, and you have chores and lots of things to learn right here. There's a boy at a farm nearby who likes you, and your mother and me are going to need you around, especially when we get older."

Ilika was enjoying his stew, trying to remain completely invisible.

"Besides," Keni went on, "all that reading and numbers and other sorts of book-learning doesn't go very far toward putting food on the table. That's what's important. You've hardly ever been hungry because me and your mother have worked hard to make our farm give us everything we needed."

"Please talk to him, Ilika," Buna pleaded.

There was a long silence as Ilika looked at each of his students. He could see the excitement in their eyes. Only Rini seemed neutral about the idea. Ilika took a slow breath. "Actually, I agree with Keni, and I don't think it would be good for her, or us, to take on Kora as a student."

A chilling silence fell over the group. Kora retreated into herself and stared at the ground. Most of Ilika's students did the same.

Keni's wife brought out a large plum pie and began to serve. She asked her daughter to get a cup of fresh cream, and Kora did so silently, without eye contact or joy. A few of the students refused the pie, claiming they were full.

Ilika, however, was determined to enjoy every bite. Keni struck up conversations on light topics, from farm animals to the weather, and Ilika responded pleasantly. When the students finished eating, they all wandered silently back to the woodshed. Ilika and Keni went over to the fire pit and the farmer soon had a blaze going.

"Thanks for respecting my wishes," Keni said. "Do you think they'll get over it?"

"I hope so. Will Kora be okay?"

"Yeah, next time the lad up the road comes by for cheese."

Ilika chuckled.

Keni left to do his evening chores, and the other family members were busy here and there. Ilika warmed his hands and gazed into the dancing flames.

Kibi was the first to join him, snuggling close on the log and putting her arms around him. "I trust your reasons for doing what you did."

"Thank you," he said, joining her in the embrace.

A few minutes later, Sata and Boro sat down at the fire. "We wanted to hear your reasons for not taking Kora," Boro said.

"I'd be happy to share them," Ilika said, "but I only want to do it once."

Mati and Rini appeared in the light of the fire and found seats. Sata whispered the situation to Mati.

Neti and Miko squeezed in, both looking glum and remaining silent.

Toli showed up. "Buna's in one of her moods. Says she isn't coming."

"It isn't optional," Ilika said in a firm but quiet tone.

"I'll see what I can do," Kibi said.

"Thanks."

Ilika gazed into the fire, trying to collect his thoughts. About ten minutes later, Kibi returned with Buna.

"Thank you all for coming," Ilika said.

"I thought we were free," Buna mumbled with an angry pout. "Kibi said this isn't optional."

"You *are* free, all of you. But there are, and will continue to be, things that are required as long as you are my students, and as long as you want to be considered for my crew."

"Makes sense to me," Boro said.

Buna flashed him a dirty look.

"I have been asked my reasons for not wanting to take Kora as a student. The most obvious is that she does not have the leave of her parents. But there are others.

"There is only so much of me. I am teaching nine when I only need five. It takes time and energy for me to figure out what to teach, how to approach it, in what order, with what materials, using what words and symbols. Most nights I lie awake for hours making my plans for the next few lessons.

"Getting a new student caught up would be a huge task, even if you all helped. And I have not tested Kora. I know, from the tests, that all of you are able to learn very quickly. I don't know that about Kora. My impression is that she is curious, and that would probably motivate her for a week or two. Then she would start slowing us down. I can already see there are some lessons she likes to avoid. As it is, it will be a miracle if we find the time for everything I want to teach you this summer. There were many slow learners in that room full of people I tested. I did not pick them. I picked you.

"But there are even more important reasons. The world is a big place with lots of uneducated ... poor ... sick ... even dying people ... everywhere. Sometimes we can help them a little bit in passing, as I have done several times since arriving in your kingdom. But as candidates for the crew of my ship, you must get it clear in your minds that our work will be to run the ship.

"Sometimes the mission of my little ship will be to help people, even rescue them. Sometimes it will be different, something even more important, and we will have to let people stay uneducated, poor, maybe even die, so that we can do what is important at that moment. Yes, it will be hard. Sometimes we will cry about it. But it is a hard, cold fact that even if we gave every copper we have, and every minute of our time for the rest of our lives, there would still be needy people in the world."

He took some deep breaths, but couldn't think of anything else to say. His students all gazed thoughtfully at the fire.

"I have a headache, and I'm going to bed. You are welcome to stay up and talk. In fact, I hope you do. If anyone is still interested in being considered for my crew, I will depart with them after breakfast tomorrow. You are all free to make your own choice."

※　※　※

Chapter 9: Travel Plans

Roosters greeting the new day woke Ilika, as they had each morning at the farm. Kibi was still asleep close beside him, so he carefully got up and tucked the blankets around her. Shadows already moved about the farm, carrying feed or milk buckets to and fro. Smoke rose from the kitchen chimney.

Ilika looked around the woodshed, and found all his students still there. Seeing Buna and Toli side by side again made him smile.

Tip-toeing out of the woodshed, he visited Tera, already working on fresh hay, grain, and molasses, then stretched his stiff body toward the sky. The farmer's wife came out of the barn and walked toward him.

"You did good last night about Kora. How soon will you all be ready for breakfast?"

Ilika looked toward the woodshed and saw his students beginning to stir. "Half an hour?"

"That's about when Keni and the children will be ready."

When Ilika returned to the woodshed, Kibi was rolling up her bedding, and so he busied himself with his own. A few moments later, he discovered Buna had seated herself on the ground nearby, and the others were standing behind her.

"We figured out what the problem is," she said, "and I was picked to tell you. We just don't know enough about what it's like on a ship. We know it will slow down other lessons a little, but we need you to tell us more about it. We're sorry we didn't trust you yesterday. Now that you told us why you won't let Kora join us, we can see it. We know we're free to walk away, but all of us want to go with you."

Ilika blinked away some moisture that had gathered in his eyes. "You . . . um . . . you're right. I'm sorry. I haven't told you enough about life on a ship. Even though I can't get into technical details until we're at the ship, I can certainly teach you the communication skills and trust a crew must have."

"We also made another decision. You tell him, Boro."

"Um ... we decided that, if it's okay with you, we don't want to mess with horses. One donkey for Mati is enough. Horses will cost a bunch of money, and take time away from lessons. We want to sell our saddlebags at the next town, except for Mati's, and get rucksacks instead, the kind we can tie our bedrolls onto. Everything will be easier to carry that way."

Ilika considered the proposal. "No one is bothered by walking a few miles a day?"

They all shook their heads.

"Okay. I agree, it will keep things simple."

Just then a clanging sound began, and they turned to see the farmer's wife banging her serving spoon against a lid as steam rose from the cooking pot on the stump.

Miko licked his lips. "Sounds like breakfast!"

✳

After eating, Buna was full of energy, so Ilika assigned her to purchase food from the family. Then he asked Mati and Rini to plan their route toward Lumber Town at the foot of the mountains. He handed them the map and they huddled in the woodshed to look at the situation.

When everyone was packed and ready to depart, Kora was nowhere to be seen, and her mother explained that she had suddenly volunteered to check on the goats. The farmer, his wife, and their three boys waved good-bye as the troop of nine walkers followed their one rider along the farm road that would take them north to the main road.

✳

"Buna, report on our food supplies, please."

"Lots of good stuff! Hard and soft cheeses, plenty of bread, and dried fruits. Porridge grains and some butter. Oh, and hard crackers that'll last a long time. Kibi got salt and herbs already. And I got a bag of shelled nuts!"

"Excellent. Hopefully we'll find more berries and other goodies in the wild."

"Of course we will," Kibi said with a grin.

Ilika ruffled her hair.

As soon as they rounded a bend and were completely out of earshot of the farm, Ilika caught up with Toli and Buna, and spoke softly. "When I give the word, lead us westward up into those hills."

He waited until they were crossing a stretch of dry, stony ground that would not easily reveal their direction. "Everyone, Toli and Buna are leading now."

The two new leaders headed off the road without saying a word. Most of the others shrugged, and quickly followed.

Mati and Rini were the most confused of all, having just planned the route for the next several days. They looked at each other as the rest of the group disappeared into the bushes.

Toli and Buna guided them slowly up a rocky ravine into the grassy hills above. On the way, Ilika caught up with Boro. "At the top, take the lead and go south along the ridge line, but stay out of sight of the farm."

Boro nodded and continued the climb.

Ilika looked back and could see Mati and Rini, last of all, slowly coming up the ravine. Tera was sure-footed, but occasionally came to piles of loose rock and refused to cross. Mati talked to her donkey for a moment, then let her choose a way around. Ilika smiled.

Breathing deeply and glowing with pride, Toli and Buna reached the top of the hill and stood gazing around at all they could see. Once everyone arrived, Boro announced he was leading, and headed south.

Walking, for both people and donkey, was now much easier, as animal paths laced the grassy hillsides everywhere. Rini caught up with Boro, and Mati found herself in the middle of the group behind Sata. Morning clouds started to disappear, and sun hats quickly came out. Occasionally the bones of an animal stood witness to the passing of the years.

At Ilika's request, Neti took the lead and guided them down along a tree-lined stream where everyone was happy to drink and refresh themselves.

Sata led them slowly to the top of a high, lone hill. The spring air was so clear they could see the capital city, now just a small gray line below a range of hills in the southeast.

Miko took them across a ridge back to the north-south line of hills, and finally Kibi led them downhill to a small creek with flat, sandy banks.

"I think this is far enough," Ilika said, setting his bedroll and saddlebags down.

Everyone else did the same, and Rini untied Mati's bedroll so she could dismount.

"What should we eat first?" Ilika asked.

"Soft cheese and bread," Buna replied firmly. "Everything else will stay good longer."

"I'm sure some of you are wondering why we are here, instead of on the road to Lumber Town."

"Yeah!" Mati blurted. "Me and Rini had it all planned. Now we're going the wrong direction!"

Most of the others gathered around with equally puzzled looks. The only ones who seemed completely comfortable with the day's journey were Kibi, Boro, and to Ilika's surprise, Buna.

"Dis-information," Boro said calmly.

"You mean . . . for Keni and his family?" Neti asked with disbelief. "Can't we trust *anyone*?"

"To take someone into our trust, we would have to explain exactly what needs to be kept private, and why. That would take a long time. And even if we were sure we could trust Keni and his wife, could we trust all his kids to keep our route secret? Even his four-year-old son?"

Neti looked at the ground. "Okay."

"I vowed to keep us all safe, and never let that high priest, or anyone else, mess with us again. I can't do that if we're completely honest with everyone we meet."

Mati struggled with hurt feelings. "It just seems like it was a waste of time for me and Rini to plan that route."

Ilika accepted a slice of bread covered with soft cheese from Buna. "You asked me to teach you what it's like on a ship. In any challenging team-work situation, we have to deal with unexpected change. That's what today's walking exercise was all about. Nothing I will ever ask you to do, as your teacher or your captain, is ever a waste of time.

"Sometimes things will change before we expect. If nothing else, our preparations will be valuable practice. Can you be happy with that situation?"

Mati squirmed a little. "Um ... I think so. It will help if you tell me beforehand if it's real or practice."

"Sometimes I will tell you, sometimes I won't. Do you want to know beforehand so you can do things less well, less carefully, if it's just practice?"

"Um ... no."

"Remember when you were learning to ride Tera?"

"How could I forget!" she said with a grin.

"You didn't just put the saddle on and head down the road. You started by practicing in the corral, around the camp, and on the nearby hills. None of that practice put any miles behind you. Was it wasted?"

"Okay, now I see what you mean."

"On the ship, we will practice many things before we ever really do them. We will plan ahead, only to change our plans — or toss them out completely and makes new ones — or just wing it because we don't have time to make plans."

Ilika fell silent and started eating his bread and cheese.

"Which way are we really going?" Kibi asked quietly.

"Port Town," Ilika said around a bite of food, "unless something comes up to change that."

Kibi chuckled. "So ... we would have the best chance of getting there if we keep it to ourselves when we meet people?"

Ilika laughed and nodded, still chewing.

"On your ship," Boro began, "can we always talk about why we did something after it's over?"

Ilika swallowed his bite. "Oh, yes, that's important. It's essential that the crew members do their jobs when the commander speaks, but it's also important they *understand* their jobs. Imagine how hard it would have been to get here if each of the leaders had to explain, on each leg of the journey, to each person, how to walk."

Buna laughed out loud. "It would be like Mati learning to ride Tera!"

Everyone laughed as Neti passed out pieces of dried fruit.

* * *

Chapter 10: Communication

As everyone was unpacking their new cooking gear and supplies, they noticed Ilika tearing small pieces of paper from a larger sheet, and writing on them.

"I've prepared a game that's all about communication on a ship." He mixed the pieces of paper and handed one to each student. "This will also introduce the idea of mathematical variables. On the little sheets you are getting, letters are variables. Think of them as little boxes that can hold any number. The goal of this game is to find the number in variable A. The only rule is that you must communicate with words — you may not show your paper to others."

Ilika fell silent as they looked at their sheets.

Sata grinned. "I have A! A equals B plus C."

"Huh?" Neti said, looking quite confused.

"We have to find B and C!" Toli said forcefully.

"B is D minus one," Rini said.

"So who has D?" Miko asked.

"No!" Toli barked. "We should look for C first!"

The game quickly became a shouting match. Ilika stretched out on his bedroll and stayed low in case anyone started throwing things. Toli and Miko both clearly wanted to be leaders, Neti and Kibi tried to be problem solvers, and Mati had her hand up. The rest stayed quiet and frowning at the confusion.

It wasn't long before the two leaders were competing for the services of the problem solvers, primarily by seeing who could talk the loudest. Mati had given up and joined the observers. As soon as Kibi realized no one could hear her, she closed her mouth and didn't open it again.

Suddenly everything stopped. Both of the leaders looked frustrated. The rest stared at the ground or gazed at the sky.

"The exact same thing happened the first time I played this game in my own training," Ilika admitted.

"So . . . you're not mad at us?" Neti asked with a worried expression.

"Of course not. I just need to teach you how we communicate on a ship. What you just experienced was the natural, human way of doing things. It only works up to a certain level of complexity, and nine people trying to verbally solve a fragmented math problem is *way* too complex.

Everyone nodded agreement or grinned.

"The first method I'll teach you is called information-driven communication. We use it on a ship when not much is happening, no stress, no emergency. Each person has one or more jobs, and the little papers you are holding represent your jobs. For example, Sata's job is to use the values of B and C, do an addition, and find A.

"But the important thing is *when* each person speaks. At the beginning of the game, Sata *cannot* do her job, she has no information to report, so she keeps her mouth shut. Only one person has something to report. Lay all your papers face up so I can see them."

$$A = B + C$$
$$B = D - 1$$
$$C = E + 2$$
$$D = 5 - F$$
$$E = 6 \times 3$$
$$F = I - 6$$
$$G = H - 4$$
$$H = I + 1$$
$$I = 5$$

"Boro is the only person who can report information. Go ahead, Boro."

"I is five."

Buna snickered. "You don't *look* like a five!"

Ilika smiled. "Now that Boro has shared his information, someone else can speak."

"It's . . ."

"No, Toli, let that person discover it."

"Oh, it's me," Mati said. "H is I plus one, so it's six."

Soon they had the idea. Ilika reshuffled the papers and passed them out again.

"I is five," Kibi said.

"H is six," Boro reported.

A few minutes later, everyone clapped and Toli smiled with pride when he finally announced the value of A.

"Now compare that to your first try, which included power struggles, hurt feelings, lots of noise, and *no* answer."

Kibi smiled. "Information-driven is much nicer."

"And it works!" Miko announced with pride.

"On a ship," Ilika said, "knowing when to be silent is just as important as knowing when to speak."

They all took a well-earned break. Several scouted for wild edibles. Mati brushed Tera, Miko started a fire, and Sata dipped water from the stream into their new cooking pot, hoping there would be something for soup besides salt and dried herbs.

✳

As Ilika soaked up the last of his soup with bread, he smiled. It had been a thin soup — just the spices they carried and a few greens and mushrooms — but it provided inspiration.

"Running a ship is sort of like making a soup. There may be a head cook, but he or she has to trust the other helpers to do their jobs. Some of you knew which edible plants to gather, someone built a fire, others collected wood, and someone made the basic broth.

"The same thing is necessary on a ship. It was scary operating my ship all alone on the way here. I was praying every minute that nothing unusual happened."

"It's hard to imagine someone sailing anything bigger than a rowboat all alone!" Miko said with big round eyes.

Ilika laughed. "Well . . . with you guys learning all your lessons quickly, I shouldn't have to go anywhere alone ever again."

They all basked in the warm glow of his compliment.

"The other method of communicating on a ship is called need-driven, and is used for critical operations and emergencies. Any crew member, if they *need* to act or report something right away, and they are missing something, can just say 'I need . . . whatever,' and the person who can get it goes to work, without delay, just as if the commander had ordered it."

Several students nodded slowly. Others were still thinking about it.

"We'll use the same problem we used earlier." He reshuffled the papers and passed them out again. "The urgent need is to find A. So someone says . . ."

"I need B and C," Rini said quickly.

"Perfect, Rini. No one should speak unless they are working on finding B or C."

"I need D," Kibi said.

"Great. Kibi is calling for more information in order to provide Rini with B."

"I need F," Neti said.

The needs and results continued until Rini could finally announce the value of A. Everyone clapped.

"What do you do if two different people ask you for something at the same time?" Sata asked.

"There's a priority on the ship based on who's work is most urgent."

Neti grinned. "I bet the captain always comes first!"

"Nope," Ilika corrected. "The captain is just a coordinator. The pilot has first priority."

Neti looked surprised, but others nodded.

✳

As the evening twilight faded, they all got comfortable in their bedrolls.

"I like the sound of the stream better than all the chickens and stuff," Mati said.

"No roosters tomorrow morning!" Miko said happily. "We can sleep longer!"

As they gazed up at the stars, Ilika talked about asteroids, comets, and other minor members of the solar system. Rini pointed to a shooting star, and was surprised to learn it wasn't a star at all, just a little rock burning up while passing through the air.

Ilika quit talking when he realized half his students were already asleep.

✳　✳　✳

Chapter 11: Vibrations

After a simple breakfast of porridge and mint tea, the group packed and slowly climbed the next hill to the south, the grass still wet with morning dew.

From the top of the hill, they could see the westward road below them in a narrow valley. While they sat and watched, enjoying the sunshine as morning fog began to clear, three different parties passed by on the road below, two with handcarts and one lone horseman.

When no one could be seen on the road in either direction, Rini began to lead the way down the grassy hillside.

Suddenly a strange chirping sound came from Ilika's bracelet. "Everyone back up to the top, quickly, no discussion!" he ordered as he turned and began striding up the hill.

Something in the teacher's voice convinced his students this was no lesson or test. Mati arrived first and moved well back from the top. Everyone else arrived moments later.

"What's going on?" Toli asked loudly, fear showing in his eyes.

Ilika sternly put his finger to his lips, then motioned for everyone to gather around the donkey. "A large group of horses on the road. Rini, crawl to the edge and see what you can see, but without being seen."

The slender lad wiggled his way forward until he could just glimpse the road between blades of grass. Everyone could hear hooves on the road below. Rini reached back with one hand and held up four fingers.

About a minute later, he stood up and returned to the group. "Soldiers. Gone around the next bend."

"How did you know?" Buna asked Ilika, her eyes sparkling with curiosity.

"My ... um ... magic box ... which works with my ... magic bracelet ... can sense ... vibrations. Back at the shack, I set it to tell me if more than one horse was walking or running nearby."

"Wow . . ." Neti said, her mouth hanging open.

Kibi frowned in thought. "Because . . . soldiers never travel alone?"

"That's what I'm hoping."

They waited a few more minutes. Ilika checked the screen on his little device, and Buna tried to see, but he closed it and slipped it back into his saddlebag.

She stuck out her lower lip for a moment, but then grinned.

They attempted the crossing of the road again, Rini still leading, and this time were able to disappear into a tree-lined ravine on the far side.

"Math game," Ilika announced as they rested before beginning the ascent. "I'll give an addition, subtraction, or multiplication problem to the next person in line. They solve it, then make a new problem using the answer and another number, and give it to the next person. This is teamwork, not competition. Kibi, four plus three."

There was silence as Kibi pictured the quantities in her mind. "Seven. Miko, seven minus two."

Everyone seemed to be in good spirits. The problems started out simple, but slowly got harder as they climbed higher up the ravine.

"Mati, three times ten," Rini said.

Ilika looked worried for a moment, but he was soon able to relax.

"Ten . . . twenty . . . thirty!" Mati answered. "Sata, thirty plus eleven."

"Forty . . . one!"

Ilika's eyes opened wide with surprise. But his students seemed to sense they were getting in over their heads, and several subtractions followed. Then Toli got another turn.

"Buna, thirteen times three!" he said proudly.

As the seconds ticked by, Buna's face grew red and silent tears gathered in her eyes.

"Toli, you messed up," Boro scolded.

"I . . . I'm sorry, Buna."

Buna dried her tears, but didn't say anything. A few minutes later they came out of the trees onto a grassy hilltop. Everyone was hot and tired, so they stopped to rest.

"From a captain's point of view, I have criticism for both Toli and Buna," Ilika began. "Toli forgot the object of the game. I don't think he was trying to hurt Buna, he was just showing off, and that destroys trust."

"It's also a good way to destroy a relationship with a very nice girl!" Neti said with vinegar in her voice.

Toli continued looking at the ground.

"I agree. Now to Buna. Instead of using her head and telling Toli she couldn't do the problem, she got stuck in her feelings. Feelings are wonderful things, but they work very slowly, they express themselves poorly, and they are *terrible* at math."

A few others smiled.

"When off-duty, everyone on a ship sometimes shows off, and sometimes experiences deep feelings. When on-duty, either one of those can get us killed."

For the next few minutes, everyone was quiet. Buna scooted close to Toli and put her arm around him. He turned to her and held her close.

✳ ✳ ✳

Chapter 12: Shepherdess Noni

After stale bread and hard cheese, tasty red berries growing by a little stream brought a light to the students' eyes. Although two students, for different reasons, were reluctant, Ilika began the math game again, with much greater success. The well-worn track slowly became a wagon road as they continued over the hills southward.

The day was nearing its end as the troop began to look for a place to camp. No large trees offered shelter on the open hills, but the warm day promised a pleasant evening and a star-studded night.

Mati was leading when suddenly Tera called out loudly in her two-toned voice and broke into a trot.

"Tera! Where are you going in such a hurry?" Mati demanded. She was about to bring Tera to a halt when they crested a slight rise and could see a shepherd's wagon, pulled by another donkey, coming toward them.

The driver brought the wagon to a stop and let Mati approach. Tera pranced right up to the other donkey and stood sniffing and squeaking.

Mati looked at the wagon, and was surprised to see a girl not much older than herself with wild curly hair. "Hi. I'm Mati. This is Ter."

"Hi, Mati. I'm Noni, and your Ter is talking to my Ri. Bringing up the rear somewhere is Bo."

Just then, two other groups approached. From behind Mati came the nine walkers. From behind Noni came dozens of sheep, with the biggest dog Mati had ever seen nipping at their heels. As soon as the dog sensed strangers, he gave a deep bark that would have frozen the blood of anyone not on good terms with his master.

"It's okay, Bo," the shepherdess said, "they look like nice folk."

"Everybody, this is Noni, and Ri, and Bo," Mati introduced. "Noni, this is our teacher Ilika." She went on to name all the others, and each smiled or waved. The sheep flowed around the gathering of humans and donkeys, then spread out to work on the new grass.

"I was about to make camp," Noni said. "If you don't mind all the critters, you can camp with me, share grub and stories."

Ilika looked around, and everyone appeared to like the idea.

"There's a good place just up here. Come on, Ri, haul the wagon up to camp, then you can go play with your new friend. She's a jenny too, so you won't get into any trouble, and she's older, so she probably won't challenge your over-inflated donkey pride."

Several of the students chuckled. Noni guided the wagon, and the sheep slowly made way.

✳

The campsite nestled in a hollow out of the breeze, with a sandy area and fire pit. Noni brought her wagon to a stop, set the brake, and climbed down to unharness Ri.

"Okay girl, go play. Come back by tomorrow morning."

"You let her run free?" Mati asked, still mounted.

"Oh, yeah. She won't go far — she prefers my company to wolves and mountain lions. Bo will keep an eye on her."

Mati thought about it as Rini untied her bedroll. "I've never let Ter run free. Do you think she'll stick around?"

"I've never seen a donkey run away from a good owner . . . as long as no jacks are around. There aren't, or Ri would tell me and . . . you know . . . get herself in trouble."

Mati dismounted and held Tera's halter. "If I let you run and play with Ri, will you stay close to camp?"

Tera made a squeaking sound.

Mati's face twisted with thought and worry. They could all see Ri prancing to and fro in the grass, and Tera's eyes sparkled with longing.

Finally Mati took a deep breath. "Okay, Ter, just remember there are wolves and things out there, so stay near camp. Go play!"

Tera dashed away. After Ri reared up in dominance, and Tera hung her head in submission, the two jennies were soon dancing and prancing together among the sheep, who bleated loudly when their serious grass eating was interrupted.

✳

For the first time, Ilika watched Miko strike sparks with the flint and knife into a pile of dry grass.

Miko looked up as soon as he had a steady flame. "You don't use flint and steel in your country?"

"Well . . . we probably know about it, but I just never learned how."

Miko shook his head in disbelief.

Before the sun set, Boro picked helpers to carry firewood from the nearest tree-lined gully. Toli looked more confident with each armload he added to the growing pile.

Sata balanced the bronze pot on rocks Miko carefully placed, and Noni brought dried vegetables out of her wagon to add to their salt and spices. Rini sliced bread and cheese with the help of Bo, who checked both to make sure they were edible.

"It's so nice having all this help!" Noni remarked, stirring the soup. "I usually have to get my own wood, water, everything. Ri and Bo are wonderful, but this is their time off."

The twilight darkened as everyone gathered around the fire. Tera and Ri lay in the warm sand between the wagon and the fire. Bo had his eyes closed as Rini scratched behind his ears.

"Don't you get lonely and scared, being all alone?" Neti asked.

Noni smiled. "I'm never alone! Ri and Bo are here, and the sheep, and the wild creatures that call to each other. The clouds, the sun, and the stars keep me company."

Neti squirmed and frowned with discomfort at the idea.

Buna, on the other hand, was sparkling with curiosity about the shepherdess. "Where did you . . . get the sheep?" she asked.

"When I was thirteen, my father died and my mother started spending time with an old soldier who had liked her for years. I decided it was time to make my own way. I had raised four sheep in our old back pasture, so I took my sheep, a little sack of food, a few coppers my mother saved for me, and hit the road."

"But . . . you've got sixty or seventy or . . ."

"Eighty-seven. Sheep have babies. Also, stray sheep just seem to find me. I can think of about ten that just showed up."

Buna chuckled. "How do you make money?"

"I learned places to sell their wool, and sometimes *them*." She noticed the cringe on Buna's face. "I know. For years I never thought I'd sell any of them. They're my friends, they keep me company, give me milk. But there just got to be too many!"

"Wouldn't you feel safer if you had a man with you?" Neti asked.

"Me, I don't care for men. I mean . . . you guys are okay, I just mean . . . for my own close, personal relationships."

Buna snickered at the thought and flashed Noni an understanding smile. "How did you get that neat wagon?"

"That's my pride and joy, and she cost me fifteen sheep. Ri cost me five more. Before that, I had an old canvas tent that was always leaking."

"Can I see inside?" Buna asked with a light in her eyes.

Noni grinned, and she and Buna looked at each other for a long moment.

✳   ✳   ✳

Chapter 13: Eighty-Eight Sheep

Against a background of soft bleating sounds and occasional donkey noises, suddenly a very different call was heard, a loud and deep note of distress.

"Did I say something about sheep having babies?" Noni began. "I think one is about to, and might need help. Damn! I haven't lit my lamp, and now I don't have time. I have to go deliver a baby in the dark. Some of you can come along if you want. Whoever stays can finish the soup. Come on, Bo, let's go find her!"

Buna was instantly at Noni's side. Ilika, Boro, and Sata followed. They worked their way through the flock, all ripping and chewing grass. The distress call came again, then a bark from Bo, somewhere ahead. Soon they were outside the flock, feeling their way under a moonless night sky.

"We're looking for an ewe laying down, probably the only one," Noni said with fear in her voice. "Bo?"

He barked again, straight ahead, perhaps another hundred feet.

"Ilika?" Buna said with urgency in her voice.

"I'm thinking the same thing, Buna. Would light help, Noni?"

"I'd give anything for a little light right now. If she isn't calling, she might be in big trouble. I hate this! Why didn't I light my lamp?"

Suddenly there was light.

"What's that?" Noni screamed.

"Just a little magic bracelet Ilika picked up," Buna said in a calm voice. "We use it all the time."

While Noni was recovering, Ilika used a bright, focused beam to scan for the ewe and the dog. "Over there!"

They all dashed to the laboring animal, and Ilika changed the light to a soft glow.

Forgetting her fright, Noni set to work. The ewe was alive, but very weak. Blood covered her hind legs and the nearby grass. The shepherdess quickly discovered one of the lamb's back legs in the birth canal.

"Silly lamb. That doesn't work very well."

She slipped her hands along the lamb's body until she found the other back leg, still inside its mother. Pushing in a little, she held the legs together, then pulled with all her might.

The lamb came sliding out into her lap, still partly covered by its birth sack, and red with blood. Noni burst into laughter and tears at the same time.

Buna was right beside her, trying to see and ready to help. "It's not breathing . . ." she said anxiously.

"That's okay," Noni said, wiping the birth sack away with the tail of her tunic. "It has a little time. The ewe would be licking it right now, but I think she's too weak. We have to trust the gods — there's not much else we can do."

"Where's all the blood from?" Sata asked with a worried frown.

"The ewe. She got torn up trying to push out the lamb the wrong way. How bad she's torn will determine whether she lives or dies."

"Maybe . . . me and the other guys could carry her back to the camp, near the fire?" Boro wondered out loud.

"Would you? She's so far from camp, she'd be dinner for some wolf if we left her. But we have to let the afterbirth come first."

Sitting beside Noni, Bo whimpered his concern.

"Everything's okay here, boy. Keep an eye on the others."

The dog whined once more, then trotted off to protect his sheep.

A moment later, the lamb began to sputter, and Noni angled its head downward in her lap and massaged its sides. "It has to breathe now, or die."

The new little creature was trying very hard to breathe, but it was not an easy thing to do for the first time. The ewe began shuddering, and a moment later something large and dark red slid out onto the grass.

"That looks bad. Is she . . . d-d-dying?" Sata asked with a trembling voice.

"No, that's normal. In fact, the more I look, the less blood I see. I know it looks like it's everywhere, but it's all thin, with no deep pools. I think her chances are good, especially if we can get her to camp."

Boro hopped up. "I'll go get helpers."

"Thank you!" Noni called.

*

An hour later, the ewe lay on a blanket between the fire pit and the wagon, and the newborn was suckling on its mother. Ri and Tera helped to block the breeze.

Noni looked down at the pair. "Did I say eighty-seven?"

Buna laughed. "Eighty-eight now!"

"Tomorrow, I want to get a bath somewhere," the shepherdess declared.

"Me too!" Boro called from the fire circle.

"Yeah!" Miko and Sata both agreed.

Noni mixed molasses and water and the new mother drank deeply. The bleeding had stopped and the lamb seemed healthy, so Noni ambled over to the fire.

"You and Buna haven't eaten dinner," Ilika said. "We saved you some."

Noni swayed for a moment. "I was wondering why I felt faint. Maybe that explains it."

The entire group laughed. Sata poured the remaining soup into wooden bowls as Rini handed them bread and cheese.

"Okay," Noni said around a bite of bread. "I want to know all about this . . . magic bracelet. I want to know where I can get one."

"It comes with Ilika's ship," Miko said with a nod.

"He's a captain," Neti explained.

"And his country is far away from here," Buna added.

"So it's probably the only one in the kingdom," Toli speculated.

"Damn!" Noni said with disappointment. "But thank you. That would have been a lot harder in the dark."

For a minute they all sat in silence, gazing at the flames.

"Okay, with ten of you," Noni began, "somebody must have a good story to tell."

"How about . . . *Mati and the Bottomless Pit*," Neti suggested.

Everyone chuckled — or shuddered — at the memory of crossing the gaping hole in the floor somewhere inside the city walls.

"Or maybe *Boro and the Underwater Passage of Doom*," Mati said with a grin.

Spooky noises showed that many wanted to hear that one. Buna, however, remained silent.

"I know!" Kibi said. "*Kodi and the Gold Piece*."

Everyone laughed nervously.

"Or *Kibi and the Fruit Basket*," Ilika suggested.

"The very best would be *Ilika and the Evil High Priest*," Toli said.

"Yes!"

"Let's hear that one!"

For the next hour, Noni listened to their stories, all of which made her laugh, or brought her close to tears. Then she took on a puzzled expression and looked at them askance. "Why do I get the feeling these aren't just old wives' tales you've changed by putting your own names in them?"

Kibi laughed deeply. "These are all the things that have happened to us in just the last few weeks!"

Noni smiled, then yawned uncontrollably.

"Noni," Ilika began, "would it help if we hung around for a couple of days? We have lots of lessons to do."

"That would be great. I could get a bath, there's enough grass for two or three days, and Bo and I can take them down to the stream each day while the mother and baby stay here. Hopefully I can get her up and eating in a day or two. What are your lessons about?"

The students looked at each other, then all said at once, "Everything!"

✳   ✳   ✳

Chapter 14: Rain, Rain . . .

"Can we learn some more astro . . . nomy tonight?" Toli asked.

Ilika looked up. "No. I think we will learn about the hydrological cycle that is probably about to dump rain on us."

Everyone looked up. Even when they shielded their eyes from the firelight, not a single star could be seen.

"What's a hydro . . ." Sata asked, struggling to remember the word.

"Hydrological cycle. Hydro is part of the word hydrogen, element number . . ." He looked around.

"One," Boro said without taking his eyes off the fire.

"Hydrogen means water-maker in your language. When two atoms of hydrogen join with one atom of oxygen . . ."

"Element . . . eight," Mati said with only slight hesitation.

". . . then two electron energy levels are completely filled by the ten electrons, creating a very stable compound called . . . water. Everyone's heard of it?"

"Yes, Ilika," Kibi said, grinning in the firelight.

"*Where* are you *from*?" Noni asked with wonder. "First a magic bracelet, now . . . I don't know what to call it!"

"Basic chemistry," Toli said.

Ilika chewed on a piece of dried fruit in silence for a minute, then described the cycle of water that begins with evaporation from the oceans, continues with falling rain or snow, and ends with rivers running back to the sea. "It's been going on for billions of years."

Sata squinted. "Ten to the ninth power?"

"Several of those," Ilika added.

"Would you draw the water molecule for us tomorrow?" Toli asked.

"Yes. And I need to go over the electron energy levels in much more detail. But I just felt a drop. You don't mind if we put our heads under your wagon tonight, Noni?"

"Just block it well! That old brake isn't too good in a strong wind."

They scrambled, and soon had all their saddlebags under the wagon. Noni took in her cooking things, and brought out a small tarp to put over the ewe and lamb. Miko and Boro put pieces of firewood around all four wagon wheels. Soon they had their bedrolls laid out with the open ends under the wagon. By that time, big drops of rain were landing everywhere around them.

"I'm going in," Noni said from her doorway. "Stay dry!"

"We will!"

"Good night!"

They were soon snug in their bedrolls, the waxed fabric shedding the rain well. They could hear the wood creak above them as Noni moved around. Bo joined them as soon as he checked for strays.

*

The group stayed with Noni, Ri, Bo, and the eighty-eight sheep for two more days. A light rain fell each night, but the days in between were pleasant, and the sheep loved the wet grass.

Buna could be found with the shepherdess whenever she didn't have lessons. After getting a bath and washing some clothes in a stream, Noni invited Buna into her wagon. Everyone else poked their heads in the door to observe the guided tour.

The bed and its straw mattress filled about half the space, with storage underneath and pegs for hanging clothes above. Opposite the head of the bed, a little iron stove straddled a small kindling box. A sturdy shelf held a copper washing basin, with a bucket on the floor for fetching water. Wooden boxes under the bed held clothes, food sacks, and crocks. Feathers, sprigs of greenery, seashells, and small bones dangled everywhere string could be tied, telling of the many places Noni had been with her wagon.

As soon as Toli got bored with the tour, he used his large boots to measure the outside of the wagon, announcing it to be three feet wide and seven feet long.

Back inside, Buna was fascinated by the little stove and its smoke hood, allowing Noni to cook and stay warm even in the worst weather. The two girls stayed and talked for more than an hour, until Buna reluctantly dragged herself away for the next lesson.

*

The ewe was on her feet the day after the birth, but didn't go far from her hungry lamb. She had many volunteers to bring water and grass.

Ilika started teaching the multi-digit arithmetic for addition and subtraction, and several could remember doing it that way in their heads with simple problems. They devoured another chapter in *The Adventures of Godi and Tima*, and took turns reading the story, from the beginning, to Noni.

On the afternoon of the second day with Noni, Toli got his wish for more astronomy lessons. With the campfire as the sun, Ilika walked thirty strides across the grass before placing a tiny pebble on the ground for the innermost rocky planet, and several more equally far apart. His students came along behind, and stared with open mouths at the little pebble representing their own world. Then he hiked another three hundred strides down the road where he placed a fist-size rock for the nearest gas giant, then continued down the road with more gas giants in hand. Mati, on crutch, waited at the last rocky planet.

On the third day, the students gained a good understanding of electron energy levels, and could draw the chemical states of water.

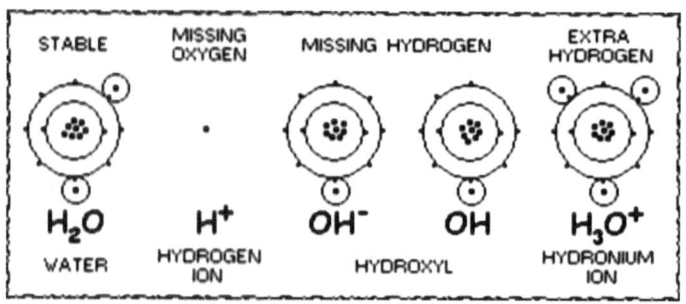

Ilika noticed several of them looking thoughtfully into their cups that evening, and carefully tasting before drinking.

*

The sheep started to wander farther and farther to find grass, and Noni needed to move her flock to a village to the north for shearing. Buna and Noni walked together in the twilight. Their laughter was heard back at the campfire, but their words could only be guessed.

Ilika and his students crawled under the wagon for the last time as the nightly rain began to fall.

*   *   *

Chapter 15: Difficult Parting

While everyone ate porridge and the two donkeys frolicked together one last time, Kibi took Ilika aside. "Noni has pitched in way more than her share of the food. I think we should give her a nice gift. Maybe . . . a great silver?"

"Good idea," Ilika said. "And I know who would love to present it to her."

"Yeah!"

They returned to the breakfast circle, and Ilika dug out the coin. "Noni, we have a little gift for you, and I'm going to pass it around so each of us can make a wish on it. Buna, you're last."

He kept the shiny coin cupped in his hand so Noni couldn't see it, closed his eyes for a moment, then passed it to Mati. Each person who received it looked to see what it was, but kept it hidden. Noni squirmed with curiosity.

Finally Buna made her wish with a big grin on her face, and handed the large coin to the shepherdess.

"Wow! I've never even touched one of these before!"

Toli suddenly looked very smug and started to pull something out of his money pouch, but Buna stopped him with a hand on his arm and a dirty look. Noni didn't notice.

"Thank you! You guys are so sweet. I'm going to keep it for something important."

All the girls shared farewell hugs with the shepherdess. The boys hugged Bo and waved good-bye. Mati hugged Ri, the second donkey she had ever known, and now the best friend of her own donkey.

Noni turned to get her wagon ready for the trail, not bothering to wipe the tears from her eyes.

Ilika helped Mati mount, and everyone else grabbed their saddlebags and bedrolls. Boro and Sata led the group southward.

Buna repeatedly turned around to glance back at Noni and her wagon, but they soon crested a slight rise. She didn't bother to wipe her tears either.

*

The wagon road wound its way south and west over the grassy hilltops for several miles, each hill a little lower than the one before. About mid-day, they sat on the last hill eating lunch and looking down into the huge green valley spread out before them. It contained not one, but two rivers that met on their way to the sea.

But the valley also contained something none of the students had ever seen. White plumes rose straight up from the ground at several points on the edge of the valley.

"What's the smoke from?" Neti wondered aloud.

Ilika got out the map. "I didn't know we'd find geothermal activity! Ah, yes, I see some symbols for springs on the map. That's not smoke, Neti, it's hot water."

"You mean . . . we could take a bath?"

"Maybe. Sometimes geothermal activity is just steam vents, like we can see here. But there might also be pools of wonderful hot mineral water at just the right temperature."

"Where does it come from . . . the Underworld?" Sata asked with a tinge of fear in her voice.

"Time for a little geology," Ilika said. "Think back to our very first astronomy lesson. Imagine our rocky planet sliced open like an apple. The skin of the apple is the crust of the planet, all the rocks we can see. The rocks of the crust are always moving around slowly because of heat and gravity. Big blocks of crust slowly crack, smash together, pull apart, or slide past each other. Sometimes the rocks melt and spew out of a volcano."

Miko shrugged. "Never heard of that."

"There aren't any in your kingdom. But sometimes, like here, pockets of hot rock heat up the water deep underground, boil it into steam, and it heads for the surface through any cracks it can find."

Although they all looked forward to hot baths, they agreed it wasn't important enough to walk the entire huge valley, so they selected a plume to the southeast that wasn't too far off their path.

Ilika took questions as they left the road and worked their way down the hillside toward the mysterious white column of vapor. Tera gave her two-toned call of happiness as they entered the shade of the forest on the edge of the valley.

"Phew! What's that rotten smell?" Toli asked, nose shriveled.

"Those are sulfur compounds, mostly hydrogen sulfide. They often come with geothermal activity. Many different minerals get dissolved by the rising hot water or steam."

"I can see something!" Mati announced from her elevated viewpoint. "A clearing . . . and the dirt is white . . . and yellow . . . and pink . . . and I don't know what else!"

❋

A few minutes later, the entire group stood gazing around them with awe. Pools of steaming water began on the hillside more than a hundred feet above, trickled from one pool into the next, and ended near their feet where the water from the lowest pools gathered into a warm stream. Many different pale colors created a rainbow all across the hillside.

"What a rare sight!" Ilika said, smiling. "Several different minerals are showing, and some of the colors are from algae."

"Algae?" Kibi inquired.

"Little one-celled plants. Some can grow in hot water up to a certain temperature. Notice how the shades of green only start about half way down the terraces? Near the spring at the top, it's too hot for anything to grow."

Neti grinned. "So . . . we could pick any temperature we want!"

"Are the minerals . . . poisonous?" Sata asked with a deep frown.

"No, not in the trace amounts in the water. I'll do a chemistry lesson when we get settled."

Almost everyone turned their attention to selecting a campsite. Miko started walking toward the hissing sound about a hundred yards farther east. "I'm gonna look at the steam thing."

"Steam is very hot!" Ilika warned.

"I know," Miko said without pausing or turning around.

❋ ❋ ❋

Chapter 16: The Gaseous State of Water

At the base of the steam vent, guarding a small dark opening, strangely-shaped rocks clustered near the ground. The white vapor plume started about ten feet higher up and sliced its way into the sky until dispersed by the wind. Between the rocks and the plume, there seemed to be nothing but air.

Mati guided Tera toward a grassy area somewhat downhill from the hot spring terraces.

Ilika set down his bags near Kibi's, and just as he looked up, saw Miko put his hand into the empty space between the rocks and the white plume. "No! Mik . . ."

Miko's blood-curdling scream cut off all other sound. He fell to the ground and held his right hand out as if it burned with fire.

"Miko!" Neti screamed and ran toward him.

Ilika dashed, and others came close behind.

When Neti landed on her knees at Miko's side, he was screaming with pain and his right hand was rapidly turning bright red.

Ilika was there a moment later. "Don't touch his hand! Don't let him hit it on anything!"

Miko started shaking his right hand to be free of it, but Neti grabbed his arm. Blisters rapidly formed on the palm.

"Boro, help me carry him. Kibi, his bedroll, in the shade. Neti, keep that hand safe. Rini, a pot of cold water, quickly."

Kibi dashed away. Ilika and Boro got on both sides of Miko to carry him, now crying like a baby, but every few seconds screaming in pain.

"Clasp arms behind his back and under his knees. One, two, three, lift!"

They moved their patient, trembling and screaming, slowly back toward the terraces. Several others went to help Kibi make a comfortable place. Mati quickly dismounted and tied Tera to a tree.

As Miko was lowered onto his bed, Rini dashed back from the nearest cold stream. Ilika quickly guided the shaking hand into the sloshing pot of water. Miko soon quit screaming, but his crying and sweating continued.

"Buna, a cup of cold water. Kibi, find that really soft ointment. Boro, you're on duty here with Neti. You *must* keep him from damaging those blisters. Nothing else matters. Sit on him, if you have to."

Boro nodded.

"Mati, a damp cloth for his head. Sata, will you plan a soup or stew? You'll have helpers free in a few minutes. Berries, too. Sour ones, if possible."

"Kibi, can you come?" Sata asked. "I don't know that much about wild foods. Buna and Rini too."

Kibi located and delivered the ointment, then left to join the foraging team.

"Neti, he's almost settled down enough to take spoonfuls of water. Go slowly."

"We need to change his clothes," she said, her nose shriveled.

"I know, I can smell it. That much pain can make the body lose control of things. But we need to get him out of danger before we can deal with it."

Toli edged near. "Um . . . what can I do?"

"Take off Miko's boots, put some folded cloaks under his legs, and massage his feet."

Toli opened his mouth, but no words came out. Slowly, with a slight frown, he did what Ilika asked.

✳

By evening, Miko had gained enough presence of mind to be ashamed of what he had done, ashamed of his complete dependence on others, and ashamed of the odor coming from his body.

He had taken some water, and was bravely sucking on sour berries. Each one made him shudder.

"Why sour, Ilika?" Sata asked as she stirred the hearty soup simmering in the bronze pot.

"The biggest thing we have to worry about now is infection."

Their faces were blank.

"Microbiology lesson tomorrow, but sour means acid. Remember the hydrogen ion? It kills, or at least slows down, the little bugs that cause infection. That's also why we have to keep those blisters from tearing. If they get torn, microbes would get in, and that kind of infection would be very hard to fight."

"How long do I need to keep my hand from touching anything?" Miko asked.

"Two or three weeks."

"I can do that, now that it doesn't hurt so bad. For a while I wanted to chop it off, but Neti and Boro wouldn't let me."

They both smiled.

Ilika said, "I know you'll be okay while you're awake and thinking about it. What I'm worried about is at night when you're asleep."

An anxious look appeared on Neti's face.

"I want to take a bath and change clothes," Miko declared.

Boro helped him stand up, and Neti got out fresh clothes. Ilika showed them how to splash water from a nearby pool, but not let the mess get into the pools or streams. Miko required Boro's strong arms for the entire bath. Neti did the splashing, then helped Miko dress.

As they settled down to dinner, Ilika thanked those who had found wild foods for the stew. "And I want to thank you, Miko, for creating a situation very much like a real emergency on a ship. I'm sorry you had to pay so high a price, but it was good for all of us. In an emergency, the commander doesn't have time to say 'please' and 'thank you,' or explain things. You all took it very well."

Many sparkling eyes met his.

"Miko came very close to going into shock, but we managed to avoid it. Shock is when the body thinks it is dying, gets very confused, and starts doing things on its own that don't help. Losing the bowels is pretty minor. The worst is when the heart slows down, the blood pressure drops, and eventually the heart stops. Toli helped avoid that by elevating and massaging Miko's feet."

Toli's smile was mixed with a little guilt.

"I trust that no one else is going to stick their hand, or any other part of their body, into the steam vent. There is a big lesson here I want you all to learn. Either that, or go back to the slave compound where it's safer."

After a long silence, Buna mumbled, "Ilika's angry."

"Yes, I am. There are a million things out there that can kill you, and about half of them are invisible. If you're going to stick your body parts into them just to see what will happen, even after I've warned you about them, then you won't live long, and you certainly can't work on my ship. I'm going to be watching to see if Miko learned this lesson well, and if everyone else learned the lesson he paid for."

Silence stretched for several minutes as bowls were refilled and those who had not yet eaten were served. Miko didn't take his eyes from his stew.

"Um ..." Rini began tentatively, "what do we do if Miko gets an ... infection?"

"Good question," Ilika said. "Port Town is closer, but we don't know if it has a good healer. From what I've seen, Doti would be our best chance. But without antibiotics, even she can only do so much."

"Anti ... biotics?" Neti questioned.

"Medicines that fight infections directly."

"And if she can't help?"

"We'd do everything we could to help Miko's body fight the infection. Sometimes a person can be saved by cutting off the body part that's infected."

Miko's face suddenly shriveled up like a prune.

＊

Before bed, Ilika coated Miko's blistered hand with ointment, then wrapped it loosely in their cleanest cloth. He set his bracelet to chime every hour, and they took turns all night long tending the fire and watching over their injured friend.

＊　＊　＊

Chapter 17: Many Hard Lessons

Everyone sighed with relief when Neti unwrapped Miko's hand the following morning to discover that his blisters were still intact. She lovingly applied ointment while Kibi used a rock to squeeze juice from a bowl full of sour berries. Miko puckered up just watching.

Ilika took the entire morning to talk about microbiology. In the process, he used smaller measurements than they had ever before imagined, millionths of an inch as he drew several types of bacteria, and even smaller units to talk about viruses.

By mid-morning, they knew the common effects of a bacterial or viral infection, how the little critters might get in, and what the body did to keep them out. Miko gained a new appreciation for the fragile layer of damaged skin that covered his blisters.

During a break for lunch, Ilika smiled when he noticed several of his students looking for microbes behind trees and between rocks.

*

On the third day at the hot springs, Ilika brought out the lice potion, and again insisted they splash water from a nearby pool. He was careful to do a very good job on Kibi's head.

As wet, clean hair slowly dried, regular lessons resumed. Ilika made two paper cones around a slender stick, glued together with tree sap, and introduced the conic sections. He had their undivided attention, as they knew geometry was only a small step away from navigation.

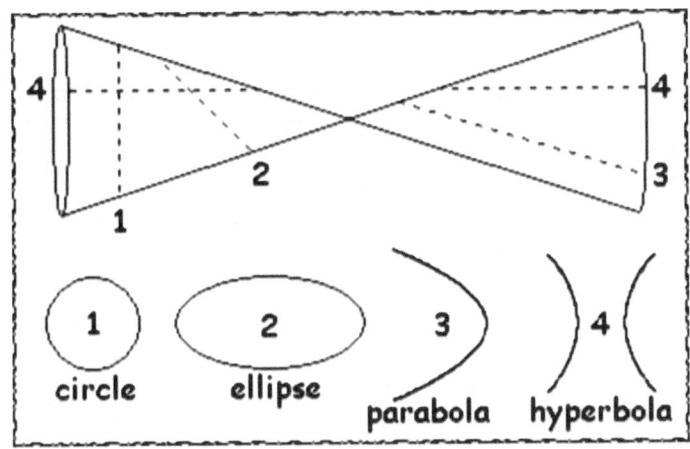

Miko's eyes suddenly grew large as he remembered the first time they had discussed ellipses — in a dark tunnel, under the city walls, when he was thinking of jumping across a gaping hole in the floor. They ended the lesson by looking for the mysterious curves as they watched each other throw rocks toward the river.

✳

The following day, when everyone gathered for lessons, Ilika just said, "Follow me."

At first they thought he was going to the terraces to do chemistry. Instead, he headed for the steam vent.

Miko had not gone anywhere near the place since the accident. Now, as he saw Ilika's destination, he started to fall to the back of the line, shuffling his feet and looking around for some sour berries to pick.

Neti, noticing his reluctance, sat at the back of the group so he could easily join her.

"I know at least one of you isn't very comfortable here. That's why I didn't do this yesterday or the day before. How's the hand, Miko?"

"Hurts just being here."

"I can imagine. Let's see what we have — something that can send a column of vapor a thousand feet or more into the air, day and night, every day for, I don't know, probably the last ten thousand years . . . and make this hissing, almost roaring sound doing it. All that tells me there's a lot of power here, and I had better respect it. What do you guys think?"

"I agree!" Miko said with a big grin.

Almost everyone laughed.

"Respect it and fear it," Sata said with wide eyes.

Ilika cocked his head. "I disagree with that. We've talked about how our minds don't think very well when feeling strong emotions. When close to something of great power, we need to be on our toes and thinking clearly. Respect, yes. Careful, yes. Fear, no."

Sata squirmed. "I think I meant . . . more like . . . careful."

"Okay. Let's see what we can learn about this, without getting hurt. We can see and hear the vent. We can see the white plume of water vapor up there. I think Miko was on the right track. He realized there must be something in between, something that connects the two. His problem was that he used the wrong instrument. Everyone know what an instrument is?"

"Like a compass on a ship?" Rini guessed. "I saw one once."

"Yes, a compass is an instrument, a device that measures something, and every instrument has its limits. If you try to make an instrument work beyond its limits, it will give you the wrong information, and probably be damaged."

"Like my hand!" Miko blurted out.

Ilika grinned. "Everyone, help me think of ways we can learn something about this mysterious thing here."

Boro raised his hand. "We can see it a little. When I look through it at things on the other side, they're wavy, like looking over a fire."

"So what quality does fire have that this might have?"

"Heat."

"Yes. More ideas?"

"We could poke a stick into it," Toli proposed.

"Sounds pretty safe. You may try that, Toli."

The nineteen-year-old looked around for a way out, but seeing none, summoned the courage to find a stick and approach the steam vent. Even though he held it with two hands, the stick was immediately jerked upward. "It's strong!"

"Water's starting to drip down the stick!" Kibi noticed with alarm.

"Very hot water!" Toli said as the drops reached his hand and he let go of the stick. It twirled away and landed near Boro.

"This is true steam," Ilika went on, "the gaseous state of water. It is invisible. Most of the time when people say steam, they mean water vapor, white cloudy stuff they can see. Vapor can be hot, but this vent is pouring out steam much hotter than boiling water, and it's under high pressure. If you ever forget the difference between the two, just ask Miko."

✳

As evening approached, Ilika decided to join the foraging team. As they headed out of camp with shovel, cooking pot, bowls, and hats, he noticed Sata and Boro down by the river having a heated discussion, but he couldn't hear their words.

The stew was tasty that evening, as they found wild onions and garlic, and shared the last of the hard cheese from Keni's farm. After dinner, Kibi proposed they climb the hill behind the camp to see what they could see, maybe discover a few more berries.

Everyone liked the idea. Sata began striding up the hill, clearly intending to walk alone. Boro joined Rini and Kibi. Mati grabbed her crutch and joined Ilika.

A quarter hour later they discovered a group of boulders on the hillside that gave an excellent view of the hot spring terraces, the vapor column from the steam vent, and the valley beyond, already deep in evening shadow. Everyone climbed onto the rocks and sat in silence contemplating the scene.

"Why are we staying here so long?" Sata asked in an irritated tone of voice.

"One of us was stupid enough to burn himself," Miko said.

Neti put her arm around him and kissed him on the cheek.

"We needed to kill our lice eggs," Rini said. "Only one more treatment, right Ilika?"

"I think so. If we can keep Kibi lice-free, the rest of us should be easy."

Kibi snarled, then rubbed her hair against his.

"And there's lots of food in the area!" Neti said happily.

"But that's all stuff we could do at Port Town," Sata said in a voice close to a whine. "Don't you guys feel something strange here? Am I the only one who thinks there's something . . . evil . . . about this place?"

All the other students remained silent.

"Sata," Ilika began, "can you tell us what it is about this place that makes you think that?"

"Something about it isn't . . . natural. I've never seen or heard of a place like this before. It smells weird, and look what it did to Miko!"

Ilika pondered her words in silence.

"I feel a lesson coming," Neti said softly.

Ilika smiled. "What you're doing, Sata, is something almost everyone does. When we're uncomfortable with a person or a place because it's strange, unknown, or difficult, we pass judgment on it, call it a bad name, and try to push it away.

"I agree this place is unusual, it has a funny smell, and it has dangers, one of which Miko discovered. But I assure you that everything here is completely natural. None of it fits any definition of evil I've ever heard. The world has many places that can make us uncomfortable. Calling them evil, or any other bad name, doesn't make them go away."

There was a long silence.

Sata looked at Boro, then back at Ilika, and sighed. "I think . . . that's what Boro was trying to tell me."

Boro shrugged. "I'm just not as good as Ilika at explaining things."

"What did you say?" Buna prodded.

"I said, 'Too bad, so sad.' She didn't like it."

"It's a hard thing to hear," Ilika said.

Kibi nodded. "Why don't we think of things Sata can do to get over her feelings about this place . . . if she wants to."

Sata took a deep breath. "I want to."

Miko scooted closer to Sata. "Sata, what happened to my hand was completely my fault. If it was normally a flower garden, and then it suddenly hissed steam just for me, I might think something was up. But it's just hot water, doing what hot water does."

Sata thought about his admission, and nodded her thanks.

"To me," Rini added, "this place is really beautiful. All the colors in the terraces are like a picture Pica would paint. The steam vent is just a pretty fountain that happens to be a little too hot for us to touch, but it's still beautiful."

Sata looked at Rini with respect, then nodded slightly.

"I hope," Ilika began when everyone else had fallen silent, "you will give serious thought to what 'evil' or 'bad' or 'weird' means to you. They are easy words to use when we don't think about what they mean. They are much harder to use correctly."

Sata did her share of the berry picking on the way back to camp, then spent the rest of the evening quietly pondering all she had heard.

✳

The next morning, Ilika asked Sata what she thought about the idea of leaving that day.

After a long pause, she said she wanted another day to try to make peace with the place.

Ilika did several short lessons that day, starting by opening their story book and teaching them all the parts of speech. They remembered nouns, pronouns, verbs, and adverbs from Ilika's test. Kibi and Sata picked up the rest very quickly, as they always did with anything about language, then helped the others.

Ilika noticed Sata wandering around the geothermal area during some free time after lunch, even poking a stick into the steam vent. It collected hot water, then twirled away, just as it had for Toli.

After dinner, as everyone else was sitting around munching on berries, Sata crept alone to the best bathing pool, removed her clothes, and slipped in.

✳ ✳ ✳

Chapter 18: To the Sea

A light rain fell early the next morning, just enough to make them stuff their blankets into their bedroll covers. Buna was on watch over Miko, and made sure he was awake before helping him do the same. The shower quickly passed as the cloudy sky brightened with the new day.

Breakfast was just a few scraps of dried fruit and whatever berries they could find. Ilika overheard comments about tasty inn food at the end of an easy day's walk. Before departing, no one could resist one more dip in their favorite hot pool. Ilika took a good look at Miko's hand, and Neti reminded him the ointment jar was almost empty.

After reluctantly climbing out of the relaxing hot water, Ilika spread out the map and selected a new emergency meeting place, a village on the coast several miles north of Port Town, on the route he hoped to follow. The morning clouds lifted but still provided shade as they departed their camp below the hot spring terraces. Rini had trouble tearing himself away, but Miko didn't look back. Sata was somewhere in between.

After they found the wagon road that came down off the hills, farm cottages began to dot the river valley, with little herds of cattle, goats, or sheep, as well as gardens and small fields of grain.

The chirping of Ilika's bracelet sent them scurrying into the trees as three soldiers came riding by, going in the opposite direction. The group waited in hiding until the armed men were long gone.

The ten wanderers ate lunch with a large farm family. The kitchen table was laden with fresh and plentiful food and drink, and the students' eyes sparkled every time one of the family members mentioned the sea, now so close at hand. After they had eaten, shared a bit of local news, and purchased some bread and cheese, they were quickly back on the road.

*

For a while as they walked, Ilika and Neti were in the lead, a bit ahead of the rest.

"What do you think Ilika's ship is gonna be like?" Buna asked anyone who cared to speculate.

"A tall ship, I think," Sata predicted, "with white sails!"

"He said it was small," Rini reminded them, "but you're probably right about the white sails."

Boro joined. "Yeah, I've heard big ships have crews of twenty or more."

"I bet it has a mermaid in front, like the one I unloaded about a year ago," Toli said.

"Or maybe a dragon!" Kibi speculated.

"Yeah!" Sata agreed.

"I wonder if we get cabins," Mati said from atop Tera.

"The ships I've seen only have a cabin for the captain and his lady," Miko informed, "and everyone else sleeps in bunks."

Several glanced at Kibi, and she blushed.

"Why don't we ask him?" Rini suggested.

"Ilika!" Buna called.

"Yes?"

"The people you pick — do they get cabins on your ship, or bunks?"

"There are three cabins on my ship, each with two beds, so we all share with one other person."

"I know who *I'm* gonna share with if he picks me!" Miko said proudly.

Neti grinned, and for similar reasons, Kibi smiled.

The rest were silent, thinking about the possibilities.

❋

About mid-afternoon they came to the north-south road. The salt air was pungent and they could faintly hear the roar of waves, but could not yet see the ocean.

To the south, the road crossed the wide river valley, then wound into the wilderness beyond and eventually to another kingdom.

To the north, according to the farmer where they had eaten lunch, just over a rise, lay Port Town.

Ilika looked straight ahead, to the west. A small hill of boulders and scrawny trees stood between the road and the ocean. "I know some of you have been in Port Town, but have you seen the open ocean?"

No one claimed the experience.

❋

Mati and Tera picked their way among the rocks, but had to stop a hundred yards short of the hilltop. Tera was happy to wait in the last sandy space between the boulders, as tasty grass grew where it was protected from the wind. Ilika and Boro helped Mati to the top.

As they all gathered on the topmost boulders, a broken cloud layer poured shafts of golden sunlight onto the open ocean about two hundred feet below. The dark water spread out before them from north to south without an island or distant shore in sight. The students' mouths opened and their eyes grew round with wonder.

After a few minutes, Sata stuttered out what most of them were feeling. "P-please, Ilika, teach us about what we are seeing so we won't b-be afraid of it."

He thought for a moment. "This is where all the water goes at the end of its journey down the streams and rivers. There are several oceans by name, but they are all connected, so it's really one big world-ocean. Since the rivers wash minerals off the land, and evaporation takes only pure water back into the clouds, the ocean is very salty. It would make you sick if you drank it. Although it may be shallow near the shore, it eventually becomes several miles deep."

"What is that roaring sound?" Miko asked.

"Waves. They move across the ocean as ridges of water pushed along by the wind, and when they hit land, they release their energy."

"Are they dangerous?" Neti asked.

"Sometimes. They can just creep up a sandy beach until they tickle your toes. They can also throw a wall of water twenty feet high against the rocks, and you had better not be in the way. The sea is very beautiful and gives us many things, but it must be understood and respected, or it will slap you just like that steam vent."

Miko swallowed, and everyone gazed thoughtfully at the vast ocean before them.

✳   ✳   ✳

Chapter 19: Port Town

After a few minutes of looking at the huge expanse of shimmering water, all of Ilika's students were becoming dizzy. When he turned his attention to Port Town, they were quite willing to do the same.

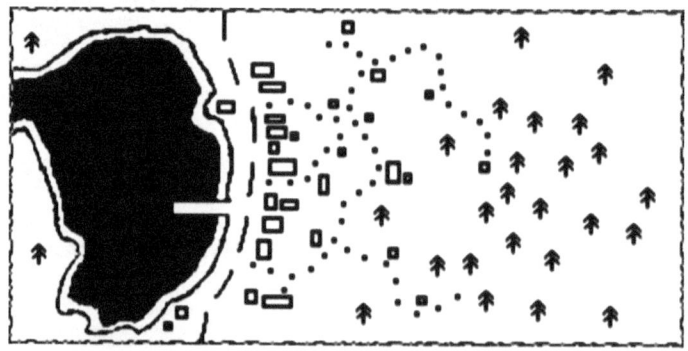

The town lay on the inside of a protected cove with only a small opening to the ocean. Stone and wood buildings lined the waterfront where most of the shops clustered, and tiny people carried burdens to and fro. No roads climbed the hillside behind, but little paths connected the many cottages and houses that perched where they could. Several small fishing boats sat at an angle on the sand north of the town. At the lone pier, slaves unloaded a large wooden sailing ship.

"That's not your ship, Ilika?" Buna asked.

"No, not my ship. Mine is hidden somewhere no one can find it. But something tells me we need to be very careful here."

"Me too," Kibi added.

The rest nodded agreement.

"It's smaller than I was hoping," Ilika went on. "I only see one inn. Any coming and going by anyone, especially a large group, would be seen by everyone."

"I see guards," Rini said.

"I see lots and lots of slaves," Buna added with a slight shiver.

"On the hill," Mati said, pointing, "that white building looks like a church. Could be the same order that's after us."

"Magistrate's house and guard station are right on the edge of town," Toli pointed out, frowning. *This* edge of town."

A few more minutes of peering with shaded eyes allowed them to identify all the buildings where they hoped to do business, and all the buildings they wanted to avoid.

"Okay, they're looking for a large group, so we're not going to give them one. Boro and I will go in for a scouting and shopping trip, and we'll take empty saddlebags. You'll all get a turn to go shopping, but I think we have to forget the inn."

"Just remember," Kibi said with a worried expression, "they're looking for *you*."

"Yes, but I can protect myself. You're in charge here. Boro and I will be back by dark. Stay off the roads and well hidden."

✳

The magistrate's house, just above the road on the south side of town, was of stone and sturdy timbers, but most other buildings made do with weather-beaten wood and thatch.

Guards with squinting eyes watched Ilika and Boro as they passed beneath the guard station, and again on the waterfront, but the pair of strangers appeared to be nothing more than horsemen who had already stabled their mounts and were in search of supplies.

Some of the buildings facing the wharf had stone fronts to better handle the weather off the sea, and in one of them Boro spotted something they needed. He entered the saddle shop and Ilika followed.

The shopkeeper watched intently as the strangers looked around.

"Here they are!" Boro said, spotting the canvas rucksacks. "But they only have four."

"How many backs you got?" the shopkeeper asked pointedly.

Boro winced for a moment. "I have brothers. We want to trade in these saddlebags." He handed his to the man, and Ilika did the same.

"I give you three for each of these."

"How much are these packs?"

"Silver."

"Silver!" Boro said in a somewhat contrived tone, "I could get this for five coppers in the capital."

"This ain't the capital," the man shot back.

Boro started to return the rucksack to its peg.

"Eight," the shopkeeper said dryly.

Boro looked at Ilika and allowed some seconds to pass.

The man sighed. "Seven."

"I'll take all four," Boro said with a slight smile. "So seven times four is . . . help me, Ilika."

"I think you can do it."

Boro started sweating.

"Seven is five and two, is it not?" Ilika hinted.

A moment later a smile came to Boro's face. "Twenty . . . and . . . eight, twenty-eight! Minus six for the saddlebags . . . twenty-two."

The shopkeeper had to do the math for himself, so they utilized the time to look over the other merchandise. Boro noticed the man counting out the proper number of copper coins of his own into a pile, taking out six, and then recounting the resulting pile.

"That'll be twenty-two."

Boro dug out two silvers and two coppers and they returned to the waterfront with four rucksacks.

"Why don't we give these to the girls?" Boro proposed. "Except Mati, of course."

"I'm sure they'd appreciate that," Ilika said as he scanned the buildings. "Up there!" He pointed to a mortar and pestle above a doorway, accessible only by a crude stone stairway that ascended the hillside. "A healer."

They carefully climbed the ancient steps and pulled back the thick woven curtain that covered the doorway of the little cottage.

A bearded gnome of a man sat at a cluttered table with his head just inches from the pages of a book. He looked up as they entered. "Customers or thieves?"

"Customers," Ilika said. "Do you get many thieves?"

"Used to, 'til they got it through their heads I don't have any money."

"Can you make us an ointment? Very soft, for a burn."

"Red, blistered, or cracked?"

"Blistered, and we've managed to keep them from breaking for five days."

"Then there's hope. Yes, I can make such an ointment. Come back in an hour."

Ilika and Boro returned to the wharf and found a fruit and vegetable wagon. Gulls called to each other and wheeled overhead as the two travelers did their shopping, then sat on a low stone wall to pack it all into two rucksacks.

"I'm starting to get the feeling we're being watched everywhere we go," Boro whispered. "And I don't mean by gulls."

"Yes. And not always by guards, either. Maybe the healer's thieves are still about."

As they climbed the stone steps again, this time with heavy packs, they sensed eyes following them.

Ilika smelled the green ointment the healer handed him, still warm in its jar.

The healer pointed with a shaking finger. "Fresh knitbone, dried mary bud, and vera juice. Have you got three coppers?"

Ilika poked in his pouch. "I do not. May I give you a silver instead?"

"Oh, my! You may . . . but not to me. Give it to the baker and tell him it's for me. That way the thieves won't get it, and I'll have bread."

After descending the old stairway, they delivered the promised silver piece to the baker, and whispered to each other about the shadow creeping along not far behind. They both agreed, out loud, that the large plum pie on the baker's counter would be greatly appreciated back at the camp.

✳ ✳ ✳

Chapter 20: The Cave

When the two scouts returned to the rocky hill south of Port Town, they found only Miko and Neti snuggling between some rocks out of the evening breeze.

"Where is everybody?" Ilika asked.

"Well . . ." Neti began with a smirk, "Kibi is probably in the kitchen, Mati and Sata were in the sitting room when we left, Toli and Buna were in their chamber, and Rini was in the library. Oh, and Tera has her own stable, *with* running water."

Ilika smiled and cocked his head. Boro had his hands on his hips.

Without further explanation, Miko led the way down through the rocks toward the open ocean. The sandy beach was currently about thirty yards wide with the tide quite low. The cliff on their left became higher and higher as they walked south, soon towering above them.

The cave entrance was completely invisible until Ilika and Boro followed Miko and Neti behind some huge boulders near the cliff face. The entrance tunnel was just high enough for a donkey with head lowered, and indeed they were welcomed by Tera's two-toned call as they entered. A little stream slithered along the side of the passage toward the ocean.

The cavern inside was easily forty feet wide and fifteen high, but the back receded into darkness and its end could not be seen. A small fire welcomed them from its ring of rocks. Small boulders naturally divided the large sandy floor into a number of smaller spaces, and several of these already contained a pair of bedrolls side by side. Tera had her own space near the entrance, with several big clumps of grass that someone had brought in from the top of the beach. She worked on one clump while Mati brushed her.

As Ilika and Boro surveyed their new campsite with delight, Rini entered with an armload of driftwood, and moments later Kibi came in with the cooking pot brimming with black mussels.

"As you can see," Neti said, spreading her arms, "when you put Kibi in charge, things happen."

Ilika nodded. "Very nice. We got fruits and vegetables, ointment, and a pie."

"Pie? Did you say pie?" Toli asked from behind them, carrying a few pieces of driftwood.

Neti received the ointment from Ilika and sat down with Miko.

"It seems to be well above high-tide level," Ilika said, seeing nothing but bone-dry sand except along the stream.

Kibi nodded. "We thought about that. Maybe we can't get in or out at the highest tides, but it seemed worth it."

"How far back does it go?"

She knelt down by the stream to rinse the mussels. "Farther than we can see. We thought about making a torch, but decided to wait and see if your bracelet was available."

"Sure. We should do that tonight. I'm sure we'll sleep better knowing if anything's in here with us."

They all gathered around as Ilika and Boro unloaded their packs. Kibi and Sata were delighted with all the stew vegetables that emerged.

As they all gathered around the fire, the rucksacks were presented to Kibi, Sata, Neti, and Buna. Boro described what they had seen and done in the town, including the evidence that thieves were afoot.

When a shaft of orange sunlight suddenly found its way directly into the cavern, Ilika jumped up. "Let's go watch the sunset over the ocean!"

As everyone dashed outside, Tera squeaked and came out last.

Ilika sat down just a few feet above the wet sand, and the others spread out beside him to watch the orange ball of fire sink slowly into the water.

"Why is the sun a different color when it's setting?" Rini asked.

"We're looking at it through a greater thickness of air." He drew circles in the sand and pointed out the difference between noon and sunset. "It's the air, especially with dust or smoke or water vapor, that changes the color. The sun, out there in space, is always shining the same color, day and night."

"How far away is it?" Sata asked.

Ilika took a moment to convert the distance. "About eighty million miles."

"Real millions, not the kind that just mean a whole bunch?"

"Yes, real millions."

"There it goes!" Toli said as the sun slipped out of sight for the night.

They sat for a few minutes in silence, just gazing at the sunset colors in the sky.

"We need to tend the stew," Kibi said, getting up.

"And then eat it!" Toli added.

✳

The first order of business, after a hearty mussel stew, was to see if anything of interest — or danger — lay hidden in the unlit depths of their cave.

With the possibility of thieves about, Ilika announced that he or Boro would be with any part of the group at all times. Mati, who already knew the back of the cave was too rough for her, sat down at the fire ring. Boro made sure the knife was within reach, then joined her. Mati suggested they practice reading to each other.

The rest of the group followed Ilika as soon as he activated the light. At the first jumble of large rocks, Miko discovered he was going to need two good hands. He grumbled, then made his way back to the reading circle.

The natural rock tunnel was smaller than the cavern, but high enough for their heads. Occasional patches of sand between the boulders held old broken crates, smashed barrels, frayed ropes, and broken jugs.

"This is starting to look familiar," Toli observed.

"Could this be . . . part of the smuggling route?" Kibi wondered aloud.

"I've heard of smugglers' caves," Rini said. "They sometimes go all the way to some building in the town."

"It's going in the right direction," Ilika pointed out.

They worked their way among the rocks for about half an hour, each person calling out when they noticed anything new. Nothing useful was found. Dozens of dark cracks could admit an animal or child, and Rini slithered into a few, but none would provide passage for crates or large men.

"I just remembered," Ilika said when they stopped for a rest, "the first building you come to from this direction is the magistrate's house, with the guard station right beside it. The house is stone, and certainly old enough to have been here during the smuggling period. Let's make sure we don't pop up in the magistrate's kitchen."

"Yeah!" Kibi said with big round eyes.

"Here's a canvas bag," Buna announced, picking it up by a strap. "Never mind — all rotten."

A few minutes later, a huge pile of rocks completely blocked the cave. They poked around, and Rini tried one crawl-hole while Ilika aimed the light, but it went nowhere and contained only a broken cup.

"Everyone find a place to sit," Ilika said. Once they did, he turned off his light.

"Wow. *That's* dark," Neti said with a shaking voice.

"There is absolutely no light deep in a cave. You could sit here for hours, even days, and your eyes would never adjust. If you bring your hand near your face, you will sense it's infrared heat and it's slight electrical charge, but you will never be able to see it."

"What's an ... electrical ... charge?" Sata asked.

"Remember the ions we've studied? When lots of them, of the same positive or negative charge, collect in one place, a measurable charge is built up. Charges can sometimes flow along a pathway, and that's how our nerves work. You've all seen lightning?"

They all nodded in the dark, then chuckled and said, "Yes."

"That's the biggest electrical flow there is on a planet. And it's way too much for our bodies, so it's very dangerous."

"Will you teach us more about it when we have light and paper?" Toli asked. "This stuff is neat!"

"Oh, yes, it's on my list. I just need to teach you how to multiply and divide first."

"Oh, goodie!"

"As far as I've seen, everything in here is from the smuggling period, at least fifty years old. Has anyone seen anything newer?"

"Fresh animal droppings," Buna reported.

"What kind?"

"Something small. Maybe ... rabbit."

"Anything else?"

No one spoke.

"Shall we return to our cozy fire?"

"Yeah!"

✳

The six who went exploring repeated what they had learned about eyesight and electrical charges to the three who stayed behind. Ilika made a few corrections before he smiled.

They ate pie, and agreed the only dangers lurking in the depths of their cave were small and furry.

"That danger is always there, every night, no matter where we are," Boro said with confidence.

Miko took a deep breath, then suggested he no longer needed to be watched over at night. Ilika looked at his hand, and was happy to see his blisters hardening and shrinking.

As several students were starting to yawn, Ilika led them down to the cave entrance. They were shocked to see that the ocean was completely full, and threatening to overflow right into their cave. Ilika assured them it would come no farther.

Before crawling into their beds, most of them put their belongings into their bags so they could move to higher ground quickly, just in case Ilika was wrong.

✳ ✳ ✳

Chapter 21: Little Thief

None of the suspected small animals visited that night, and Miko's hand fared well. The tide was rising again as they ate breakfast, so they quickly gathered more firewood, and grass for Tera, before the beach was flooded.

Ilika took the morning, around the fire in the cavern, to introduce the arithmetic for multiplication. They rejoiced, freed at last from making tedious and boring rectangles of dots.

Soon after mid-day, the tide began to retreat and the sun came out to warm the beach. Ilika went into town with Mati and Sata to sell the two unneeded saddlebags. Mati easily found a crock of molasses for sale, but Ilika had to ask in several shops before locating a small stack of writing paper.

By the time they came to the cheese maker on the northern edge of town, the trio knew they were being followed. Ilika remained calm as they acquired a wheel of hard cheese, then added bread and a berry pie from the bakery. Sata glanced around constantly, and mumbled something about how safe she felt in the wilderness.

When the shoppers returned to the cave, the tide was low and everyone was outside seeing what the ocean had left behind. At many places on the beach, laughter and squeals of delight came from the students as they discovered strange shells and mysterious creatures with tentacles. Sata helped Mati dismount, and the two friends went down to the water's edge to see what they could find.

Ilika joined Kibi, prying mussels from a rock.

"We've had fun here," she began, "but we might have our own thief. I'm sure there were more carrots last night, and Buna can't find her comb."

"Sounds like a small thief."

"That's what I was thinking. Some critter now has a comb in its nest somewhere, and a belly full of carrot."

They both looked at each other in silence for a long moment, half-smiles on their faces ... then turned their attention to some gulls squabbling over a morsel nearby.

*

"Addition and subtraction are opposites. Multiplication has an opposite too. Can anyone guess what it might be?"

Toli fidgeted to buy some time. Ilika could see a sparkle in Rini's eyes. "Rini?"

"I imagine a loaf of bread. When we multiply, it's like stacking up several slices. So the opposite would be taking a whole loaf and slicing it."

"Can everyone picture that?" Ilika asked.

Most heads nodded, Toli and Sata most vigorously.

"Slicing is a good name. It's actually called division. It is *not* commutative, *cannot* be done in either direction, just like subtraction."

$$\text{whole} \ / \ \text{slices} = \text{slice}$$

"The first number is the size of the whole, the second is how many equal slices we want, and the answer is the size of the slice, in the same unit as the whole."

The rest of the evening around the fire was devoted to drawing and discussing pies — plum pies divided into two, four, and eight equal parts, apple pies divided into three, six, and twelve, and finally berry pies divided into five and then ten. The last division into tenths would be just right for their group, Neti pointed out.

With a grin, Sata brought out the real pie.

*

After getting their bedrolls ready, everyone carefully packed all their small belongings into rucksacks or saddlebags. Ilika sat by the fire a little longer, then began looking around with a worried expression.

Boro noticed. "Sata? She's out looking at the ocean," he said, putting another piece of driftwood on the fire.

Ilika wandered outside. The tide was most of the way in, but not yet high. By the light of the waxing moon, he could see his youngest student sitting on the sand just above the reach of the waves. He joined her.

She smiled at him but didn't say anything.

After a few minutes, he said, "The ocean is very powerful, has many dangers, and some funny smells. Different, but also similar to the steam vent and hot spring terraces. How are you doing with places like this?"

She rolled the question around in her mind for a moment. "Slowly making peace with them. I've always had walls around me, and parents nearby. You do some of the things my parents did, and Kibi too, but you know when to let me ... be grown up and take care of myself. It's scary sometimes."

They both took a moment to scoot farther up the beach to avoid a wave.

"Personal power is the ability to stand on your own two feet, with a smile on your face, in the middle of a universe that contains a million ways to crush you."

Sata cocked her head thoughtfully. "Please say that again."

He did, and added, "I didn't make it up. It's a well known saying in my country, especially in the Transport Service."

"I'm working on the two feet. Maybe when they don't feel so shaky, I'll try the smile too. Is that the real million, or just a whole bunch?"

"I think in this case, it's closer to the real million."

They sat in silence for a few more minutes.

"I'm going in," Ilika said. "Good night."

"Good night. I'll be in soon . . . or else the ocean will push me in."

Ilika chuckled and headed for his bedroll.

✳

"My pack is gone!" Neti gasped as soon as she crawled out of bed the next morning.

Everyone scrambled to check on their own, then help Neti look for hers.

After a quarter hour of searching, even with Ilika's bracelet light, they remained clueless. Not even a scrape mark in the sand, where it might have been dragged, could be found.

"So much for thinking it was just a small animal," Miko grumbled as they gathered back at the fire ring.

Kibi and Rini started passing out things to eat.

"Only a person could make off with something that big without a sign," Boro stated.

No one disagreed.

"All your stuff was in it?" Rini asked.

"Yep. Clothes, comb, ointment . . . one pencil, and my hat. Luckily I keep my coin pouch in my bedroll at night!"

"Cloak?" Boro asked.

"No, it's my pillow. And I have the clothes I'm wearing. Hey! That's still more than I ever had as a slave!"

Ilika smiled. "Let's consider our options."

"Leave today?" Sata suggested, but quickly scrunched her face, clearly not happy with her own idea.

"Go back to having someone on watch all night," Kibi proposed.

"Set a trap and catch the thief!" Buna asserted dramatically.

No one could think of other possibilities, so they discussed the pros and cons of each. Sata spoke against her own plan. In the end, feelings were split between setting a watch and setting a trap.

"I'd like to try Buna's idea," Ilika finally said.

Buna looked almost shocked, then grinned with happiness.

"It has the advantage," he continued, "of possibly getting Neti's stuff back, if the thief just has them hidden in one of the crawl-holes nearby. I have a strong hunch our thief thinks we are easy prey and will be back. And I have the means to render him harmless." He tapped on his bracelet.

"I *knew* that did more tricks!" Buna said with sparkling eyes.

Ilika put his finger to his lips. "So I'd like to ask Neti to wait a couple of days to replace her stuff, see if we have any luck."

"Okay. Anyway, this is exciting!"

"We'll talk about our plans more out on the beach this afternoon. I don't want to talk in here because you-know-who could be listening. Tide is coming in now, and it's Boro's turn to lead a shopping trip this afternoon. Toli and Buna, you want to go?"

"Sure!" they both agreed.

"We need potatoes," Kibi said.

"Carrots," Neti added.

"Pie," Mati suggested. "Or sweet biscuits."

"Yeah!" many voices agreed.

After they finished eating, Ilika had paper and pencil out.

"You're all getting good with numbers. I'll teach you the arithmetic for division soon, but let's play with it now that you know about both multiplication and division.

"First of all, it's important to remember that numbers, all by themselves, are just abstract concepts. To be of use, they need units attached to them. If I say 'five,' you know how many that is, but we aren't talking about anything yet. If I say 'five apples,' all of a sudden it's something real, something interesting."

"Especially if you're hungry," Mati noted.

Ilika smiled. "But you have to be careful when adding or subtracting, and make sure the units are compatible. If I have five apples plus three plums, I have eight something, but it's not apples or plums."

"Fruit?" Kibi suggested.

"Good thinking. Sometimes you can find a word that applies to everything. What if I had three feathers plus two mushrooms?"

After the chuckling died down, Rini said, "Five things?"

"Yes, sometimes we have to resort to very vague words. With addition, we can still do it. Not with subtraction. If I have five apples and I subtract three plums . . ."

They all looked at each other.

Miko grinned. "If you can do that, you've been drinking too much ale."

Everyone snickered as Neti elbowed him to be quiet. "So for subtraction, the unit has to be the same?" she asked.

"Yes. Now let's switch to multiplication and division. They can actually combine units in useful ways. Today you are going to learn your first mathematical formula that describes how reality works and allows us to measure, analyze, and predict real events in the world."

He looked around. Seeing that he had their complete attention, he picked up paper and wrote.

$$S \times T = D$$

"Speed, multiplied by Time, equals Distance."

All his students stared with big round eyes as if he was revealing a magical incantation that would allow them to rule the world.

"Each variable in the formula has a unit, and they have to make sense. Speed is in knots, Time is in hours, and Distance is in nautical miles. These make sense together because knots *means* nautical miles per hour, so all the units match."

He looked around. Rini nodded understanding, but the rest needed a few examples.

Once they were comfortable with the formula and the correct units, Ilika's eyes sparkled with mischief and he gave them a few more examples. The students enjoyed pointing out to their teacher that apples were NOT a unit of time, and cups were NOT a unit of distance.

✳

When Boro, Toli, and Buna returned from town, they reported being questioned by the guards. Boro had remained very quiet, since he had already had a similar experience. A couple of silver pieces from Toli's pouch, with trembling hands, made the guards bid them farewell. Buna hugged Toli again, as she had done on the road, pride showing on her face.

The three shoppers unpacked vegetables and sweet biscuits, and Boro held up the extra knife he had purchased, just in case something happened to the one they had. Buna had a new comb, and passed out lengths of colored ribbon to the other girls, with hers already shining from her tangled hair.

✳

During afternoon lessons, all their belongings came out to the beach with them. Smoothed sand, with a bedroll cover and several sheets of paper, made a workable writing surface.

Knowing the dagger-grip his students used in the capital city would not allow them to truly learn to write, Ilika showed them a more delicate hold. They tried, but the pencils tended to spring away as if they had minds of their own. After many tries, Miko and Buna were nearly in tears. Rini had no better luck and couldn't stop laughing.

With the passing of the first hour, some control was achieved. With finger muscles quickly cramping, most had to rest their hands after each letter. Suddenly a snapping sound came from Boro's direction. The large boy sighed.

Ilika handed him another pencil.

By the time they came to the letter Z, they were ready to burn their papers and throw their pencils into the ocean. Ilika collected the supplies and shooed them away to run on the beach or collect driftwood. Kibi stayed behind with Ilika, as others were in charge of dinner that evening.

"Will it get any easier?" she asked with a sad face.

He started massaging her shoulders. "Of course. It's a physical skill, and our bodies take time learning new things."

She relaxed and let her mind drift over the sea. "Is there a job on your ship I can learn to do?" she asked with her eyes closed.

"Oh, yes. I can already see which job each of you would do best."

"Thank you. I know it will be a hard decision."

"Actually, after the experiences we've had together, I could almost pick my five right now. I'm sure I'll have no trouble by the end of summer." In the silence that followed, he kissed her neck.

Kibi glowed with happiness. She knew Ilika couldn't yet announce a final decision. She also knew he was telling her anyway, in hints and touches that her heart could understand clearly, even if her mind was still unsure.

✳ ✳ ✳

Chapter 22: Kit

The trap was set.

The camp had been rearranged, with packs and saddlebags all near the center. Wide avenues, where no one was sleeping, led to both the entrance and into the depths of the cave, as they had no idea from which direction the thief would come.

All evening long, by the fire, they ate mussel stew, reviewed the rules of logic, savored sweet biscuits, and talked about all the units of measurement they had ever used, or Ilika thought they could understand. But not a word was spoken about thieves, missing items, or traps.

After getting comfortable in his bedroll, Ilika checked the programming of his little handheld device. Everything looked good, so he snuggled close to Kibi and drifted off to sleep.

*

A tingling sensation from his bracelet nudged Ilika awake. He strained to listen, but could hear nothing over the constant sound of the ocean. His hand felt for the little device and found it a few inches away. Touching the screen control, at its dimmest setting, he could see the eleven dots that were his students, himself, and Tera. Another dot, hotter by its color, represented the coals of the fire. One more dot, about three hundred feet deeper into the cave, moved slowly toward them.

He knew he was well hidden from that direction by boulders, so he carefully sat up and slipped into his boots. Then he pulled gently on the ropes that went in one direction to Boro's bed, and in another direction to Miko's. The three of them formed a triangle around the packs and bags. Ilika glanced at the screen and saw the intruder still slowly approaching.

Now they had only to wait. Boro had one knife, Miko the other, and Ilika his bracelet.

Ilika crawled forward a few feet to be closer to the bait as the mysterious dot on the screen passed the one-hundred-foot mark. He breathed slowly. No sight or sound revealed the locations of his helpers.

Suddenly Ilika realized that the thief had picked up speed. Fifty feet, forty, thirty, twenty. He set down the device, waited two more seconds, then sprang from his hiding place, tapping a code into his bracelet even as he jumped.

He landed near the packs at the same time the light came on. Boro and Miko, seeing him spring, were a heartbeat behind, knives raised.

The bright light revealed a hand grabbing a pack strap, then a little boy who squinted and howled with pain and confusion. The three were instantly around him, the others only seconds behind, not bothering with boots.

"Dim your light," Kibi said firmly as she took charge of the situation, going to her knees in front of the boy who was dressed in nothing but tattered shorts. She put her hands on his bare shoulders. "You're okay now. We're not going to hurt you. You're safe with us."

Ilika gave Kibi and the boy some space. "Boro, Miko, please build up the fire. Sata, make a bowl of food for the boy. Everyone else, relax. Morning is not far off." Then he perched on a nearby boulder where he could oversee the situation.

For the next several minutes, the boy's eyes shifted every possible direction, looking for a way out, but the grown-up girl in front of him continued to hold him firmly while saying things to him.

"My name is Kibi, and the man sitting on the rock is our teacher Ilika. Over here is Buna, and this is Neti. What is your name?"

The boy's lips opened several times as he slowly began to relax, but at first no sound came out.

Kibi waited, seeing that he was trying to speak. About six years old, he appeared quite wild with hair that had not seen a comb in a very long time, if ever.

His mouth moved slowly, as if searching for an old memory. "K . . ."

Kibi again pointed to herself and those around, saying their names. Then she pointed to him.

"K . . . it," he intoned slowly.

"Kit?"

A tiny smile flashed across his eyes.

"Kito?" Buna asked.

He frowned, then repeated, "Kit."

At that moment, Sata arrived with a bowl of bread, cheese, and fruit, and passed it to Kibi.

"Kit, this is Sata. She brought you some food."

Kit jerked the bowl from Kibi's hands, huddled into a defensive crouch, and started eating rapidly.

"You were hungry! I know how that feels. I used to be a slave, and often didn't have much to eat."

The fire was beginning to illuminate the cavern. Kibi continued to hold

Kit firmly, talk to him, and name the people within sight.

Ilika relaxed, seeing that Kibi had everything under control.

Kit soon finished the food. "Neti, we have a sweet biscuit left, don't we?" Kibi asked.

"Yep. Two of them."

"I'm going to let go of you now," Kibi said to Kit. "You are not my prisoner. You can run away if you want to. But also you could come and sit by the fire, be our friend, and have a sweet biscuit."

Buna, Neti, and Sata went over to the fire. Kibi took the empty bowl and went that way too, glancing back with a sparkle in her eyes, and leaving a space between herself and Buna on the sitting log.

"His name is Kit, and he seems to understand a lot, but I don't know if he can talk except to say his name," Kibi reported.

"I wonder why he has an animal name," Buna questioned.

Ilika shrugged. "It may have been given to him when his parents, or whoever raised him, realized he was different."

Soon Kibi and Buna noticed Kit peeking over the log between them.

"Let's give him plenty of time," Ilika said. "He may have had no human company for years, surviving on stolen scraps and wild foods."

"Fr . . . iend?" Kit asked unexpectedly.

"We will all be your friends," Boro said, "if you will be our friend."

Cautiously, he moved forward and sat between Kibi and Buna, looking up at each of them to check their reactions.

Neti reached across and handed him a sweet biscuit. His eyes lit up when he tasted it.

※

Ilika discouraged his students from questioning Kit too much. The boy was most comfortable with Kibi and Buna, and seemed to feel safe with all the girls. He looked at Mati with special interest, seeing her crutch and her handicap, but remained shy of Ilika and the boys.

Kit had no lack of appetite at breakfast, and tagged along with the girls, helping them carry things as they were cleaning up and tending the donkey.

When Ilika brought everybody together for lessons, Kit had no idea what was going on, so he snuggled close beside Kibi and peered out from under her arm.

"You may have noticed that your first formula, Speed times Time equals Distance," he said, laying the sheet down so they could all see it, "was in the correct form if we already knew Speed and Time, and were looking for Distance.

"Now we have to learn to transform the formula so that we can find Speed if we know Time and Distance, or Time if we know Speed and Distance."

"Seems like we would usually know Time and Distance, not Speed," Toli said.

"I'll do that one first. Since both sides of an equation are the same, if you add, subtract, multiply, or divide the same number on both sides, the equation remains good. So we look at our formula. To get to the version Toli suggested, we need to get Speed alone in the equation. So we need to get rid of Time on that side.

"Remember what you get anytime you divide a number by itself?"

Rini waited a few seconds for anyone else to answer. Finally he said, "One."

"And remember the identity factor, the number you can multiply or divide anything by without changing it?"

"One," Sata said, grinning as she saw the connection.

"So if I divide the left side by Time, then we have Time divided by Time, which is one, the identity, so we can toss it out. But we have to also divide the right side by Time to keep the equation good. There it is. Speed equals Distance divided by Time."

$$S \times T = D \qquad \frac{S \times T}{T} = \frac{D}{T} \qquad S = \frac{D}{T}$$

It took about half an hour for Ilika to work through enough examples for all his students to understand the new formula. By that time, Kit had slipped away.

Kibi stood up and looked around, then took some deep breaths and sat back down.

✳ ✳ ✳

Chapter 23: Brainwork

Everyone agreed that Kit was not the one watching and following them in Port Town. Their precautions, therefore, remained in place. As soon as high tide backed away enough to let them pass along the beach, Ilika left with Kibi and Rini.

Those who remained at the beach used the middle part of the day to collect wood, bathe, play in the sand, and wade in the retreating tide. Not yet knowing where they stood with Kit, they brought all their things out to the beach with them.

As lunchtime neared, Kit came out of the cave and approached the group on the beach slowly, dragging Neti's pack behind him, ready to run if anyone raised a hand against him.

Instead Neti hugged him, slowly and gently. "Thank you very much, Kit. Would you like that other sweet biscuit we saved?"

He nodded.

"And now you are a true friend, and welcome to eat lunch and dinner with us."

The boy's eyes sparkled, but he wasn't finished. He opened his hand and held out Buna's comb.

She hugged him, and didn't tell him she had already replaced it.

No one said anything about the carrots.

✳

The three shoppers arrived soon after. They shared their finds, including two more canvas rucksacks, which they presented to Toli and Miko.

Kit was amazed at the bounty they brought out of their packs, including more spices, several pieces of fruit, fresh bread, and a pie. With the addition of the last of their cheese, they feasted on the beach as seagulls eyed them from the cliffs.

Moans came from several students when Ilika brought out writing paper.

"Now you can appreciate the work that went into our hand-written book about Godi and Tima."

"*Really* appreciate it," Mati agreed, nodding.

"Today we are doing the same thing, but using our *left* hands."

"Won't that be like starting all over?" Toli whined.

"Yes, but each hand is connected to a different side of the brain, and both sides need to express themselves."

With thoughtful frowns, they got their writing surfaces ready. Kit looked over their shoulders awhile, but soon vanished again.

Most of them had an easier time than the day before, even using a different hand. Ilika went from person to person, making suggestions about holding the pencils and constructing the letters.

When they all arrived at Z, Kibi took a deep breath. "Since Kit has disappeared again, we have something we want to talk about . . . you know . . . about him."

"Yeah," Buna jumped in. "We don't want to get any big ideas without hearing your side, Ilika . . . like we did with Kora."

"Okay," Ilika said, collecting the pencils and paper.

"As I remember," Neti began thoughtfully, "the main problems with Kora were . . . she didn't have her parents' permission, and she would slow down our lessons."

"With Kit," Mati continued, "there *are* no parents, and he's not interested in lessons and could *never* catch up."

"So we're just wondering," Sata added, "if he can travel with us."

Ilika lay on his back, hands behind his head, gazing up at the scattered clouds. "He seems to be bonding quickly, learning to help out, and has promised, by his actions, not to steal from us anymore."

"We know he'd have to be free to choose," Kibi said.

"Yes. And when we split into two groups in the fall, his only option would be staying here."

"We understand," Mati said.

"Let's all sleep on it, decide tomorrow. So far, I don't see any big problems with the idea."

Several students let out the breath they had been holding.

Kit was back in time to help clean mussels, dig grass clumps for Tera, and carry driftwood for the fire. Everyone saw the look of sheer contentment on his face as he ate stew and bread, and later on, plum pie.

"Please teach us about our brains," Rini begged after all the dishes had been washed and the fire built up.

Kit snuggled close beside Buna to listen.

"What we call our brain is really three large brains, each divided into several working regions."

As Ilika talked about each, he pointed to its location in his skull.

"The most primitive, which all complex animals have, is the cerebellum, connected directly to the spinal cord. It controls many things without conscious thought, like breathing and blood pressure."

"Even when we're asleep?" Miko asked.

"You'd *die* if you didn't breath at night!" Toli blurted.

Miko gave him an icy stare. Toli dropped his gaze.

Ilika waited another moment, then went on. "Above the cerebellum are the two halves of the cerebrum. The left half does most of our thinking and short-term memory. It's the brain that's working the hardest when we're doing lessons. The right half does feelings, intuition, creativity, and long-term memory."

"So that's why we remember best when we feel things!" Kibi said with sudden understanding.

Ilika grinned at her. "The connections between the brains are almost as important as the brains themselves. Some people, mostly men, have poor connections between the left and right brains. That's why men are better at simple tasks that need focus. Most women have much better connections, giving them the ability to do several things at once. Also, men tend to develop the left brain, and women the right."

"So . . . are women's brains better?" Rini asked.

"In a sense, yes. Their right brains are more developed, and their connections are better. But you must remember that 'better' is a tricky concept. Right now, in your kingdom, the ability to focus on simple tasks, combined with men's bigger muscles, gives them all the political power. On the other hand, in the Transport Service where I come from, most of the ship captains are women, because women are better at paying attention to many things at once."

There was a long silence. All the girls looked very proud.

"I must point out that we are only talking about typical men and women. Rini, Boro, Miko, and Toli are not typical men. They have well developed right brains and good brain connections. They wouldn't have passed my tests otherwise. Same for you girls and the left brain."

All the girls glanced at their favorite males and smiled. Miko received a kiss.

Kit stayed through the entire lesson and the discussion that followed. Kibi, Buna, and Neti made a bed for him with their cloaks in an unused sandy space, and it made him smile, but for the moment he was content to sit by the fire with the others.

Eventually the students started yawning and getting ready for bed, and still Kit sat listening to conversations, or gazing into the flames.

* * *

Chapter 24: Mommy

When morning light crept into the sky, the fire was nothing but warm ashes, Kit was nowhere to be seen, and his bed was untouched.

They checked their belongings. Nothing was missing.

"I haven't thought of any reason he can't come with us," Ilika said. "Have any of you?"

They shook their heads.

"He certainly has a mind of his own, so even if he comes along, we have to be ready to let go of him at any time."

"We know," Kibi said, nodding. "He's a free spirit."

Kit pranced into the cave entrance just as they were preparing breakfast, with wild flowers for all the girls. His appetite was as good as ever.

"Kit, we have decided to invite you to come with us," Kibi said as they were nibbling pieces of fruit at the end of the meal.

"Go?" he said with a confused look on his face.

"We are leaving soon, probably tomorrow," Buna explained.

Ilika nodded. "We're traveling north up the coast, then into the mountains. Have you ever seen the mountains?"

Kit was frowning.

"If you come with us," Neti added, "you can eat every meal with us, and we'll get you some clothes and blankets and a little pack . . ."

"But you will always be free," Kibi said. "You aren't a slave and we never want to make . . ."

"NO!" Kit yelled suddenly. "Mommy!" he said in a defiant voice.

"Mommy?" Ilika questioned. "This changes things."

"Where's Mommy?" Neti asked Kit.

Kit pointed toward the town. Then he jumped to his feet and grabbed Neti's hand and tried to pull her up. "Go Mommy!" he begged.

"Well, Neti, it's your turn to go into town," Ilika said. "It looks like you,

Miko, and Boro should visit Mommy and see what the situation is. High tide isn't until almost noon, so you could get out now if you wanted."

"Sounds like we should," Boro said. "Shopping?"

"Vegetables."

"Soft cheese or butter."

"Sweets."

"Sell those two extra saddlebags."

The three students were soon ready, and Kit was clearly excited. The rest waved good-bye as the foursome headed up the beach toward the rocky hill.

*

As the tide was coming in, those who remained at the camp hurried to do anything outside that needed to be done. Since they would be trapped in the cave at lunchtime, they decided to make hot soup.

After lunch, Ilika did some reading with Buna, math with Kibi and Mati, and writing with Toli and Rini, all of whom were a little weak in those subjects.

Sata knelt at the cave entrance when the tide reached its peak, breathing deeply. Sometimes her face bore a smile, at other times a frown.

When Mati finished her math review with Ilika, she wandered out to see what her friend was doing, and overheard Sata mumbling, ". . . with a smile on your face . . . with a smile on your face . . ."

"Hi," Mati said.

"Hi, Mati. Welcome to Sata's Test."

Mati looked puzzled.

"I'm doing good at all the lessons. The ocean will decide if I can be on Ilika's crew or not — and other things bigger than me that make me want to run back to my parents' inn and wash tables."

Mati nodded. "I think my big test is Tera, and I don't think it's over just because I can ride."

*

As soon as the shoppers trudged into the cave, Miko flopped onto his bed without a word. Boro looked very glum as he unloaded food. Neti had obviously been crying.

"Where's Kit?" Buna demanded.

"Oh . . . visiting Mommy," Boro said with a strained voice.

"I thought being a slave was the worst thing that could happen to someone," Neti said, tears returning. "I was wrong."

"Mommy must be pretty bad," Toli speculated.

"Mommy is DEAD!" Boro roared. "We were in the stupid GRAVEYARD on the hill!"

"And Kit has old blankets stashed there," Miko said from his bed. "He SLEEPS on her grave every night, VISITS her every day!"

Everyone was silent. Neti curled into a ball on her bed beside Miko. Boro sat down at the fire, chin in his hands.

"I'm sorry," Ilika said softly. "How long ago?"

"It's a peasant's grave," Boro muttered, "just an old piece of wood that says 'Mira.' But the grass has grown up. I'd say two years, maybe three."

"What was Kit like when he was there?"

"Seemed completely happy!" Miko blurted out.

"It's off in a corner, behind some bushes," Boro explained. "He lives there. No one will ever know. He even stacks his broken crocks in a neat pile behind a tree. It's his little world, him and Mommy."

"Were you guys . . . respectful?"

"What do you mean?" Neti asked with an edge to her voice.

"There is certainly a lot wrong with this situation, a lot to be sorry about. But Kit is dealing with the loss of his mother, he appears to have no one else, and he is surviving. He invited you into his secret place. *Were* you respectful?"

"I . . . started crying," Neti said, getting up and coming to the fire. "But I didn't yell at him or anything."

"Miko and I kept our thoughts to ourselves," Boro said.

"Do you think he will come back here tonight?"

"I think so," Boro said. "He curled up in his blankets like he wanted to take a nap. We told him again that he was welcome to come with us, and then we left. I see now that we could have been more respectful."

"I think you did pretty well," Ilika complimented, "considering how unexpected it was."

※

The tide was very low as they collected mussels and a few clams for dinner.

"If Kit comes back," Rini said, "but doesn't want to go with us, I think we should give him a gift."

"I wonder what he would like," Sata thought out loud. "A bedroll with new blankets?"

"A bunch of copper pieces so he can buy food?" Kibi suggested.

"I like both ideas," Ilika said, "but if he starts spending money, the thieves will take an interest in him."

"Not good," Kibi said.

"I know!" Boro burst out. "Remember how we paid the baker what we owed the healer? We could do the same for Kit, but more than a silver!"

Kibi smiled and nodded.

"Boro, did he walk through town freely this morning," Ilika asked, "without any fear of the guards?"

"Yeah. And they took no interest in him."

"Okay, we have a plan, and everyone can get him a gift as we go through town tomorrow."

Moments later, Kit toddled up the beach, ready to help with dinner. They all greeted him warmly, and those who had seen his mother's grave were very respectful.

※

Dinner was tasty, and at Ilika's suggestion, they told stories from their adventures. Several had been shared with Noni, but two new stories were told for the first time — *Mati and the Stubborn Donkey*, and *Miko and the Steam Vent*. Miko even showed Kit his burned hand, harder and pinker than the other, and the little boy's eyes widened.

Kibi invited Kit to have breakfast the following morning, and then walk across town with them as they began their journey northward.

He nodded and everyone could see the sparkles in his eyes, but he disappeared as soon as they were done telling stories. The tide was rapidly rising.

✳ ✳ ✳

Chapter 25: Farewell to Port Town

A dark, overcast sky the following morning made Kit a little late for breakfast, but they waited. The travelers and their guest ate a last meal together in the cavern, sharing little memories about mussel stew and squabbling seagulls. Kit mostly listened, sometimes nodding or smiling.

Finally Ilika and Boro sat down to pack their gear, and the others took the hint. Those with rucksacks cut lengths of rope from the coil to lash on their bedrolls.

Ilika, Sata, and Mati left first, climbing up to the road by the shortest route. Their job was to make sure the town looked safe for the others, reporting back quickly if not.

Toli, Buna, and Rini departed the cave half an hour later, going around the hill to the cove, then along the beach to the town.

Next came Miko and Neti, again along the road, appearing to be a young farmer and his wife, shovel over his shoulder.

Boro and Kibi followed their resident guide. Kit led them an easier way into the town and directly to the bakery.

"I would like to buy three hundred loaves of bread," Kibi said to the baker.

"I can't make that many, even if I have my oven going all night long."

"But I only need one or two a week."

"Ah! That I can do. Are they for little Kit here?"

"You know him?"

"Sure. See him just often enough to know he didn't run off when his mother died."

"Yes, they're for him."

"You got three great silvers?"

"I'll give you four if you'll give him a treat with each loaf, a sweet biscuit or a tart."

"You've got a deal!"

"I'll be checking," Kibi said and looked the baker in the eyes.

"I'm an honest man, and you can't say that about many around here."

"So I've heard."   Kibi handed the man four great silver pieces without letting anyone else see them.   Kit received his first loaf of fresh bread, clutched to his chest like a beloved doll.

On the way to the meeting place, Kibi explained to Kit that if he got a loaf about every three days, he could get them for three years.

He smiled, tore a little piece off the end of his loaf, and ate it.

*

At the junction north of town, one road went east into green hills toward the capital city, another north across grasslands to Lumber Town, and a narrow trail wound its way through scrubby bushes and trees toward the beach.   When Kit and his two companions arrived, the entire group of eleven walked a little way down the trail.   A dry, sandy place witnessed their final moments together.

Kibi told them about her success with the baker, and Kit held up his loaf to prove it.

Buna presented him with her extra comb.

Kit smiled with happiness as he stuck it in his hair, so tangled it stayed right where he put it.

Sata handed him a bedroll cover, complete with two new blankets inside.

"Kit dry!" he said, making a simple sentence for only the second or third time.

Neti handed him a small cooking pot.

Inside Kit found a wooden spoon, a small knife, and a piece of flint. "Stew!" he said and grinned.

Mati opened a cloth bundle to reveal eleven sweet biscuits, offering the first to Kit.

"Mmmm!" the boy said with gleaming eyes.

When they finished eating biscuits, all the girls lined up to give Kit farewell hugs.   Their faces and wet eyes showed their longing to ask, just one more time, if he would come with them.   But Ilika had already reminded them that he had made his decision and given them his answer.   If he changed his mind of his own accord, he was still welcome.

The boys offered warm handshakes, and after a moment of hesitation, Kit accepted.

Finally they prepared to depart, shouldering packs or saddlebags, boosting Mati onto Tera, and taking up the shovel and rope.

"Bye, Kit!"

"Stay dry!"

"We love you!"

"Bye!"

"Remember bread at the bakery!"

Kit stood with his bedroll under one arm, and his cooking pot and loaf under the other, watching his friends leave on their journey.   Having friends was very nice, and gave him the same warm feeling that Mommy gave him.

When they were out of sight, he turned his feet to the trail from this end of town to Mommy's place. He wanted to show her his new things, and maybe take a nap.

But later, when the tide was low, he wanted to go down to the cave and pry mussels with his knife, and make a fire like he had seen his friends do. That would make Mommy very proud of him.

* * *

Chapter 26: Real Thieves

Ilika and his students had only walked a few hundred yards along the trail to the beach when three men stepped out from behind a bush and blocked the path. Dressed as deck hands or laborers, they wielded knives and clubs. More men, dressed and armed the same, appeared at the sides and behind them, bringing the total to at least eight.

Ilika's group instinctively huddled closer together. Tera gave her two-toned call loudly and tried to run, but Mati held the reins.

"Looks what we gots here!" one of the men at the front said. "The ones who've been spendin' money in town like it was beach sand!"

"Mati, dismount," Ilika said firmly.

"But Tera . . ."

"Now!"

Boro was near and lifted her over the bedroll. Tera bolted toward the beach almost before Mati could get her left foot out of the stirrup.

The men made way for the frightened donkey and laughed.

"We figures if you got so much money to spend, you've probably got lots more. And even if you don't got that much, the pretty girls'll be fun to play with, right guys?"

"Yeah!" several of them called, laughing and jeering.

"Boro, get Mati on the ground," Ilika ordered.

Mati was confused, but Boro acted, lowering her to the sand firmly.

"Ways I figures it, you boys got two choices. Drop yer bags and take off them nice clothes and walk away, or the birds can pick yer bones when we're done with you."

"Everyone down on the ground!" Ilika yelled as he tapped a code into his bracelet. A strange high-pitched sound filled everyone's mind, students and thieves alike, while Ilika turned a complete circle, aiming his bracelet at those standing.

Ilika turned once more to make sure. All the thieves had crumpled to the sand and were completely still.

"Yes!" Miko cheered, raising both fists. "But you got Toli, too."

"Don't worry, he's just asleep."

Kibi jumped to her feet and wrapped her arms around Ilika.

"Can I get up now?" Mati asked.

"Yes. Everyone can get up," Ilika said over Kibi's shoulder. "Sata, walk with Mati. Boro, help me carry Toli. Everyone's going to wake up in about a quarter hour, and I want us . . . let me see . . ." He kissed Kibi, then extracted himself from her embrace. ". . . on that little hill by the beach."

"What about Tera?" Mati asked with concern while getting her feet back under her.

"I'm glad she ran," Ilika said softly. "She could have hurt someone as she fell."

"Don't worry, Mati, we'll find Tera," Rini said, touching her on the shoulder.

✳

Boro and Ilika carried their limp cargo as far as they could, then Ilika climbed onto the highest boulder as Toli and the thieves started waking up. He cupped his hands and projected his voice toward the thieves. "HAD ENOUGH?"

The men, still wondering what happened, could hardly get back to town fast enough. They knew sorcery when they saw it, and figured they were lucky to be alive.

When the others described to Toli what he had missed, he looked ashamed. Mati sat on a nearby rock and admitted that she too had been confused, worried about Tera, and hadn't responded to Ilika's commands very well.

As soon as Toli could stand, Ilika urged them all toward the beach to look for the donkey. Mati hobbled along as fast as she could with her crutch, worry written on her brow. The trail took them between grassy sand dunes and finally to the water's edge.

✳

If Tera had turned right, she could have run up the coast to her heart's content. But she had turned left, and the beach soon ended in a sand bar at the entrance to the cove. She had run as far as she could and then stopped. While she stood there, dealing with her fear as well as a donkey can, the tide continued to rise, and the sand bar was rapidly becoming an island.

Mati called.

Rini and Neti pleaded.

Miko and Boro yelled.

Tera stood where she was and called back with her unique voice.

Ilika, Boro, and Toli waded out to Tera's shrinking island. They talked to her, pulled her halter, and slapped her rump.

But wading through swirling water was just not something this donkey was ready to do. At least, not until some greater danger came along.

Ilika arranged for one. He explained to Boro and Toli that his bracelet could make a variety of sounds, and one was especially designed to scare off just about anything made of flesh and blood. They got Tera pointed toward the beach, then waded into the water as far behind her as possible. Ilika tapped in the code.

The roaring, snarling, snapping sound they all heard caused hearts to race and muscles to tense, but since no beast was visible anywhere, the students mastered themselves.

Tera did not have so much self-control. Mati wasn't sure her donkey even touched the water as she came flying back to the beach.

Tera ran back toward the road until she was tangled in bushes and face-to-face with a rocky hill. There she stood, eyes swirling with fear, head turning from side to side looking for the gigantic donkey-eating monster that must be close behind.

When the three rescuers returned to the beach, they collapsed onto the dry sand, unsure whether to laugh or cry.

* * *

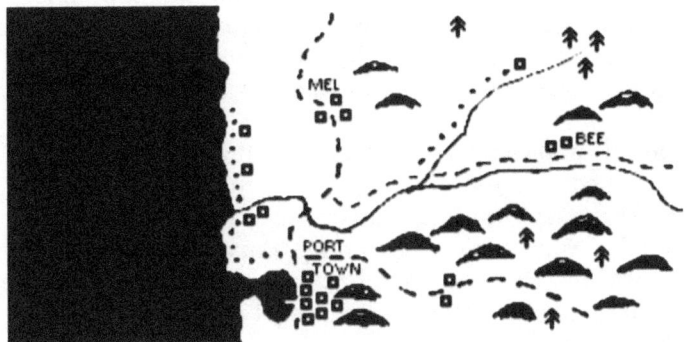

Chapter 27: The Edge of the Ocean

This part of the coast, Ilika and his students discovered, was much more populated than the rocky beach south of Port Town. Every time nature left a bit of land between the high-tide line and the cliffs, a fisherman's cottage nestled among the stunted trees. Occasionally, when the cliff was low and gentle, a crude stairway climbed the rocks to a simple dwelling at the top. Mati looked at those stairs and shook her head.

Almost without exception, the fisher folk were friendly, and the group took lunch at one cottage where the young wife, baby at her breast, had a big pot of fish stew always going on the stove. She was amazed and delighted to receive the silver piece Kibi handed her.

As they sat on the log seawall just below the cottage, frothy waves nearly splashing their boots, the students had questions about recent events.

"Ilika, what would happen to someone like Kit in your country?" Neti asked.

"As soon as anyone was aware of it, a companion would be assigned. That person would be with him while he dealt with his mother's death, and would help him make the transition to a new family. People foster each other's kids all the time. No one goes unloved or uncared for in my country."

"Wow. Where do these companions come from?" Sata asked.

"All citizens of my country are available for companion assignments. In the Transport Service we don't do a lot of it, because we're moving around all the time, but once I was called to spend a couple of weeks with a guy about my age who was having emotional problems. During that time, the healers figured out what was bothering him and found him a new home where he would be happy."

"Amazing . . ." Kibi said quietly.

As the tide went out, they continued their journey northward along the beach. A rickety wooden bridge spanned the mouth of a roaring river where it cut through the cliffs. Tera was nervous, but allowed Rini to lead her, both of them following Mati on her crutch. Once on solid ground again, Buna walked with Ilika, a mischievous smirk on her face.

"Let me see . . . your bracelet can make bright or dim light . . . feel horse vibrations . . . chime the hours . . . see when someone is coming . . . put people to sleep . . . and roar like a dragon. Anything else?"

Ilika only smiled.

"Can it make money? It seems like we never run out!"

He chuckled. "No, it can't make money, Buna. I brought thirty-two great gold pieces with me, and each one breaks down into so many copper and silver pieces that it just seems unlimited. My biggest expense so far has been six great gold for slaves."

"Slaves!" she blurted out with wide eyes. A moment later she relaxed and smiled. "Oh, yeah . . . us."

*

As the sun started descending toward the ocean, they came to a cottage and asked if they could camp above the high-tide line.

The old fisherman and his wife welcomed them, but were unable to offer a meal as they had next to nothing themselves. The man's hands were getting very stiff, he explained, and he was having trouble fishing.

Kibi immediately invited the old couple to join the group for dinner, and they gratefully accepted.

The students collected driftwood and pried mussels from the rocks, just as they had back at the cave. A few vegetables, some spices, chunks of bread, slices of cheese, and they were ready to share a feast.

The old couple wondered what brought such a group to the ocean so far from the nearest inn.

"Ilika's a ship's captain," Miko explained, "and we're his students. Some of us are going to be his crew."

"That reminds me," Mati said, looking at her stew, "I'm sorry for questioning your command this morning."

Toli looked at the ground. "Me too."

"Apologies accepted. What did you, or anyone, learn from it?"

"It's like what we talked about before," Boro began. "We can ask questions later, but when you give a command, it means *right now*."

The old fisherman and his wife ate their stew quietly.

"Boro is right," Ilika said, "but this is a little different. Mati thought she knew something that made the command seem wrong. She knew Ter was thinking of bolting, and knew that if she dismounted, she wouldn't be able to keep that from happening. Am I right, Mati?"

"Yep."

"What she didn't know, and I didn't have the time to tell her, was that I *wanted* Ter to bolt, considering what I had to do next."

Boro nodded. "I see."

"So what should we do in a case like that?" Rini asked.

"Right now, you know almost nothing about how the ship, and how my . . . um, tools . . . work, so you have to have lots of trust in me. However, in most cases I still want to know your thoughts and observations, whenever there is time. So you should carry out the command, and share your thoughts as soon as possible."

Rini nodded.

"When the five of you who become my crew know your jobs very well, this will change a little. It is possible for me to give a bad command. I'm human — I can make mistakes. If you're *very* sure something's wrong with my order, then it's your responsibility to delay carrying it out until I explain it. In an extreme situation, it's even your responsibility to refuse the order, maybe even remove me from command, by force if necessary."

They were all silent and thoughtful as his words lingered in the air.

"Sounds like you are training your students well," the old fisherman said. "My wife and I are going in now."

"Good night!"

When the couple had gone, Ilika brought up another subject. "Toli, you experienced something back there that none of the others have experienced. Can you describe it?"

"You mean what it felt like, or how embarrassed I was afterwards?"

Several people chuckled.

"Both."

"Everything just faded to gray and then black. I never even felt myself hit the ground. Next thing I knew, I was up in the rocks. Then I remembered what happened. I remembered standing there hearing what Ilika said, and thinking that I wanted to discuss it first."

Nearly everyone laughed. Ilika was grinning from ear to ear.

Boro said what others were thinking. "When eight men with knives want to rob us, kill us, or rape us, it's just not a good time for talking."

Toli squirmed. "I know that now. I'm really sorry."

"You paid the price," Ilika pointed out firmly. "But there's something I want all of you to remember. My bracelet can put people to sleep. What if the person is on a horse or donkey, or standing on the edge of a cliff?"

"They could get hurt," Mati said with big eyes.

"Yes. Even just standing, someone could hit their head on a rock and die. It's a defensive weapon, but it can be deadly."

✳

The following morning, the old fisherman went out in his little boat very early.

His wife ate breakfast with the group, then went to her garden to scratch at the ground and try to make something grow.

As the students were packing to leave, Ilika proposed an idea. They all checked to make sure they still had great and small gold pieces in their pouches, then smiled and nodded.

*

When the aging man returned with the rising tide, he had two small fish in his boat. His heart was heavy with worry, for this was one of the best times of the year for fishing in these waters. It took all his strength to pull the little boat back up the beach.

When he got to the old stump where he always tied the boat, there, on top of the stump, was a great gold piece gleaming in the sun.

He looked around. The travelers were gone, and his faithful wife was at work in the garden. His heart suddenly felt lighter than it had in years.

* * *

Chapter 28: In a Pinch

After putting several miles between themselves and Port Town, Ilika slowed the pace and left plenty of time each day for lessons. Fewer and fewer cottages lined the coast as they moved northward. The cliffs became higher and the beaches more rocky.

For the next three days, Ilika concentrated on writing lessons, first with one-inch letters, then half-inch, the smallest they could easily make with their thick pencils and inexperienced hands. As soon as they were doing well, he set them to copying passages of text from their story book. This they enjoyed, and would talk about the beloved scenes as they worked.

On the fourth day Ilika began slowly dictating simple sentences while they wrote, and the thorny issue of spelling reared its ugly head. He spelled difficult words for them, and as he did, he pushed their memories from two letters at a time, to three, to four, and finally to five. Miko, Buna, and Boro had trouble beyond three.

When not writing, they learned more formulas, starting with the perimeter, area, and volume of the geometric figures they already knew. Rini thought the mysterious number pi was pure magic and quickly memorized twenty-three places. The rest were satisfied with three or four.

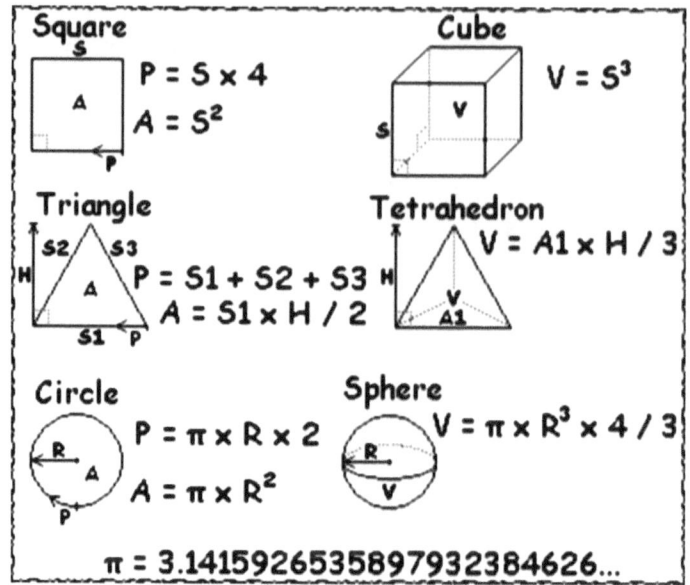

Square

$P = S \times 4$

$A = S^2$

Cube

$V = S^3$

Triangle

$P = S1 + S2 + S3$

$A = S1 \times H / 2$

Tetrahedron

$V = A1 \times H / 3$

Circle

$P = \pi \times R \times 2$

$A = \pi \times R^2$

Sphere

$V = \pi \times R^3 \times 4 / 3$

$\pi = 3.141592653589793238 4626...$

On the morning of the sixth day out from Port Town, they tried their hand at written composition for the first time. Ilika kept it simple — write about what you can see, hear, and smell right now.

As easy as the task sounded to them at first, they found it very difficult. They could talk about the things around them, but today that was not allowed. Instead they had to direct those thoughts into their hands, pencils, and papers.

Ilika smiled at the crude sentences he received.

As several hours remained before high tide, they continued their journey. As they walked, they exchanged elaborate sentences about their environment, with rich adjectives and adverbs, and wondered why they couldn't get those onto paper.

✳

With the arrival of early afternoon, and the day's high tide only another hour away, they all became a little worried. For the past hour the beach had been narrow and rocky, with no dry sand above the high-tide line. Ilika called a conference.

"If we dash back now, we can just make the last dry place before the tide gets too high."

"But it's two or three days back to the last place we could get up the cliff," Mati pointed out with frustration.

Ilika nodded. "Going forward is a risk. Are we all willing to take it?"

They looked at each other for a moment.

"Working on a ship will have risks all the time, right?" Boro asked pointedly.

Several nodded.

"Yes," Ilika confirmed, "but not risks walked into blindly or without need."
Thoughtful looks were exchanged.

"It's not *that* big a risk," Miko said with a wave of his hand. "I've seen lots
of places we could go above high tide. Not camping places, just little places."

Others agreed with nods.

"I think we should go forward," Kibi proposed, "unless anyone sees a big
danger."

Ilika looked around. No one spoke. "Okay, I accept Miko and Kibi's
proposal."

The group moved forward at their best speed, all eyes on the rocks and
cliff, looking for a bit of dry beach or cave.

The beach became narrower and the tide continued to rise. The cliff was
sheer and dangerous, offering no hope for a donkey or a crutch. Shallow
caves were common, all dripping wet and obviously pounded by waves at
high tide.

*

An hour later, though they hurried along as high up the beach as possible,
the rising tide lapped at their boots and hooves. Miko and Kibi looked
worried, and a little guilty.

They pressed on even as Tera became frightened and hard to control.
Ilika and Boro walked with her, one on each side with a hand on her halter,
urging her to keep moving through the surging tide.

Rini blinked after a spray of salt water drenched him, then glanced
around to get his bearings. The slender cleft in the face of the cliff was hard
to see, a narrow slit through the loose rocky dirt, with a hollow bowl behind
into which a small waterfall cascaded.

Standing in swirling water two feet deep, Ilika heard Rini's call above the
sound of the surf, then looked in the direction he was pointing. Before
making a decision, he took another moment to peer ahead along the beach,
and saw nothing but the rising surf starting to pound the cliff face in many
places.

"Boro, climb in there and take a look. Mati's next if Boro gives us a sign.
Everyone else, get ready as soon as Tera is clear. Kibi, keep an eye on
everyone."

No one proposed any sort of discussion or delay.

Boro thrust himself through the cleft. His eyes darted about, taking in the
small pool at the bottom and several natural ledges in the rocky soil above. A
wide shelf on the left, just a couple of feet above the pool, looked accessible to
a determined donkey.

"MATI, DISMOUNT!" Boro yelled as he came back through. "It's not wide
enough for your legs!"

Ilika grabbed her waist and lifted her off, then Sata waded close and put
the crutch into her hand.

Boro grabbed the donkey's halter.

"GO, TERA!" Mati commanded with her firmest do-or-die voice.

With the angry ocean behind, Tera went willingly. Her ribs scraped the stony soil on both sides of the cleft, but between the ocean pushing and Boro pulling, she didn't stop to notice.

Ilika helped Mati through the cleft and onto the shelf with Boro and the donkey, then turned to help the others. One by one they climbed through the cleft and found places to sit on the sides of the bowl.

Kibi came last out of the swirling water, by that time up to her waist. Ilika took her hand and pulled her up, then gave her hand an extra squeeze of gratitude.

Finally he was able to look around. The donkey stood on the widest ledge, with Boro and Mati pouring a constant stream of reassuring words into her long ears. Sata and Rini were sitting together on a small ledge, and Neti and Buna shared a large rock. Everyone else perched on tiny ledges wherever they could.

For a few minutes, all was calm, and the walls of the cleft muffled the roar of the ocean. The students looked at each other. Rini cracked a smile, and Buna joined him. Neti started giggling. Toli laughed out loud. Soon almost everyone was either laughing or smiling.

Ilika chuckled, but noticed that Miko wasn't finding anything funny in the situation.

As soon as the tide rose a little higher and found its way through the cleft, the laughter quickly came to an end. The narrow slot caused each wave to speed up, smash into the far wall of the little bowl, and splash several feet straight into the air. As the tide deepened, each wave shot higher and higher, and soon everyone was drenched again and again.

"Tera's going crazy!" Boro shouted, barely able to keep hold of the halter. "I need more help over here!"

Sata, on the opposite side, looked at the water, only two or three feet deep in the bowl, maybe four when a wave came in. She took a deep breath, waited for a wave to pass, and let herself slide to the bottom of the waterfall bowl.

She stood in the icy cold, churning water for a moment with a smile on her face, then pulled herself onto the donkey's ledge. Exchanging glances with Boro, she used her body to shield Tera's head from the spray on the side Boro and Mati couldn't reach.

Ilika saw all this and smiled to himself.

"MIKO! What are you doing?" Neti screamed.

Everyone jerked their heads in his direction and saw him clawing his way upward from his perch.

"I'm getting out of here!" Miko yelled in full panic. "I hate this place!"

The wall was, in a pinch, climbable, but Miko was causing loose dirt and rocks to rain down, some of them hitting Rini. Neti's face was filled with worry and deep disappointment.

Suddenly Miko's handholds and footholds all gave way at once, and he made a pathetic wailing sound as he slid to the bottom of the bowl.

Ilika jumped into the water, and a second later a wave filled the bowl with spray. Ilika wrapped his arms around the crying, shaking youth and braced his feet against the undertow.

The two stood together in the surging water, braced against the waves by Ilika's firm grip, frozen in place by Miko's panic.

* * *

Chapter 29: What Comes In Must Go Out

Long minutes passed as Ilika stood with his arms around Miko in the bottom of the waterfall bowl at high tide. Occasionally the others said reassuring things, or offered to hand them anything they needed.

Eventually the waves became smaller, and with their waning power, the spray ceased.

Not too long after that, the tide finally retreated from the little bowl.

Miko made some attempt to collect himself. His arms were scraped and his face scratched, but luckily his hardened blisters had not been torn open. The saddest sight to behold was the shame clearly visible in his eyes and shoulders.

As soon as the top of the beach was free of water, Ilika guided Miko down through the cleft. Boro, Sata, and Mati coaxed Tera to come next, and the rest followed after.

The sun was nearing the western horizon. Kibi, crouching in the wet sand, opened her pack and cut big slices of cheese for everyone.

Neti, a resolute look on her face, got out pieces of dried fruit, but made no move to comfort Miko. Ilika stayed with him, looking at his scrapes and bruises.

"Even though we've just been through . . . you call it Hell, I believe . . . we should go on," Ilika asserted. "It will be much easier to find a good campsite if we do it before dark."

Everyone agreed as the sun touched the horizon.

"Toli, would you lead at a fast pace, please? Everyone, eyes open for dry caves."

Toli began striding along the beach proudly.

For a few minutes, Miko found himself walking alone, head bowed. Eventually Neti slowed down so he could catch up, but she didn't yet have any words to share.

The shore continued to offer nothing dry and accessible above high tide for about another mile. Suddenly they came to a cape jutting into the open ocean, and in the fading light saw a huge bay several miles across in front of them.

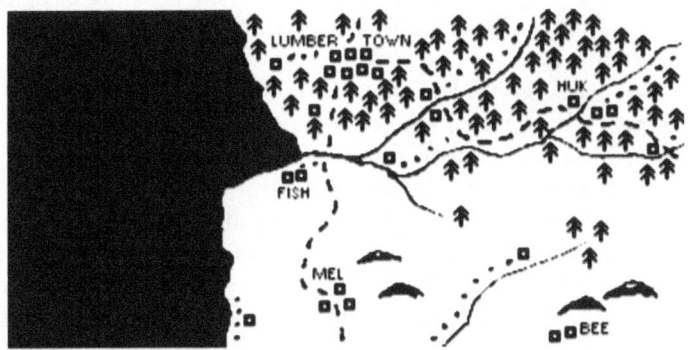

Ilika got out the map, then smiled.

"Looks like the cliffs come down quickly," Rini said, scanning with his eagle eyes. "The beach looks wide too — should be good camping."

"Hurray!" everyone cheered who still had a little energy. Miko tried to smile.

Ilika looked out at the dimming sunset colors over the dark water. "This is where we say good-bye to the open ocean, with all its glory, and all its fury."

"It's given us a lot," Kibi said with a far-away look in her eyes. "Mussels, clams, our friend Kit . . ."

Sata took a deep breath. "It's taught us a lot, too . . . about standing on our own two feet."

Miko looked at the sand.

"I'll miss it," Rini said with a hint of sadness. "It's big and beautiful."

"Let's find a camp before dark," Ilika urged. "The next high tide is early tomorrow morning, and I want to sleep in."

"Yeah!" Toli agreed, and led them along the wide beach.

A good campsite, in the dunes above the beach, was easy to find in the twilight. Even though clothes and boots were completely soaked, most of their blankets had remained dry. They sat around the campfire like zombies, then fell into their bedrolls with little conversation.

Everyone slept so long the following morning that Tera made squeaking noises of concern. Eventually her people started rising and staggering into the nearby trees.

Lunch was their first meal of the day, and Ilika declared two layover days to dry everything and recover from their recent ordeal. Kibi put ointment on Miko's scrapes, but little sympathy came from anyone.

Once the afternoon sun began to warm them, Ilika got out pencils and paper, avoiding some sheets that needed drying. "An experience like we just had is similar to things that can happen on a ship. Sometimes there's no perfect choice, so we do the best we can, then take a break to rest and learn from what happened.

"One thing that helps people deal with narrow escapes is to talk about them. Another is to write. We will do both, but since you're learning to write, we'll start there."

He passed out the materials.

"Just as with verbal reporting, writing about an event is most useful if you focus on yourself. Let other people deal with their own weaknesses."

All afternoon they wrote. When their cramping hands could write no more, they took breaks to turn wet clothes or gather firewood, then returned to writing, all struggling to get their thoughts and feelings onto paper.

Once their brains were completely fried by the effort, they went down to the water and dug up huge clams, several times larger than those on the ocean beach.

After dinner they read their writings to each other. Boro and Toli shared accounts that were mostly factual. Kibi, Mati, and Buna had stories full of personal feelings and concerns for unnamed others. Sata wrote about her new relationship with the forces of nature she once thought were evil. Rini was in a class by himself, seeing the joyous dance of the waves and the spray, and suspecting the presence of unseen spirits, gathered as if for a party.

Miko and Neti both shared their dark writings with difficulty. Miko was confused and tormented by his efforts to make his life go in one direction, only to find that the more he tried, the further from his goals he seemed to be. Neti was distressed that all the love she gave did not seem to be enough. It was painful for both of them, but after reading their papers to the group, they were once again in each other's arms, sharing tears and apologies.

The others had many things to discuss late into the evening. With the issue of Miko's panic out in the open, other thoughts could be shared. Mati wondered aloud how her beloved donkey would have survived without the help of Boro and Sata.

Ilika shared his writing last, done as if reporting the event to his commander. It contained the factual events, his feelings and fears, and some thoughts about possible spiritual influences.

"Is it really okay to put ghost and fairy stuff in a report to a commander?" Boro asked with wide eyes of disbelief.

"Where I come from, it is."

✴

On the second day in the beach dunes by the large bay, with their clothes and boots quickly drying, the entire group felt much more alive.

Ilika began teaching the finer points of writing. The difference between the past tenses gave most of them trouble, but Sata and Kibi once again caught on quickly.

> **Simple:**
>   Tera ate grass.
> **Progressive:**
>   Tera was eating grass.
> **Present perfect:**
>   Tera has eaten grass.
> **Past perfect:**
>   Tera had eaten grass.

"If we're talking about some time in the past," Kibi began, pointing over her shoulder, "and at that time Tera had already eaten grass sometime before *that*," she continued, fingers getting tangled up, "then we use the past perfect. Right, Ilika?"

He smiled and nodded.

＊

The following morning, the nine students and their teacher walked the last few miles along the wide beach to the innermost part of the bay. A small village allowed them to take an early lunch of fish stew and bread, and then buy dried fish, hard crackers, and soft goat cheese.

The local people were surprised the travelers had come from the direction they did, knowing the dangers of the beach just south of the cape. The students nodded and grinned knowingly.

Tera climbed quickly and happily up the winding road from the beach. The rest had mixed feelings as they turned and looked out over the sparkling bay for the last time.

＊ ＊ ＊

Chapter 30: Ancient Beings of Light

The main road from Port Town to Lumber Town snaked its way out of higher hills in the south, met the road from the village of Fish, then crossed the river on an old bridge of crumbling stone. Though summer was at hand in the lowlands, the travelers could see on their map that the swift muddy water came directly from the mountains, still white with snow.

Within sight of the bridge, the road disappeared into the dark evergreen forest that cloaked the lower slopes of the mountains and the northwestern corner of the kingdom.

Even though the ocean had given them a good supply of mussels and clams, little else along the beach had been edible. As they lingered on the road just outside the eaves of the forest, berries of several kinds dangled within easy reach. Neti, in a burst of sympathy, handed Miko one dark, sweet, juicy berry, but made sure his bowl was mostly filled with small, sour, green ones.

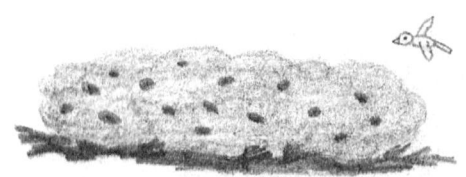

The group had only been in the area for a few minutes when Ilika's bracelet chimed its warning tone and they scrambled deeper into the bushes. Five soldiers on horseback galloped by, heading north toward Lumber Town.

When the group retook the road and entered the forest, none could resist looking straight up at the towering giant trunks all around them. At first the trees were only about a hundred feet tall, and some light slipped in from the edge of the forest. Before long, the only light was filtering down from the tops of the trees, somewhere in the dizzying heights two hundred feet or more above their heads.

They knew from the map that this part of the forest formed a triangle bounded by the southern edge of the forest and two of the roads to Lumber Town. Ilika proposed they go cross-country, as he wanted to give the soldiers plenty of time to do their business in town and hopefully depart. Everyone agreed.

So little sunlight penetrated the green canopy that almost no undergrowth shared the forest floor with the huge trunks. The going, therefore, was easy, and the few bushes they passed bore tasty red berries. Even Tera seemed comfortable in the new environment, finding plenty of tender leaves and a little grass.

Miko and Toli had been on work crews in the forest, carrying tools, food, and water for loggers. The rest admitted they had no idea such trees existed.

mireille Powers

"These trees are hundreds, maybe a thousand years old," Ilika began to teach as they walked. "I don't know if there are any in your kingdom, but the oldest living beings in the world are trees almost ten thousand years old."

Kibi frowned. "It seems wrong to cut them down."

"In my country, large or very old trees have more rights than slaves in your kingdom."

"Now I *know* I'm going to your country," Kibi announced, "even if I have to walk the whole way."

Ilika smiled. "I haven't explained photosynthesis yet, have I?"

Their blank faces answered his question.

"Plants are the original magicians. They can do something that no animal can do, including people. They can make food out of sunshine."

Several mouths opened in surprise. Rini looked fascinated, but not surprised.

Ilika continued. "Most plants need to put roots into the ground so they can also get to rocks and water, but some just need air. It's the green stuff in the leaves that does the magic, a complex, wonderful organic molecule, with a hundred and thirty-six atoms, called chlorophyll."

"Can you draw it for us?" Toli asked with excitement.

Ilika thought about the request. "It would take a long time, and not really do you any good. It's mostly carbon, hydrogen, oxygen, and nitrogen, like other organic molecules, plus one little atom of magnesium."

"Isn't that a metal?" Sata asked.

"Yes. Remember what makes your blood red?"

Her face twisted as she tried to remember.

"Iron," Boro said after Sata shook her head in surrender.

"Yes, another metal. In the process of photosynthesis, plants leave behind millions of different organic molecules that only they can create. That's why most medicines come from plants, and that's how animals live, by eating plants. No animal, anywhere, including people, can live without plants to eat."

"But what about people who eat nothing but meat?" Miko asked.

"What do the animals eat who provide the meat?"

Miko slowly nodded.

"Any food chain can be traced back to plants. Animals *cannot* make food from rocks, water, and sunshine, like plants can. Entire kingdoms of people have died because they cut down all their forests, and their lands became deserts with almost no life."

"Like the desert east of our kingdom?" Kibi asked, remembering the map.

"That one's natural, caused by the hills and mountains of your kingdom catching the rain. We'll see it after crossing the mountains."

Kibi's eyes sparkled at the prospect.

"A man-made desert is much uglier."

Her eyes lost their sparkle.

＊

They walked for another hour, then made an early camp on a gentle rise of land, clear of overhanging tree branches, and soft with needles. A trickle of a stream, just a short walk down the hill, provided water and rocks for a campfire circle. Parties spread out in twos and threes for firewood, berries, fresh greens, and to their delight, mushrooms in the moist places near the stream. Toli took the shovel, but had no luck finding edible roots, so he brought back some firewood.

All of them, as they worked or played, often stopped to look up at the giant trees all around. Sometimes they became dizzy and found themselves falling to the ground, or being caught by a friend.

Once they all gathered back at the camp, Ilika introduced their next topic of study. "You are ready to learn a new kind of number system for the measurement and calculation of angles. This will give you the basic tools you need for navigation."

As they cooked dinner, Ilika laid out a large compass rose on the ground with their campfire in the center, true north correctly placed, pine cones every ten degrees, and rocks every forty-five. When everyone had eaten, they followed him around, discussed the major divisions of the compass, and learned the difference between the direction a ship was pointing, the direction it was going because of currents and winds, and the direction they might be looking.

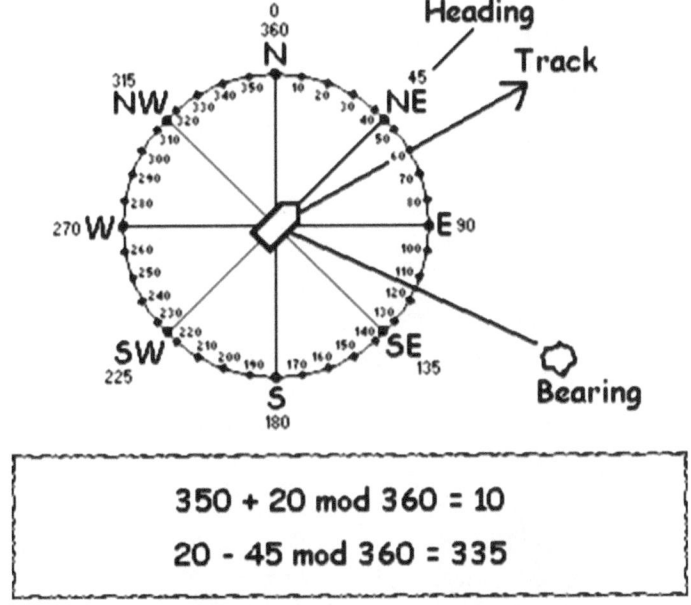

$$350 + 20 \bmod 360 = 10$$

$$20 - 45 \bmod 360 = 335$$

Faces aglow from learning actual seafaring skills, they absorbed modulus arithmetic in mere minutes, allowing them to pass over due north in either direction.

As evening descended upon the forest, they gathered back at the fire, and with many drawings, Ilika described how the compass was projected onto the planet from two different directions, allowing any point on the globe to be identified with numbers.

The longitude lines, with the compass projected down from the poles, were fairly easy for them to grasp. The latitude lines, projected onto a constantly moving surface, gave a little more trouble.

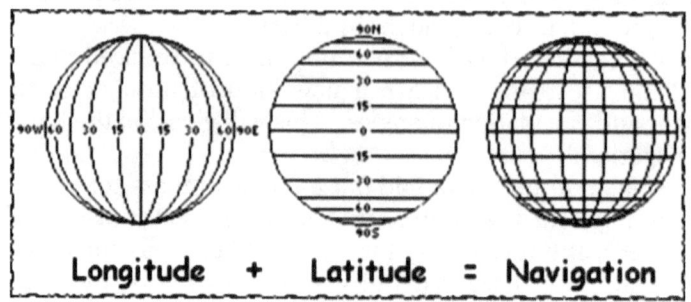

Longitude + Latitude = Navigation

The lesson over, they became quiet and thoughtful. Ilika started massaging Kibi's shoulders, and others got out combs or ointment. Bowls of berries came around, and everyone started feeling that their visit to the great forest was going to be wonderfully pleasant and uneventful.

✳ ✳ ✳

Chapter 31: Gleaming Eyes in the Dark

At least, they thought their visit to the great forest was going to be uneventful — until Rini spoke.

"We're being watched."

"Report," Ilika said in a soft voice.

"It comes and goes, about dog size. Sometimes on one side, sometimes another. Never gets close enough to see more than gleaming eyes, about fifty feet away."

"I think I've seen it," Buna whispered.

"This is a forest," Boro pointed out. "We're the visitors."

"Yes," Ilika agreed. "Looks like we need to set a watch. Wood supply?"

They looked, and agreed it was enough for the night.

"Magic bracelet to chime the hours?" Buna inquired with a smirk.

Ilika smiled. "I'll get it ready now."

Sata helped Mati tie the donkey to a little tree within the light of the campfire. Boro collected a small pile of fist-size rocks.

*

When Buna shook Boro awake for his watch, dawn light was already in the sky. She whispered that the watcher had disappeared at first light, but she had caught a glimpse of its shape and size, too small to be a wolf.

Boro nodded as he put up his hood against the cool morning air. As Buna disappeared into her bedroll, he strolled around the perimeter of the campsite, rock in hand, but saw nothing.

As soon as Kibi awoke in the morning light, she and Boro went to look for tracks, especially on the soft ground near the stream. They soon found what they were looking for, and both spoke the same word at once.

"Fox."

*

At breakfast, Neti proposed they try to make friends with the fox, and give it something to eat from the stew pot each night. The other students liked the idea, but Boro felt a watch was still needed.

Ilika remained neutral about the idea, and plunged ahead into the measurement of angles, especially as they applied to common shapes.

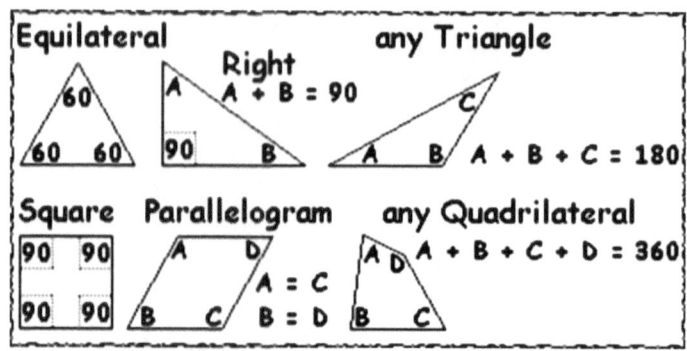

During mid-day free time, when not gazing up at the towering trees, those who were weak at math made sure they reviewed with someone who was stronger. Buna was always mixing up equilateral and right triangles, and Toli tried hard to straighten her out. Kibi and Mati wouldn't let Rini out of their sight until they had the difference between heading, track, and bearing firmly in mind. None of them wanted to let a bit of it slip past them if it applied to navigation.

* * *

"I was stopped by the fiery breath of the dragon," Ilika read from his sheet of paper that afternoon. "See how the passive voice gives power to the dragon, and makes the fact that I stopped seem unavoidable, instead of a choice I made?"

Most of them nodded.

"You try it. First an active verb, then passive."

They started writing. After a minute, Mati burst out laughing. All eyes turned to her.

"Please, share!" Ilika begged with a grin.

She cleared her throat. "I ate the tart. I was eaten by the ..." She doubled up with hysterical laughter.

Ilika smiled.

Sata's hand shot up. "The tart was eaten ... when I smelled its delicious fruit filling!"

"That works a little better. But thank you for sharing the funny one, Mati."

After another hour, they were getting the idea, and their sentences became much more interesting. Ilika ended by having them write a paragraph about something they saw, heard, or felt during their watch shift the night before. Most of them wrote about the gleaming fox eyes that had observed them from the darkness.

That evening, a little way from camp, Ilika came upon Miko looking at his scabby knees, crying softly from the burning itch and the shame. Ilika sat quietly with the lad for a few minutes, until Neti arrived with ointment and a bowl of sour berries.

Ilika didn't see any signs of infection, but kept that fact to himself.

※

The students and their teacher stayed at that campsite for two more days, taking their first steps into the world of trigonometry. Ilika started with the simplest and most useful function, the tangent of forty-five degrees. As soon as they discovered that a triangle made from paper would allow them to pace off the heights of the trees, no bush or tree anywhere near the camp went unmeasured.

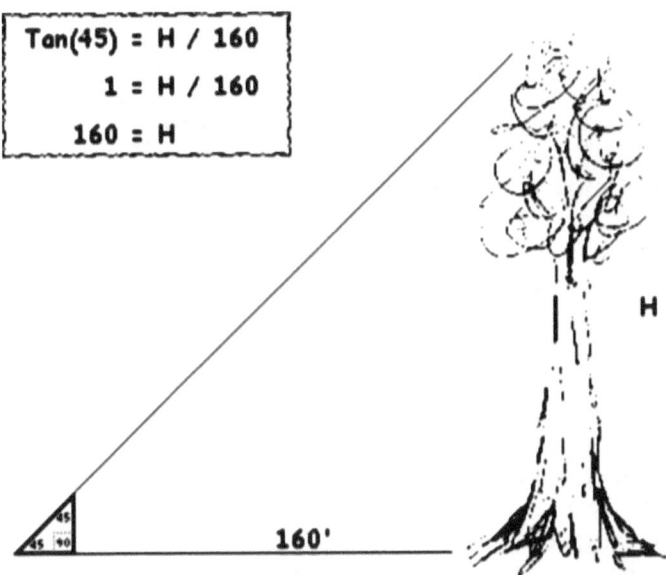

$$Tan(45) = H / 160$$
$$1 = H / 160$$
$$160 = H$$

160'

H

In the afternoons, Ilika taught more of the tricks of writing, starting with personification, then moving into exaggeration and irony. Kibi and Sata were in their favorite element, and Mati and Rini also enjoyed themselves. Boro, Neti, and Buna tried hard, but it didn't come easily. Miko and Toli would rather collect firewood.

Also during those two days, everyone became excited about the possibility of taming the fox. They all agreed not to throw rocks at it as long as it wasn't hurting them, and they left a portion of their stew on a piece of bark each night.

The fox never ate the stew, which by morning was covered with ants. On the second morning, it waited through dawn and disappeared just before sunrise. On the morning of their departure, it sat in plain sight and watched them as they ate breakfast.

※   ※   ※

Chapter 32: Trial by Teeth

"I was awakened by a mischievous dream!" Kibi announced as they sat around the unlit campfire circle eating crackers and dried fruit. "But . . . I can't remember it."

"Anyway, nice sentence!" Ilika declared. "Passive voice and implicit personification."

Sata joined in the game. "I dreamed that Death came out of the ocean, and flowers bloomed everywhere He went."

"Wow! Explicit personification and irony, not to mention some interesting spiritual concepts."

The rest joined in the process, with various degrees of success.

"I'm so hungry, I could eat a bear!" Miko said with a grin.

"Excellent exaggeration for emphasis, Miko."

When the language game was over, Sata brought up the concern they all shared. "What are we going to do about the fox?"

Ilika glanced at the beautiful creature, still sitting beside a tall tree, both fur and bark of a similar reddish-brown. "Are you sure we need to *do* anything?"

"Well," Boro began, "since we offered it food, even though it didn't like our stew, it's gotten more friendly . . ."

"So we have to decide if we want to invite it to come with us . . ." Sata continued.

"And," Mati jumped in, "we have to think about what to do when we go into a town."

"Foxes eat meat," Neti explained, "and all we've had were fish and mushrooms and things like that."

Ilika looked thoughtful. "So it would probably want to hunt its own food. Do any of you object to inviting it to come with us?"

They all shook their heads.

"Do any of you object to *forcing* it to come with us?"

They all slowly nodded.

"I feel the same as you. Invite, yes. Force, no. Same deal we offered Kit. I can't imagine it wanting to go anywhere near a town."

"I agree," Kibi said. "If it did come with us, we'd have to go around the towns, and send small groups in for shopping, like we did at Port Town."

*

By mid-morning they had refreshed themselves at the stream, packed everything, and were ready to go. The fox continued to sit about fifty feet from the camp, watching every movement with keen eyes.

Mati mounted her faithful donkey. Almost everyone spoke to the fox in a friendly voice, inviting it to join them on their journey. Only Toli and Miko were too embarrassed to add their voices to the invitation, but they smiled.

The group began walking as close to northward as the terrain allowed, Mati and Toli at the front, the rest spread out in a loose line behind. Those at the rear soon passed word up that the fox was indeed following, about a hundred feet back. This, combined with the good weather and the easy traveling among the towering trees, put them all in a happy and carefree mood.

*

The fox had never seen people like these before. They didn't appear to be in the forest to cut down trees or trap animals, like all other humans in her experience. They ate differently too, with not a whiff of the usual burnt meat or rotten fruit juice. They were interesting, and she remained curious enough to follow at a safe distance.

*

By now, Miko had noticed that his scrapes and scratches, though still itching, were starting to heal, and he too was happy. Neti still handed him sour berries whenever she found them, and he grumbled a little, but then smiled and kissed her . . . and ate the berries.

The great forest was proving to be the safest, most gentle place they had yet visited in their travels, perhaps in their entire lives, with no one to steal from them or arrest them, nothing to burn them, and no high tide. Even the creatures of the forest seemed merely curious.

With Miko and Neti bringing up the rear, those in the middle of the line of walkers began to frolic, play little games of tag, speak in passive voice, or personify the most unlikely things, including some that Tera left behind on the ground. Peals of laughter repeatedly echoed through the trees.

The forest floor gently rose and fell as they moved north, and sometimes the lead pair would be out of sight for a moment. As they played and joked with each other, those in the middle tended to dally, or even stop to share something funny. No one noticed when the fox gave a little yip and disappeared.

Rini's full attention was suddenly captured by the sight of Toli running back over the next rise and cowering behind a big log, gasping for breath.

Rini couldn't see Mati. His heart started pounding as he dropped his bedroll, slipped off his saddlebags, and ran forward.

*

None of those in the lead were prepared for the huge snarling timber wolf, easily half the size of a donkey, that sprang into their path. Tera leapt back a yard when the beast appeared, then tried to turn and run for her life. Mati immediately pulled the reins tight and commanded her to stop and stay.

As soon as Rini could see over the rise, he veered to the nearest tree and ripped a low branch from the trunk with one determined heave.

After fighting her own panic for a moment, words came to Mati, words spoken by her teacher weeks before. *Both your lives may depend on YOU keeping your wits . . . maybe running . . . maybe calling for help . . . maybe attacking the predator.*

Somehow she knew that turning her back on the wolf was not an option. The present stalemate existed because an even larger creature was facing the wolf, without showing fear.

Mati opened her mouth to call for help, then closed it, remembering that she was over a hill from the others. She had no idea where Toli had gone.

Growling and showing huge yellow teeth, the wolf took a measured step forward with its ears laid back.

Suddenly Rini appeared at Tera's side, the jagged end of his broken branch thrusting forward.

Mati knitted her brow and urged Tera forward a step.

Tera was halfway between courage and terror, her lungs heaving with deep, forceful breaths, when she felt the command to move forward. On shaking legs she took a step, then pawed the air with one front foot and opened her mouth, letting all her teeth show.

*

This was what the wolf hated. He knew very well that a pack had great power. He knew because he was once part of a pack, and they always had plenty to eat. Then he accidentally broke some silly taboo and the alpha female chased him away. Now he was alone, and could hardly find anything to eat. For a moment, when the tall human ran away, the wolf thought he might have an easy meal, maybe even a feast if he could bring down the donkey.

Now there were two of them again, and this male, while small, showed no sign of running. Even the stupid donkey was getting courageous, and the wolf glimpsed other humans running up behind. It was now or never.

The desperate wolf leapt toward the female on the donkey.

About three-quarters of the way to the prize, something caught him in the shoulder and sent him flying off to the side.

The wolf knew this hunt was over, and fully intended to run as soon as he landed, but suddenly a high-pitched sound pierced every muscle in his body. A heartbeat later, everything was dark.

* * *

Chapter 33: Different Strokes

Rini was instantly over the wolf, broken end of his branch poised and ready to spear the animal, his face red and his chest heaving. But he went no further.

Boro had Mati off the donkey a moment later and Sata joined them. Mati clung to Sata with one shaking hand, but continued stroking Tera with her other hand while reassuring the donkey that it was over and they were safe.

Neti and Buna also surrounded donkey and rider with comforting words and caresses.

Ilika stood back, taking in the entire situation, looking for any dangers they had missed, and making sure all needs were covered. He noticed Rini's decision to not harm the sleeping animal.

Kibi went to the wolf where Rini continued to stand guard. She could see the large animal's bony ribcage rising and falling slowly. She knelt down and felt his legs to see if any had broken when he landed. "He's fast asleep, Rini."

Rini waited a moment more, then thrust the branch away into the woods, revealing blood on his hands and arms.

"How long do we have, Ilika?" Kibi asked.

"About a quarter hour, maybe a little more."

"Everybody! I want all the dried fish we have left!" Kibi yelled.

"I have two!" Neti called.

"Two ... or three ... in my b-bags," Mati said with a weak, shaky voice.

Boro started digging into Tera's saddlebags.

"Everyone else, head up the next rise, meet just beyond it!" Ilika ordered.

At that moment Miko arrived carrying Rini's things. Toli, at his side, looked quite embarrassed. "Mati ... I'm so sorry ..." Toli squeaked in a voice close to tears.

Mati gave him a blank look, nodded slightly, then let Boro help her remount.

Buna noticed that Toli felt terrible and needed comforting. Instead, she joined Kibi and stroked the fur of the sleeping wolf before heading up the hill.

Kibi received all the dried fish the others could find, placed it near the sleeping creature, and backed away.

"Good thinking, Kibi," Ilika said. "Please go look at Rini. I'll bring up the rear."

Kibi nodded and dashed up the line of walkers to see how badly Rini was bleeding.

Ilika waited until everyone else was moving, then kept one eye over his shoulder as he put distance between himself and the sleeping timber wolf.

✳

The fox was fascinated. These were definitely strange humans. They had been confronted by the wolf, who was hungrier than ever before, and had somehow put him to sleep. But the strange part was, they didn't hurt him, but instead left a pile of food! It was something the fox would expect another wolf to do, but had no idea humans were capable of such compassion. The fox watched from a good distance as the humans disappeared over the next hill.

Soon the wolf started waking up. At first he was confused and frightened, and wanted to get away. Then he smelled the fish, and it was more food than he had seen in the last month. He was unwilling to leave it behind.

But he felt vulnerable, with some of his muscles still a little numb, and his mind not yet fully awake. He circled, trying to get his weak body to respond while protecting the pile of food.

He could smell the fox and kept an eye on that direction. No one was going to touch his food — it was all that stood between him and starvation.

He could also smell which direction the humans had gone. They were a strong pack, and the wolf had no intention of following them, especially in his weak condition.

The fox watched as the wolf finally settled down to his meal. Then, giving him a wide berth, she headed off into the woods to see what the strange humans would do next.

✳

The students and their teacher sat on the ground in a tight circle on the top of a rise more than a mile away.

Miko swallowed, noticing Rini's calmness while ointment was applied to his hands and arms where the rough bark had cut and scraped him.

Ilika explained that he couldn't use his bracelet at first without dropping Mati and Tera. It was Rini's blow that knocked the wolf into the clear.

Several of the students commented that sparing the wolf, then feeding him, was not what most people would have done.

"Never, ever, limit yourselves to what other people would do," Ilika advised. "Cruelty is cruelty, and it doesn't matter how many people do it. Boro said it well a few days ago — we are the visitors here. This forest is the wolf's home, he was alone and very hungry. We can't blame him for trying to eat some meat that came walking by."

Buna snickered. "You mean us?"

Ilika smiled. "By feeding him, we reduced the chance of him following us and trying again, and we did a kindness to a fellow creature. Cruelty and revenge have no place in the Transport Service."

A thoughtful silence lingered for a minute.

"I . . ." Toli started, but became choked on his own shame and couldn't go on.

Mati scooted over next to him and took his shaking hand. "I know what it's like to be scared. I used to be scared all the time. I could never get away from anyone or anything that was hurting me. I only quit being scared when I learned to ride Tera, and Ilika made it clear that only strong people who can handle their fears can be on his crew."

"I . . . think I blew my chances," Toli muttered, looking at the ground.

"Maybe," Ilika replied firmly. "It will depend on what you do with this experience, and the experiences you have during the next few months. I'm not going to make any decisions until the end."

Toli nodded and dropped his eyes back to the ground.

Buna grinned — from the opposite side of the circle.

✳ ✳ ✳

Chapter 34: Lumber Town

After witnessing the humans put an animal to sleep, the fox followed at a greater distance and did not allow herself to be seen again. As the group approached the town, they believed the fox was gone for good. Some of them turned and said good-bye out loud just in case it could hear them.

✳

The day became quite warm as Ilika and Buna picked their way downhill through the trees. Their cross-country direction first joined an animal track, which then crossed a path, which finally met a cart road.

The dusty town of wooden buildings nestled in a ravine completely surrounded by the great forest. Trees marched right down to the back doors of the houses and shops. A creek tumbled through the town, flowing westward to the ocean, sometimes behind the buildings on one side of the ravine, sometimes the other side, and sometimes right beside the main road, requiring little bridges to get to the shops.

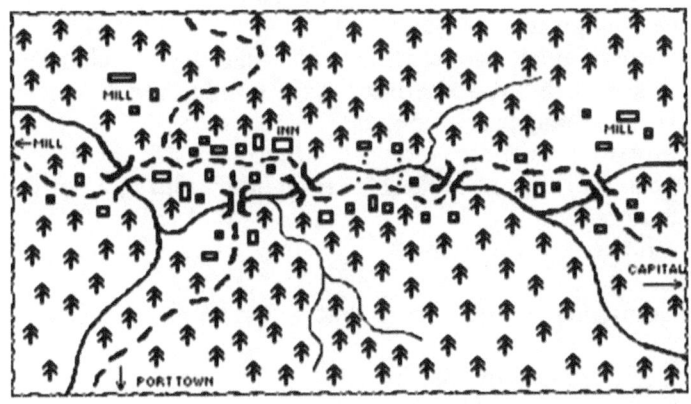

Many of the buildings boasted sturdy logs and shake roofs, but the poorer houses were nothing but rough, weathered boards. Buna spotted the large inn, on the north side of the ravine, and Ilika noticed the stables right next door. The money changer was just down the road, as well as the baker, fish seller, produce cart, cheese maker, and dry goods store. At least three mills surrounded the town, with the constant sound of saws going back and forth. No visible presence of guards or priests was to be seen anywhere. Ilika and Buna both smiled.

Before returning to their companions, the scouts purchased a fresh loaf and a crock of soft cheese.

✳

"I think our best defense against those who would like to arrest me for my evil deeds . . ." Ilika paused to let the laughter die down. ". . . is to continue to avoid the public appearance of a large group. So we'll make three small groups. We can all get together in our rooms at the inn, but the three groups will pretend to not know each other in the common room and in public."

"You think they're still looking for you?" Toli asked.

"I can't think of any way to find out . . . except the hard way. But if we all keep our ears open, maybe we'll learn something."

Several nodded agreement.

"Let me see . . . Buna, Mati, and Rini are with me. Miko and Neti are with Kibi. Toli and Sata are with Boro."

Kibi smiled at Boro, who had become the trusted third leader of the group.

"I have a little question," Sata said hesitantly.

Ilika gave her his attention.

"In your country . . . or on Transport Service ships . . . do you ever have . . . birthday parties?"

Ilika smiled. "Is someone I know turning eleven?"

"Um . . . yeah . . . a few days ago . . . but it didn't seem like a good time to say anything."

Ilika started clapping and everyone joined him.

Sata looked delightfully embarrassed.

"In my country, most people choose a special day to celebrate their life. Sometimes it's a birthday, sometimes it's a holiday that's special to them. Shall we have a birthday party for Sata?"

"Yeah!" everyone cheered.

"But if we do that, I want to do it for everyone. Who's had birthdays since we've been together?"

Buna was obviously squirming.

"Buna?"

"Mine's sometime in the spring, but I don't know exactly when. I'm fifteen now."

Everyone clapped and she blushed.

No one else volunteered, so Ilika asked each. Kibi would turn seventeen in early fall. Rini and Neti were born in the winter. The rest had no idea.

"Okay, we'll have parties for Sata, Buna, and . . . Miko while we're here, and Kibi and someone else when we get to Cattle Town in the northeastern part of the kingdom. What are your traditions for a birthday party?"

None of them, other than Sata, had the slightest idea.

"Um . . . some good food," she began, "with dessert of course, and the person gets little gifts from everyone!"

Kibi smiled. "So I need to shop for three birthday gifts!"

"Remember to keep them small . . . or edible," Ilika reminded them.

＊

The stable master was not used to feeding a donkey as well as he would a high-ranking soldier's horse, but the crippled girl was very clear that *this* donkey got grain and molasses every day, and she had the copper to back it up.

"She's a fine looking animal," he said to make conversation. "Not too stubborn?"

"She helped me fend off a timber wolf this morning," Mati said with a very straight face.

The stable master looked at them both with wide eyes and deepened respect.

Next door at the inn, the innkeeper was amazed at the good business he was having. Within an hour, three different groups of young travelers, rather well-off by their speech, had rented rooms for several days. The group of four had even taken a room that would hold eight, saying they liked lots of space. He was not a man to pass up good silver.

The remainder of that afternoon and evening was dedicated to recovering and relaxing. The birthday trio reserved bathtubs at the inn. Before Kibi went into her bathing stall, Ilika opened his shoulder bag and handed her the lice treatment bottle, now almost empty. She grinned, and pretended to pick something out of her hair. Ilika and the rest went to the public bath house, where the water was not very warm, but at least it was clean.

＊

Back at the inn, as dinnertime approached, Ilika assigned Toli to treat Miko and Rini with fresh ointment. Toli's hands shook as he doctored Rini.

At three separate tables, they partook of a hearty dinner of fried fish, stewed greens, and fresh bread and butter. Being so near the ocean, fish was plentiful, the innkeeper explained, but much less red meat was available than in the capital city.

"But for a few extra coppers, if you tell me ahead of time, I can get good mutton!"

Ilika shriveled his nose, but noticed Miko at another table listening and licking his lips.

"You folks are quite lucky, you know."

"How so?" Ilika inquired.

"There's talk of a band of sorcerers coming up the road from Port Town.

People say they used a spell to put the whole town to sleep. Had a beast with them too, three times the size of a man. Dragon, maybe."

Ilika had a slight smile on his face. He could see Rini trying hard not to laugh. Mati's eyes were sparkling, and Buna seemed to be putting the pieces together also.

"Lucky for us we didn't come up that road!" Ilika said loudly to cover up any temptations his students might be feeling.

With a wrinkled brow, the innkeeper agreed and went back to the kitchen.

After finishing their dinners, each group took leave of the common room at a slightly different time, then all of them gathered in the largest sleeping room.

"We had a close call today," Ilika began. "Several people had to make important decisions quickly. Tonight, we relax. Tomorrow, we'll write about our experiences in the forest."

Some of the students took on thoughtful looks as they pondered what to write. Others moaned slightly, hoping their teacher didn't hear.

"I went by the money changer," Ilika continued. "He also sells paper and pencils, and I stocked up, but he *doesn't* like breaking great gold pieces, and charges two tenths."

They all emptied out their coin pouches, and Ilika made sure they were supplied with coppers and a few small silvers, in addition to their emergency gold.

"It looks like the options for birthday dinners are fish or mutton here at the inn," Kibi announced, "or we buy stuff and make our own."

As darkness began to cloak the town, no one had energy for lessons or conversation. They didn't even bother to get candles from the innkeeper. Instead, as the light faded, they went to their separate rooms, crawled into clean sheets on real beds for the first time in several weeks, and were soon fast asleep.

✳   ✳   ✳

Chapter 35: Happy Birthdays

The following day began warm and clear as the morning sun angled through the trees spreading a dappled light through the waking town.

But as soon as feet and wheels began moving up and down the roads, and two-man saws started biting wood in the mills, a fine dust rose and began to coat everything anew.

After porridge, the students got comfortable in the large sleeping room to try to capture their experiences of the previous day in writing.

Mati found the words flowing from her pencil in a way she had never before experienced. She wrote of a deep gratitude toward one person, and an unbreakable bond she now felt with the donkey who had somehow found the courage to stay with her . . . and if necessary, to die with her.

Rini's writing was all about the amazement he felt at being able to do something heroic for the first time in his life, finding strength in himself he didn't know he had.

Kibi related her initial moment of seething anger, almost hatred, toward the wolf for attacking her friend. But she also shared her happiness, upon reflection, at being able to let go of that anger when the wolf was no longer a threat. Perhaps, she wrote, it was her many years as a slave that allowed her to relate to the desperate, starving animal.

Toli, to Ilika's disappointment, wrote a vague factual account of the event, without any soul-searching.

The rest were not so directly involved, and their writings reflected a more detached point of view.

*

Sata's birthday party was planned for that evening. Neti and Kibi volunteered to get the food. Within an hour, they had commissioned the baker's wife to make a pot of savory stew, with very little meat, like Sata's mother made. A fresh loaf and two berry pies were reserved, and then the two girls went shopping for gifts.

Boro resigned himself to looking for gifts with Toli, who was very proud to find the three rucksacks they still needed. Boro discovered a box of tiny animals carved from bone in the dry goods store, and from these they selected gifts for both Sata and Buna.

Ilika and Mati discovered a little shop of odds and ends in one room of a house. The floor was so cluttered with iron tools, wooden boxes, and chipped pottery that Mati could hardly move. Ilika spotted a book from across the room, the first he had seen in the town. He picked his way carefully toward it, and finally held in his hands a small volume of mathematical tables and formulas. Opening it randomly, he quickly spotted several errors, but was able to purchase it for a small silver piece.

"Don't tell anyone," he said to Mati as they left. "It might be for a birthday gift."

Mati grinned, and put a finger to her lips.

✳

Neti and Kibi found the perfect place for the party, a sandy level spot right beside a small stream, not far from the town but completely hidden.

When Kibi opened the covered pot and Sata smelled the delicious stew, with just enough mutton fat for flavor, she closed her eyes and a smile of contentment filled her face.

Between bites, she received her gifts of trinkets and ribbons, sweet biscuits and candy, and the most perfect fresh plum she had ever seen.

Ilika suggested that birthdays should be a time of sharing compliments, and forgiving and forgetting any mistakes or weaknesses from the past. Everyone had experienced Sata as a completely reliable member of their group, and compliments came from everyone. Mati especially remembered how she had jumped into the water to help with Tera back on the coast. Boro had kind words and a special smile for her that made her blush.

When it came time for dessert, Sata was torn. She couldn't decide whether to eat berry pie, a sweet biscuit, a piece of candy, or her perfect plum.

When others, with big grins, volunteered to help, she quickly slipped the other items into her rucksack, and asked for a serving of pie.

✳

Next morning, Ilika taught them the arithmetic for the division operation, step by step.

They were quite relieved to be learning a method that would work in every situation. Some could do a few simple divisions in their heads, or by trial and error, but were painfully aware of how limited those methods were.

By lunchtime, they all had the basic idea. Toli picked it up quickly, and was beginning to look happy again. He volunteered to go into the woods to gather sour berries while Ilika looked at Miko's and Rini's scrapes and cuts. Others went out to do more gift hunting.

After selling the last three unneeded saddlebags, Ilika was about to leave the dry goods store when he happened to glance up toward the highest shelf, near the ceiling, in the darkest corner, behind the door. There it was, the shape he had been looking for ever since they entered the forest. He had, until that moment, found nothing even remotely similar, except a wasp's nest hanging from a tree branch that was quite well guarded.

The short man got a rickety little ladder and brought it down. As he placed the smoothly stitched leather ball in Ilika's hands, a smile appeared on the teacher's face. A silver piece later, Ilika left the shop with the only spherical object likely to be found outside the capital city.

*

The innkeeper shook his head, wondering why all three groups of travelers wanted fish and wine that night, and mutton and ale the following night. Maybe it had something to do with the moon.

The fish was tasty, the bread was fresh, the cheese was creamy, and the wine was sweet. Buna took delight in all the flavors and textures of the meal. She was fifteen, and this birthday party was not just for this year, but all fifteen years. She was free now, and she was happy. She had friends and she was learning new things every day. And for the first time in her life, she had hopes for the future. Her first cup of wine was soon empty, so she asked for another.

Ilika let Buna indulge herself. There was plenty of other heavy drinking and loud talking in the common room to mask whatever she might do.

Her second cup went down just as easily as the first, but she didn't get far into the third. As soon as she started to change color and get strange looks on her face, Ilika helped her up to the sleeping room where a copper basin awaited.

She didn't make it to the basin.

When the others came up, Buna was on her hands and knees in the middle of the floor, adding to the puddle of wine and fish she had begun a few minutes before. Mati rubbed her back while Ilika and Rini gathered all the towels and rags they could find.

After a while Buna was able to drink a cup of water, but it was immediately added to the puddle. They wiped her face and helped her remove her boots. The basin was placed beside her bed as she was tucked in. The birthday girl was soon fast asleep.

Ilika and Rini set to work cleaning up the mess, with Mati helping as she was able.

*

Buna was a little afraid to admit that she was awake the following morning. In contrast to the night before at dinner, she now felt worse than she could ever remember feeling.

But since everyone else, from all three groups, was standing around in the large sleeping room, obviously hungry and ready for breakfast, she opened her eyes. Soon she started overhearing whispers that included words like 'tickle' and 'pinch,' so she gathered her courage and threw back the covers.

Boro's group went down to the common room, and a little later Kibi's group went down. After some effort figuring out how to put on her boots, Buna finally declared herself ready.

Luckily, the innkeeper provided plenty of sweet tea, as nothing else looked interesting to the fifteen-year-old.

She had a very sheepish look on her face, back in the sleeping room, as people presented her with sweet biscuits, candies, fruits, and pretty trinkets.

"Are you mad at me, Ilika?" she asked when the gift giving was complete.

"Well . . . next time there's something to clean up, I'll remember that you owe me one . . ."

Rini smiled. "And me."

Mati waved her hand. "And me."

". . . but you didn't hurt anyone, except yourself, or avoid any responsibilities, so . . . no, I'm not mad at you. I've had a hangover before, when I was about fifteen, as I remember. I didn't like it much, so I don't make a habit of it."

"I feel so terrible right now . . . I don't *ever* want to do that again!"

"That's good to hear. You'll have your next opportunity to get drunk . . . tonight at dinner."

Buna moaned. "Do you think they'd make me some tea?"

Everyone chuckled.

Ilika brought out the leather ball, which now had longitude and latitude lines, numbers, and a rough outline of the continents.

"Finally, we have a globe. Here is your kingdom . . ."

They all got close to take in this new perspective on their home.

"It's so small!" Sata said with wide eyes.

"Yes, compared to the whole planet, your kingdom is very small. This tiny dot is the capital city, and this speck is Lumber Town, where we are now."

Each student took a good look at their little corner of the world. Ilika gave them plenty of time to work with the globe and ask questions. Then he gave each a point on the globe for which he wanted the coordinates, and coordinates for which he wanted the point on the globe.

Buna discovered how difficult it was to think with a hangover.

At lunch, Buna possessively guarded her mug of cool, sweet tea.

Afterwards, Ilika set aside an hour for shopping, then gathered everyone back in the large sleeping room.

"Now that you all know the basic arithmetic operations, and plenty of logic, I can give you some realistic problems that require listening, writing, selecting, organizing, and calculating. Each person works alone. I will read the narrative three times. I recommend you just listen the first time.

"Poki is eighteen years old and lives three miles northwest of the capital city, on a little twenty-seven-acre farm that includes a two acre garden, four cows, ten goats, and twenty-two chickens. He is courting a fifteen-year-old girl who lives one mile west of there, weighs eighty-five pounds, and wants to have four children. Poki's three friends came over yesterday to help him cut two cords of firewood on his twelve-acre wood lot. Poki spent a copper piece last Tuesday to buy his girl a piece of candy, and she gave him the best three apples out of the thirty-seven she picked from her apple tree. On Wednesday he sold two goats, as he decided ten was too many for his five-acre goat pasture. He got three silvers for the nanny and one for the billy. With the money, he bought fence boards to keep the cows out of the acre around his house and chicken yard. If he and his girl get married next September, how many acres will each cow have for grazing?"

Miko, Neti, and Boro gave Ilika rather blank looks.

Kibi looked daggers at her teacher.

Rini, however, handed Ilika a little folded piece of paper.

"Having heard the whole narrative, you now know what the problem is. The next step is to write down the needed information from the narrative, and filter out anything that is not needed."

Ilika read the narrative again.

That was sufficient for Toli, Sata, and Mati, who all handed him the correct answer after a few minutes of calculation.

Kibi looked very frustrated, even though she had an entire sheet full of notes.

Ilika read it for the last time. He could see what was happening to Kibi. She was such a people-person that she couldn't ignore the human dimensions of the narrative. As a result, she was missing some of the important facts . . . about cows and acreage.

Boro, Neti, and Buna handed him correct answers.

Miko, never very good at doing math in his head, was trying to use the division arithmetic they had just learned, but was getting the steps mixed up.

Tears ran down Kibi's cheeks. She didn't have enough information in her notes to solve the problem, and now she had no way of getting it.

Everyone took a break and Ilika surrounded Kibi with his arms.

"I feel so foolish," she whimpered. "I was just so touched by the boy and the girl."

Ilika kissed the tears on her cheeks until she was giggling. "If you'll help Miko with his division, I'll read it to you again."

"Okay," she said, smiling shyly.

By dinnertime, with Kibi's help, Miko had untangled his division steps. After two more readings, by sheer force of will Kibi made herself ignore everything in the narrative that didn't tell her about the cows or the acreage of the farm. They both handed Ilika slips of paper with the answer. He smiled.

✳

Miko was in a good mood for his birthday party, and thoroughly enjoyed the mutton. Ilika found a very small piece, scooped some cooked greens onto his plate, and got a big chunk of bread when Mati passed the loaf to him. He noticed that Buna had pushed her ale into the middle of the table for anyone to take who wanted it.

Miko was thirsty and drained half his ale as soon as he sat down. Then he glanced at Buna, pushed his mug a little farther away, and didn't touch it again until he had eaten a fair amount of bread and meat.

Back in the large sleeping room, Miko was presented with candies, fruits, and trinkets, but he was most deeply touched when Neti handed him a leather necklace with a tiny cougar carved from a yellow stone. He let her put it over his head, then held her close for a long time.

Miko received good thoughts and wishes from everyone, but was most surprised by what Ilika said.

"You have kept a little bit of childlike openness that allows you to scream when you are hurt, cry when you are sad, and run when you are afraid. Most grown-ups have lost those abilities. You're like the willow tree that bends in a storm instead of standing up straight and breaking. Those abilities will serve you well, as long as you don't let them rule you."

Miko swallowed, looked into the eyes of his teacher, and finally nodded.

✳ ✳ ✳

Chapter 36: Whispers

Most of the students didn't sleep very well. The mutton was delicious, but they had eaten so little meat in their lives that it churned and growled in their bellies all night long.

Sometime in the early morning hours, Kibi awoke to the vague memory of hearing a voice. She lay on her cot, gazing up at the sloping roof logs above her, trying to remember the dream. Suddenly she heard the voice again.

Kibi, lead your people into the wind!

She quickly sat up and looked around, the room dimly lit by pre-dawn light. The voice was definitely female, but as far as she could see, Neti was fast asleep.

Remember Kibi, into the wind!

No, it wasn't Neti's voice. Kibi crept to the open window and looked out, but saw no one in the street below.

✳

In the other small sleeping room, Boro lay awake, wishing he could throw up like Buna had.

Boro, go into the wind, even if it looks dangerous!

He sat bolt-upright in bed, looking for the source of the voice. It wasn't Sata's.

Remember Boro, into the wind!

At the same moment, Boro caught a whiff of an odor he recognized. Smoke.

"Sata! Toli! Wake up! Get your boots on!"

✳

In the large sleeping room, Ilika climbed out of a dream, vaguely remembering a familiar female voice. Once awake, rubbing his eyes, he heard the same voice again.

Ilika! Arise and lead your people into the wind!

"Everyone wake up! Emergency! Boots on! Packs ready!"

❋

Kibi lay in bed wondering about the voice, and pondering why someone would want them to go into the wind, which would be west toward the ocean. Then she too smelled smoke and jumped to her feet.

"Miko! Neti! We have to go!"

❋

With an urgent voice, a bright beam from his bracelet, and some shaking, Ilika had his trio wide awake even before he smelled smoke and understood the nature of the problem. Rini quickly helped Mati with her saddlebags.

Soon Mati smelled the smoke too. "We have to get Tera!"

"We will," Ilika promised as he closed his pack and went to help Buna. "Whatever happens, follow my directions, even if they seem wrong."

❋

Caught in the first rush of people down the stairs, Kibi, Miko, and Neti were forced to slip out a side door or be trampled. Once outside, everyone around them saw the fire coming from the west and ran eastward. Miko took one step in that direction, then felt Kibi grab his shoulder with a fierce grip.

"We can't outrun the fire!" Kibi yelled. "We go west!"

Miko's eyes swirled with panic for a moment, but when he felt Neti pull gently on his hand, he let himself be led westward, behind the cheese maker and across a footbridge.

To their right the bakery was ablaze, throwing sparks and embers high into the air. A moment later the roof of a nearby house burst into flames.

Kibi pulled Neti and Miko a zigzagging course through the burning town, always west, into the smoke and among the buildings that had been burning longest. Miko was constantly on the raw edge of panic, and Neti began coughing deeply.

An eternity later they somehow found themselves in woods that were blackened and smoldering, but no longer ablaze.

❋

By the time Boro succeeded in convincing Toli to hurry, smoke was coming in the window and making them cough.

"I know where we need to go," Boro said. "Stay right with me, or you're on your own. We won't be able to come back."

Toli frowned, fumbling with his boot laces. "But how do you know . . ." he began in a whiney tone.

"Just put on your damn pack!" Sata yelled after packing it for him.

"Follow me! Stay close!" Boro commanded, and led them out of the room.

❋

Mati screamed when Ilika picked her up, but he had no choice. Rini took up Mati's saddlebags and Buna grabbed her bedroll, then they clasped hands to keep from losing each other as they followed their teacher out into the smoky corridor. Yelling, coughing people bumped into each other constantly on the stairs and in the common room. Once outside in the open air, the crowd bolted eastward.

The fire rapidly marched through the woods on the north side of town behind the inn, spreading quickly with the wind from the west. Even as they watched, a burning tree fell from the hillside above, landed just behind the stable, and ignited its back wall and roof.

"My horse!" a man yelled.

"Tera!" Mati screamed.

Ilika set her down, Rini got the crutch under her arm, and both Rini and Buna held onto their worried friend.

No one else was making any attempt to get into the burning stable. "Stay here!" Ilika ordered and ran forward.

Several people watched as Ilika pulled the big door open and went in. Against a glowing orange background, silhouettes of animals could be seen, flinging themselves about in their stalls as they screamed in distress.

Suddenly the stable was filled with a blue light and the fire almost completely died out. A moment later, a horse came running out, followed by a donkey that wasn't Tera, another horse, a cow, and finally Tera led by Ilika. As he stepped out of the building, the blue light disappeared and the fire returned to its work.

"Sorcery!" the man said whose horse had just been saved.

"Witchcraft!" a woman accused with narrowed eyes while holding her precious cow tightly.

Ilika grabbed Mati, planted her on Tera, and quickly led the donkey westward at a fast walk, toward the smoke and fire, the direction everyone else was trying to flee.

＊

Boro, Sata, and Toli veered into the kitchen of the inn to avoid a screaming knot of people, found the side door, crossed the road, and scrambled down into the streambed where the air was slightly better. Boro led them westward through the town, crawling under bridges and often pausing to splash the cold water on their faces and clothes.

Above them on the right, smoke poured from the windows of the dry goods store, and flames began licking the roof just as they passed. On the left, a burning house collapsed, sending ash and embers everywhere. The last bridge over the stream was starting to smolder even as the three crouched low to pass underneath.

Soon the stream began to descend into a narrow ravine, so they climbed out and found a road that wound westward through the smoking trees and bushes. Sata poked and prodded to keep Toli moving so Boro could concentrate on leading the way.

About an hour later, coughing and blinking, they came to a clearing in the woods west of town. The wind off the ocean was strong, the fire had burned itself out, and most of the smoke had cleared. Once a mill, it was now just a gutted building surrounded by stacks of charred wood and piles of drifting ash.

✳

Kibi was completely lost.

Smoke swirled everywhere, and Neti couldn't stop coughing.

"My eyes are burning!" Miko yelled with a shaky voice close to panic. "I can't see a thing!"

"Hold onto Neti's hand!" Kibi yelled through the smoke.

"I am!"

Kibi had Neti's other hand, trying desperately to do what the voice commanded. The wind, however, was gusting every which way, making a straight course impossible.

Follow me, Kibi!

The voice again. Kibi looked ahead with stinging eyes. A few yards ahead, and somewhat off to the right, a floating green ball of light danced in the air, but was not blown along with the smoke. After coughing and swallowing once, Kibi followed the green light, pulling Neti and Miko along behind.

✳　✳　✳

Chapter 37: Fish Stew

Boro and Sata poked through the smoldering ruins of the mill. Toli followed, sometimes silently, sometimes complaining about the lingering smoke, or about his empty stomach.

Boro stopped and slowly looked around, shielding his eyes from the bright morning sun. Green trees still stood near the clearing on the west, north, and south. "The wind is steady off the ocean. There's no way the fire could have gotten here. It had to *start* here."

Sata nodded. "And with this wind, it didn't take long to get to Lumber Town."

Just then, a quiet whimpering sound made Sata cock her head. She glanced at Toli, but he was silently sitting on a rock rubbing his eyes. "There's someone else here," she said, moving toward the trees on the south side of the clearing.

The sound came and went, but after a few minutes of looking and listening, Sata began to pick her way over logs and branches toward a cluster of boulders not far into the unburned trees. Boro followed closely, and Toli dragged himself along, coughing. Sata scrambled up the first boulder and looked down.

The girl of four or five years screamed with fear for a second, then changed her mind and reached up, crying with relief and letting Sata pull her up and embrace her.

✳

The four sat together in the woods as the little girl, still in Sata's arms, wordlessly poured out her grief. The ash smudges and tear stains on her face told her story well. When she eventually ran out of tears, Boro told of their own flight from the inn. Toli found a little dried fruit in his pack and passed it out.

The girl did not try to speak, but eventually started looking toward the clearing where the mill had been. Boro offered to let her ride on his shoulders, and after a moment of hesitation, she put her arms up to accept. With sad eyes, she gazed at the burned building, and more tears rolled down her cheeks. Whenever Boro or Sata suggested they look elsewhere for her family, she shook her head.

*

As mid-day passed and no clues about the girl's family came to light, Boro explained that they had to go south to find their friends. The girl cried until Sata mentioned that the meeting place served a delicious fish stew. She relaxed and wiped her tears, but still spoke no words.

Boro, with their new charge on his shoulders, set a straight course through the woods south and east. Walking became easier as they gained more distance from the ocean and the undergrowth thinned out.   By mid-afternoon, they came upon the main road to Port Town, and discovered they were not alone.

A family moved southward slowly, the woman limping, the man carrying a boy with burns on his face, and the little girl tagging along behind, dragging a scorched doll.

A cart, partly charred by the fire, bore a few belongings as an elderly couple struggled to make the wheels turn. Boro and Sata added their strength to the effort.

A man walked alone, openly grieving some loss and struggling to breathe.

"Um . . . compared to other people, we're pretty lucky!" Toli said.

From the back of the cart, Sata flashed him a dirty look. "When we find our teacher and our friends . . . then we'll know if we're lucky or not."

*

The other people on the road turned off when they came to a track that wound through the trees westward. The old woman explained that the family down the trail, although not rich, could be counted on to share what they had. The way was downhill, so the elderly couple nodded their thanks and headed down the track with their little cart.

The three students talked and agreed that a reliable food supply, and the possibility of finding their friends, was more important. The girl on Boro's shoulders mumbled something that might have been "fish stew."

Another hour of walking brought them to the village on the bay. A few refugees from the fire sat about with glazed eyes as they ate stew and bread.

Boro set the girl down before he and Sata went off to search the village and question everyone they could find.

Toli rubbed his eyes again, then looked down at the forlorn little girl. "Want to help me carry bowls of fish stew?"

She nodded vigorously and almost smiled.

*   *   *

Chapter 38: Leadership Lessons

Kibi, Neti, and Miko sat on a bluff overlooking the ocean. The blue sky before them and green trees behind showed no trace of the smoke or fire. The dancing green light had led them out of danger, then disappeared. Neither of Kibi's charges made any mention of having seen it, so she said nothing, still not sure if it was anything but her imagination.

Neti tried to speak, paused to cough several times, then found her voice. "Where do we go now?"

"To the emergency meeting place," Kibi said, still gazing at the open ocean, "the village of Fish at the inside of the bay, five or six miles south of here."

"But that was the meeting place when we were at Port Town!" Miko protested.

"It still is. We haven't made another one, and it's close."

"But Ilika wouldn't have gone that way! That would be going backwards!"

Neti sat quietly, just listening to the exchange.

"Going backwards a few miles is the price of finding our teacher and our friends," Kibi explained using every bit of her remaining patience.

"Ilika would go the way we were planning to go!" Miko asserted in a strained voice.

Kibi had no more to say.

"He would go up the north road into the hills," Miko said, trying very hard to sound sure of himself.

"The tide will be high soon," Kibi announced, standing on a rock and shielding her eyes. "It looks like a creek cuts through the bluff not far from here. We should be able to get down to the beach there, and then we'll have all day with the tide out."

"*We're* going up the north road," Miko said flatly.

Neti looked at him for a long time, her expression changing slightly every few moments. "I'm . . . going with . . . Kibi," she said softly.

Miko turned away, clenched his fists, and roared. For the next few minutes, he stomped up and down the edge of the bluff and threw rocks toward the ocean. Finally, he could find no more loose rocks, so he ripped a small bush out of the ground.

All the while, Kibi and Neti sat silently, gazing out over the ocean, careful not to look in Miko's direction.

About a quarter hour later, Miko suddenly sat down by himself, hugged his knees, and didn't let anyone see his face.

Neti walked over and sat down beside him. "I love you, Miko. But Kibi is right. Do you want to earn those three great gold pieces?"

Miko peeked out with tear-stained eyes and looked at the ocean. "Yeah."

"Me too. And I want to marry you, and follow you anywhere you lead, and have your children. But right now, I am Ilika's student, and Kibi is our leader. I know you're scared. I am too."

"When Kibi tells Ilika, he'll kick me out."

"Will you tell, Kibi?" Neti asked without turning her head.

"Nope. Don't like snitches. Not gonna be one."

Neti stood and held out her hand to Miko. He hesitated, then took her hand and stood up.

After a moment to reflect and deal with her own feelings, Kibi announced that she was tired, and asked Miko to lead to the bottom of the creek, and Neti along the beach.

Miko immediately brightened as he shouldered his rucksack.

※

Thinking it through step by step and announcing his decisions, Miko took his new task to heart. He led them slowly and carefully, not wanting to arrive at the beach until the tide was part-way out. They drank at the creek, but found nothing in their packs to eat.

Since none of them knew the wild foods of the area, both Kibi and Neti tried different berries as they descended toward the beach, spitting before the terrible taste got anywhere near their throats. But not far from the beach, Neti found a dark purple berry, a little dry but quite tasty, and they all started picking their first meal of the day.

With the sun out in a clear sky, and no more creeks or berries to refresh them, the miles of walking southward seemed to take forever. Twice, where the surf pounded against sheer rock walls, they waited for the tide to recede farther before continuing their journey.

Dinnertime was at hand when the three walkers finally dragged themselves along the beach toward the innermost point of the bay. From a distance they could see four figures sitting in the sand beside the eatery. As they crossed the narrow wooden bridge over the mouth of the river, the figures stood up and waved.

But Kibi knew, from the color of their hair, that Ilika was not among them.

※　　※　　※

Chapter 39: A Strange Guide

Ilika and his small group, one mounted and two walking, worked their way westward for several minutes after leaving the burning stable. Rini's eyes stung so badly he could do little but stumble along behind Buna. Tera was already skittish from the smoke, fire, falling trees, and frightened people. When the glowing green ball appeared in front of her, she gave a loud two-toned scream and stopped dead in her tracks, eyes swirling, ears flat.

"I'm surprised you can see that," Ilika said, holding the donkey's halter and talking to her with a soothing tone of voice.

"But Ilika, I can see it too!" Mati pointed out.

"Me too," Buna said, her eyes wide with wonder.

Rini just stood blinking, unable to focus on whatever they were talking about.

"I'm surprised any of you can see it. There must be a reason. That's our guide, Tera, our friend. We need to follow it to . . ."

Suddenly the light changed color slightly. To Ilika's complete surprise, the donkey walked forward and stood face to face with the strange glowing ball. She took deep breaths and made subtle squeaking sounds of curiosity.

"I think I understand," Ilika said. "We can all see it because we're going to *need* to see it. Let's be on our toes."

"But, Ilika!" Buna protested, her eyes still wide. "What *is* it?"

"It's a friend, Buna, and will guide us well. I can't explain any further right now. I need you all to trust me, and if anything happens to me, trust the light."

At that moment, the glowing ball began moving off through the smoke, back eastward and somewhat to the south. Without a word from Mati, Tera followed. Ilika came next.

Buna and Rini looked at each other, shrugged, and followed.

The light guided them out of the smoke and into a narrow ravine that threaded its way south into the unburned forest. A trickle of clear water and nearby berry bushes brought smiles to faces smudged with soot and red with irritation. Tera drank deeply from a small pool and began pulling at the grass along the brook.

Soon after faces were washed and a few handfuls of berries eaten, the light moved off again, this time back toward the smoldering town. Ilika looked puzzled, and the others would have ignored it, except that Tera immediately began following the mysterious orb.

Ilika ran, caught the donkey by her halter, and held her. Tera protested with squeaks and the stomping of her hooves as Mati hobbled to catch up.

As soon as Mati was mounted, neither she nor Ilika could do anything to stop Tera from following the shimmering ball, which had waited within sight.

"I think . . . we have work to do," Ilika said.

Again Rini and Buna looked at each other, then followed.

✳

A few minutes later, Tera twitched her ears and the others began to hear a sound they knew, a sound not too unexpected under the circumstances. Somewhere in the smoke, in the unburned woods on the south side of Lumber Town, a child was crying.

They soon found her, barely three years old, not far from a tiny house on the edge of town that had burned to the ground. The little girl continued crying and tried to speak as Ilika picked her up, but her voice was raw and incoherent. She fell silent, however, when placed on Tera in front of Mati.

To Mati's surprise, Tera didn't mind.

✳

Luckily the light guided them back to the brook and the berries, as the place would have been nearly impossible to find again on their own. The little girl resumed her crying as soon as she was put down, even while drinking water and stuffing her mouth with berries. The others picked as fast as they could, fearing they would soon be called away again.

They were right. As soon as the glowing orb decided it was time to resume the task at hand, Ilika put Rini in charge of the sanctuary and Buna helped Mati to mount.

Rini looked glum as he sat by the brook, blinking his stinging eyes and handing berries to the crying child.

✳

The fox watched from a cluster of boulders uphill from the brook. She wondered how humans could possibly survive the dangers of the world when they had such noisy children. One of her pups, years before, had been a little yippy, and had attracted a hungry hawk. The rest had grown up to be quick on their feet and quiet as mice.

To get away from the noise down at the brook, she began to trot farther south into the woods. Suddenly a little glowing green ball appeared in front of her. She leapt back and was about to run when it changed color. The glowing light now fascinated her, and she couldn't resist the temptation to follow.

As she trotted through the woods after the light, she wondered why it was leading her northeast, toward the burned part of the forest. Then she remembered that one of her daughters had her den in that area, and was expecting her first litter about now.

✳

Three more times that day the strange guide led donkey and people back into the smoke, each time finding a child petrified with fear or howling with grief, not daring to venture closer to the devastated town, not willing to leave. A seven-year-old girl was barefoot so Ilika carried her on his shoulders. A crying four-year-old boy relaxed into a soft whimper as he rode back to the sanctuary on Tera. A girl of six years had moccasins and was anxious to walk once she had somewhere to go.

Between each rescue, the light led them back to the comfort of the ravine. The seven-year-old helped pick berries, but the four-year-old boy immediately began to compete with the little girl to see how loudly they could cry and scream.

The sun dipped below the western horizon just as the last rescue mission returned to the sanctuary. The children all knew each other, but could take no joy in each other's company as long as the youngest pair continued crying. Holding them did no good, and berries only muffled the sound temporarily.

Mati volunteered, but Ilika would not let her give donkey rides in the dark. Eventually the youngest two fell asleep on blankets spread out on the forest floor, and all the others breathed a sigh of relief.

✳

Ilika and his three students sat with the two older girls, telling little stories from their recent adventures as they nibbled on berries and sipped water.

When the girls started yawning, Rini and Buna laid out more blankets and checked on the sleeping little ones.

When all their new charges were finally asleep, Ilika, Mati, Rini, and Buna gathered near Tera to talk. The donkey paused in her twilight grazing to glance at her people.

Buna lay back in the grass. "I'm exhausted."

"I wish I knew how the others were doing," Mati said with a forlorn voice.

Ilika let a moment pass. "The light . . . our guide . . . is helping them too."

Mati took a slow breath. "Good."

"Ilika!" Buna said with sudden realization. "I bet you really miss Kibi!"

"Yeah. How are you feeling about . . . Toli?"

Buna twisted her face, then just shrugged.

"I think we'll see them all again," Rini said. "Soon."

Ilika remained silent.

"Can you," Buna began, "you know, have your bracelet warn us if any wolves come around, or anything else big?"

"Yes. That would be best tonight."

After the day's experiences, no one even suggested they build a fire.

        *

Buna slept near Ilika so she could hear his bracelet if it chimed a warning. However, she slept as if dead, and didn't awaken until the sun was up and everyone else was picking berries. She sat in confusion for a moment, wondering why two little children with berry-stained faces were looking at her. Then she remembered all the events of the previous day. "How did you get them to quit crying?" she asked.

"They got a good night's sleep," Mati said from the edge of the berry bushes. "And Rini had berries ready as soon as they woke up."

Rini grinned from deep in the berry patch, handing filled bowls out to Mati.

Buna, her stomach growling, hopped up to get some.

        *

About mid-morning the glowing orb returned, but the children obviously couldn't see it. Although he wouldn't say why, Ilika got all the children ready to depart. Tera, as usual, couldn't be held back.

The crying and screaming by the youngest two quickly resumed. Placing one on Tera did the trick, but the other made up for it by screaming louder, even when carried by Ilika or Buna.

Their guide seemed to know that some of them were barefoot, and led them very slowly deep into the woods south of the ruins of Lumber Town. After more than an hour of ambling, the group entered an area of the forest where several huge trees had fallen. The glowing ball of light stopped over a massive hollow log lying on the ground. Ilika set his rider down and looked in.

A pair of frightened eyes looked back at him.

Ilika, Buna, and Rini all tried coaxing the child out, but without success. After a while they gathered around Mati, still mounted, to talk about the situation.

The seven-year-old barefoot girl crept to the log and knelt down. "Hi, it's

Misa. You can come out now, Rosi."

Rosi shook her head and refused to budge.

Over the next half hour, the six-year-old tried, Rini and Buna begged and pleaded, and eventually Mati dismounted just in case she had the magic touch. Rosi remained petrified with fear.

Soon their guide was ready to move on, with Tera not far behind.

Ilika sighed. "Okay," he said in a loud voice. "We're leaving. The hungry wolf should be along soon."

Rini brought up the rear, and when they had gone about a hundred yards, he glanced back to see little five-year-old Rosi picking her way behind on bare feet.

*

About two hours later, far to the west near the north-south road, the green orb stopped at the base of a large broad-leafed tree. Ilika, his three students, and four of the children gathered around and looked up. Rosi sat on the ground about twenty yards back and hugged her knees.

"Hi," came a voice from above.

It took those on the ground several moments to spot the boy's face among the forking branches and thick leaves.

"Hi, Kamo!" the six-year-old girl with moccasins said. "Want to join us?"

"Um . . . if there are no . . . wolves around."

Everyone looked, just to be sure.

"Anyway," Rini said, "we can handle wolves. It's crying children we don't know what to do with."

Kamo, about nine years old, climbed out of the tree slowly. He was lucky enough to have boots, but his arms and legs showed deep scratches from the rough bark.

"Where are we going?" the boy asked as soon as he was on the ground.

Rini shrugged. "We don't know."

"There might be more kids to rescue," Buna added.

Ilika switched children on Tera, and the little boy immediately began screaming.

*

The mysterious glowing guide disappeared as they approached the homestead on the far side of the road. The log house was large but not rich, the roof sturdy but old. The yard contained vegetable gardens, animals pens, and wood sheds. It also now hosted a dozen or more little campsites with simple lean-to tents protecting the few salvaged possessions of the refugees.

All those who were able worked in the gardens and pens, or carried supplies in and out of the house. A man with an axe, standing watch against wild animals and thieves, challenged the group as it approached, but threw down his weapon when he saw the three-year-old girl riding with Mati.

"Daddy!" the girl screamed as he reached up to receive her.

Little Rosi, when she finally wandered into the yard, was quickly spotted by her older brother and sister, but they knew nothing of the fate of their mother. The lad, about fifteen, showed by his mature speech that he was ready to take on his new responsibilities.

The crying four-year-old boy became happy and content when he felt his mother's arms around him, not yet aware she had been blinded by the fire. Rini breathed a sigh of relief when he saw a man drop an armload of firewood and run to join them.

The girl in moccasins wandered among the people in the yard for several minutes before recognizing an aunt and uncle. They spoke in quiet tones, and the girl burst into tears. Buna lingered long enough to see them comfort her, then share their loaf of bread.

✳

Nine-year-old Kamo and seven-year-old Misa searched every corner of the yard and talked to the people in the house. Rumor placed Kamo's uncle in the woods north of town, but nothing else was known. Misa found no one.

They both looked at Ilika.

"We're going down to the village on the bay to meet our friends. You are welcome to come with us."

Both children tried to smile, but finally just nodded.

✳ ✳ ✳

Chapter 40: Dreadful Waiting

After Kibi, Neti, and Miko drained mugs of cool mint tea and had bowls of stew in hand, the six students sat around sharing stories.

Boro told of finding the source of the fire, and Sata described their search for the whimpering sound in the woods. The little girl sat quietly, listening, only answering simple questions with nods or shakes of her head.

Miko and Neti told their story of trudging through the smoke, then along the beach, but not a word was spoken about a certain discussion that took place on the bluff.

As the setting sun neared the ocean, they bought a loaf and some cheese, walked down the beach until they came to a little stream, and followed it into the trees to camp.

*

Six thoughtful students lay awake the following morning, wondering what they would do if they couldn't find their teacher and friends.

The little girl, who had shared blankets with Sata, got up and went into the bushes. When she returned, she brought everyone out of their thoughts with two simple words.

"I'm hungry."

The students began throwing blankets back and stretching. Neti tore bread and sliced cheese. The seven lost souls sat in a circle on the cool sand to eat and talk.

"We should wait at the village," Miko asserted, trying once again to find his leadership voice.

"If Ilika . . . or anyone . . . makes it there," Boro said, "they'll stay awhile, so we don't need to sit there all day."

"I agree," Sata said. "But I think we should go in every day."

"Yeah," Neti joined. "Maybe . . . lunchtime and dinnertime. I want to wash in the stream before we go. Me and Sata can help our new friend clean up."

The little girl's mouth was full of bread, so she just nodded.

"How long will we have to wait?" Toli asked with a hint of impatience.

Kibi breathed a tiny sigh of exasperation. "When we were talking about this back at the healer's house, Ilika said it could take a week to find each other if there were problems. The town we were in burned down. If you ask me, that's a problem. We wait at least a week."

Boro nodded.

✳

After washing some clothes, they hung the wet things on trees, packed everything else, and walked the half-mile back to the village.

No sign or word greeted them about their friends.

But several more refugees from the fire had arrived, all looking quite lost, some of them still coughing, most of them penniless. Kibi approached the matron of the eatery and arranged for fish stew for anyone who arrived without money.

"What now?" Sata asked after they had been in the village an hour and had done everything they could.

Kibi was gazing out to sea. "Lessons."

Toli looked at her with disbelief. "Lessons?"

"That's right," she replied a bit forcefully. "We're not going to forget the things Ilika taught us. We're in this group to learn, remember?"

Toli cowered slightly, then nodded.

✳

Sata took them through a review of all their mathematics, drawing in the wet sand near the ocean with fingers or sticks.

Kibi pressed them to remember everything about geometry and navigation. She wanted it fresh in her mind in case she had to look for Ilika's country by herself.

Using shells for subatomic particles, Toli walked them through all their basic chemistry, including the structure of water and the dissolved salts of the ocean.

While sitting in the dunes above the beach, Boro reviewed the rules of logic, but often found his students gazing toward the village instead of paying attention.

The little girl fell asleep in the sand.

✳

As they silently ate fish stew at dinnertime, Kibi's eyes were moist and her shoulders drooped with defeat.

Just then a pair of shaggy donkey ears appeared over the first rise in the road, with Mati just behind. Next came a girl riding on Ilika's shoulders, then Buna, and finally a boy walking beside Rini.

Bowls of half-eaten stew were left for the gulls as Kibi dashed up the hill, ran right past Tera, and surrounded Ilika with her arms, kissing him with all the feeling in her heart.

He returned her kiss with just as much feeling.

When they finally separated enough to look into each other's eyes, they heard a voice come from above their heads. "I think she likes you, Ilika."

"Yes, Misa, I think she does. And I like her just as much."

A little farther back in the line, Toli and Buna stood facing each other.

"I . . . really missed you," Toli said softly.

Mixed emotions visited Buna's face for several long moments. "Toli . . . there are things about you . . . I don't like . . . but . . . I missed you too."

They carefully put their arms around each other, as if handling something fragile.

"Okay, lovebirds," Mati said from the front of the line. "Is there anything to eat? We've had nothing but berries for two days!"

Everyone started chuckling.

"Come on!" Boro called. "Plenty of fish stew right down here!"

That evening, the group was again happy and animated, and quite willing to do anything Ilika wanted. Boro and Miko collected plenty of firewood to prepare for the telling of many stories. Misa and Kamo knew the little girl from Boro's group, revealed that her name was Tati, and took over taking care of her.

With cheese and plums to munch on, Ilika asked Buna to relate their adventures. She told about their flight from the inn and the rescue of Tera and the other animals from the burning stable. Then she described the glowing ball of light that Tera insisted on following.

Kibi's mouth dropped open.

Misa and Kamo rolled their eyes and figured it was something adults made up to keep kids in line.

After Buna finished sharing the rescue of the six children, Sata told of finding the source of the fire and little Tati, and Miko related their flight from Lumber Town and trek along the ocean.

Many questions about the green light followed, but Ilika would say little, except that it was a friend. He changed the subject by asking all his students to report any problems because of the fire, or any supplies that had been lost.

Neti cleared her throat. "I could hardly stop coughing the first day, but it's getting better."

"I . . . um . . . forgot the shovel," Miko admitted with a slight cringe.

Toli squirmed for a moment. "I . . . left the rope."

"I forgot the globe," Ilika admitted with a hint of sadness. "We'll have to continue navigation lessons with paper."

"We have no idea where Tati's family might be," Boro said, "but we haven't been to the house west of the road."

"Kamo has an uncle who was working in the woods north of town," Ilika explained. "We just have to find him."

"I was up on the hill playing, and saw my parents running away from the fire, toward the capital road," Misa announced, trying to act grown-up like the others who had just made their reports.

Miko put a few more sticks on the fire to give a little extra light, and everyone made their beds. Ilika asked Kibi to walk on the beach with him.

*

"I was really worried about you," Kibi said. "If I never found you, I was going to travel until I found your country."

Ilika took her hand as they walked. "You can't get there from here . . . except in my ship."

Kibi was thoughtful for a moment. "Looking for it would have been better than staying here."

"I understand. I was worried about you too. Things like this will happen sometimes. Are you okay with that?"

"I don't want to lose you. But as long as we have a meeting place . . . I'll be okay."

"We'll always have a meeting place, usually two or three. I heard you had your hands full."

"You know what happened in my group? I mean, the things that weren't in Miko's story?"

"No details. Just that you were well-challenged, and you handled it."

"How did you know?"

"The same voice that spoke to you, speaks to me. She spoke to Boro too. It's not very hard to guess what you had to deal with. That's probably why you weren't asked to rescue children at the same time."

Kibi smiled, stopped walking, snuggled close to Ilika, and gave him another kiss he wasn't going to forget any time soon.

*   *   *

Chapter 41: Reunions and Hard Choices

The next part of the journey began by purchasing all the food they could carry, and a small coil of rope, from the people at the fishing village. Ilika explained that they needed to be as self-sufficient as possible when they passed through the burned area. Little or nothing would be for sale, at any price.

Kibi paid for the meals served to poor refugees, all of whom had now moved on. They needed homes and work, and the village offered nothing but fish stew.

After saying good-bye to the ocean once again, the teacher, nine students, and three children headed north on the road toward a town that no longer existed. Tati glowed with pride atop Tera, Misa rode Ilika's shoulders, and Kamo walked.

As they entered the forest once again, several wondered aloud how the fox and the wolf had fared. Mati led the group off the road westward when she recognized the track to the house and refugee camp.

A young woman flew out of her simple lean-to tent when she saw her daughter approach on the donkey.

"Tati!"

"Mommy!"

Boro lifted the excited child to the ground, who dashed into her mother's waiting arms.

Buna and Rini walked around with Misa and Kamo once more, just in case.

Suddenly Boro was surprised by Tati's mother pressing a copper piece into his hand, a grateful look on her face. After a moment of thought, his lips curled slightly with an idea. As she watched, he put the copper piece into his pouch and pulled out a small silver piece in one smooth motion, as if performing a magic trick. He handed the silver coin to Tati and kissed her on the forehead. The mother smiled and kissed Boro on the cheek.

Soon the group, smaller by one, was on its way again.

✳

Ilika, and those who had left the inn with him, were very familiar with the charred ruins of Lumber Town. The rest stared in amazement. No roofs had survived. Only a few blackened walls still stood. Most buildings could only be located by the presence of charred posts and smoking rubble. Neti started coughing again, and Rini's eyes stung.

Ilika led them silently eastward through the town, past the sites of the stable and the inn, toward the road to the capital city, the way Misa's parents were last seen running. One of the bridges had burned, forcing them to scramble through the streambed.

About a quarter mile outside the town, they spotted a horse-drawn wagon ahead on the road. It stopped and two men jumped out wearing rags over their mouths and noses. They picked up a body that lay beside the road and tossed it into the wagon, where several others were already piled.

A hundred yards from the wagon, Ilika asked everyone to wait.

Seeing Ilika approach, the men met him half way, glad for an excuse to get away from the wagon and remove their masks.

"Hello!" Ilika called in greeting.

"You're the one who saved some of the children."

"I had lots of help."

"Find any more? There are still some missing."

"One of my companions did, a little girl named Tati, and she's now with her mother at the house on the south road. I still have Misa and Kamo. Misa saw her parents running this way."

The man lowered his voice. "Then they're gone. No one lived who went this way. Between the smoke and the fire, the capital road was a death trap for five miles out. If they weren't on fast horses, the fire got them."

Ilika was silent for a moment. "Are there any other places where people are gathering?"

"Yeah. Village about two miles north of town, on the mountain road."

"We'll go there. It's a good bet for Kamo, at least. I'm surprised there are no soldiers helping out."

"No one could get out to summon them. I think someone finally left yesterday, the long way through Port Town. They'll strut around a little, but won't help much. Those of us with roots here will rebuild."

Ilika opened his pouch and found two silver pieces. "For your work."

"Thank you," both men said, bowing their heads with gratitude.

As Ilika steered his group back toward the town, he didn't repeat what he had learned. So it was that Misa remained in the dark a little longer about her parents' probable fate.

✳

As the group of unusual humans slowly climbed the steep winding road north of the ruins of Lumber Town, the fox watched from a nearby hill. With her sharp eyes she spotted the new additions, a half-grown female, and an almost-grown male. Somehow the situation felt familiar.

Just then the five pups crept forward to see what was so interesting. She looked at them sternly, but they remained quiet as mice as they lined up beside her to peer over the top of the hill.

The two who had survived of her daughter's pups still looked a little weak. Two others, older and larger, would be able to help her hunt soon, and she was glad. She worried most about the last pup the strange green ball had found. Its singed fur was ugly at the moment, but it seemed to have a strong spirit.

She took one last look at the humans, rounding a bend in the road and going out of sight, then turned and led her new adopted family back toward the stream were mice and other small animals were plentiful.

✳

The village north of Lumber Town, several hundred feet higher in elevation, contained six houses, their gardens and animal pens, and a small mill. It currently hosted about four times its usual population.

The group found a shady place beside the road to rest and eat some bread and cheese. Ilika took Misa on his shoulders and Kamo at his side. They wandered among the people who huddled in make-shift camps near the houses.

Many eyes looked their way, dull with sadness over the loss of their loved ones, their homes, or both. Many heads shook, not knowing where the missing parents or uncle might be.

Just then a large man stepped out of one of the houses.

"Uncle Boti!" Kamo called.

The man and the boy faced each other.

"Do you . . . know where my mother is?" the boy asked with all the hope in his heart.

"My sister . . . your mother . . . the smoke got her. I'm sorry."

The boy looked at the ground.

Uncle Boti cleared his throat. "I guess you're my responsibility now."

"I don't want to be any trouble . . ." Kamo mumbled without looking up.

"You won't be trouble, because there won't be time to be trouble. You can stay with me if you want to, but life will be hard now. I still have my tools, and the clothes on my back, but that's all. With your mother working at the bakery, making money, you could play. That's gone now. We'll have to scrape up food, every day. We'll have to build a house. There won't be any more time for play. You'll have to be a man now."

Nine-year-old Kamo looked up at his uncle and spoke through his pain. "I'll be a man. I'll work hard."

"Good to hear. I've been doing some carpentry for these people, so there's a bowl of stew in here for you."

Ilika watched as Kamo disappeared into the house, then continued his rounds with Misa.

After talking to everyone they saw, and not finding a soul who had any knowledge of her parents, they returned to the group and ate bread and cheese in silence for a few minutes.

"Misa, would you please go across the road to those berry bushes and pick yourself some? I need to talk to my students for a few minutes."

Misa's face showed that she wanted to cry. Instead she nodded, hopped up, and worked her way across the road, avoiding as many sharp rocks as possible with her bare feet.

"There is very little chance that her parents are alive," Ilika explained. "As far as she knows, she has no other relatives in the kingdom. The guards will be here soon, and anyone who can't take care of themselves will become . . . you know."

"We know," Mati said flatly.

"That leaves the possibility of inviting her to come with us. What do you think?"

"We're buddies already!" Buna declared.

"Tera likes her," Mati added. "I do too."

All the others nodded.

"What about shoes?" Rini asked.

"We'll get her something as soon as possible, and hopefully a small pack and blankets. But not here — everything is scarce here. Buna, would you get her, please?"

✳

Once Misa returned and sat down with the group, tears rolled silently down her face as Ilika shared what they knew. A frown was added when he explained what would happen if the soldiers found her alone. Then he invited her to come with them on a long journey through the mountains and down to the capital city.

She sat silently, at the first major crossroads of her life, with seven years of experience to fall back on, face twisted with grief and indecision.

✳ ✳ ✳

Chapter 42: A New Companion

Misa was not yet able to put her decision into words.

The group lingered in the little mountain village for a couple of hours, gathering all the information they could, and handing out a few coins to those who had lost everything.

When they couldn't think of any more reasons to stay, they looked at each other, and without a word from anyone, began to shoulder their packs and get Mati mounted. As soon as they stepped onto the road, Misa hopped up and planted her bare feet beside their boots, pointed in the same direction, north.

Ilika smiled at Kibi, and Boro offered the seven-year-old a shoulder ride.

*

The mountain road continued to wind through the forest into higher and higher elevations. Kibi suggested an early camp, and it wasn't long before water, berries, and a level place were all located close together.

The trees here weren't as large as those at lower elevations, and included more tall, slender trunks reaching up into the sunlight with rustling leaves. In a much better mood than earlier in the day, the students fanned out to explore, gather berries and wood, and see if any other wild foods were at hand.

Misa, lacking shoes, stuck close to camp, so Ilika got out the map so she could see their route. She was intensely curious about the roads around Lumber Town, and seemed to understand which way the fire had gone, having seen it sweep through the town with her own eyes. When tears started flowing again, Ilika held her close until Buna returned. "Here's your friend Buna," Ilika said over the girl's sobs, and Misa quickly grabbed Buna and didn't let go.

Eventually the aroma of mushroom soup, simmering on the fire, allowed Misa some distance from her grief and confusion. The other students were laughing, talking, and eating berries. She peeked out from under Buna's cloak and opened her mouth when Rini offered her a ripe, juicy berry.

✳

That evening was a story-telling marathon.

They started with some of their old favorites, like *Mati and the Bottomless Pit* and *Miko and the Steam Vent*. Soon they moved to tales that had not been told before.

Boro tackled the sad story of *Kit and Mommy*, which Misa could relate to very well. But she frowned at the part about Kit still sleeping on the grave two years later.

Buna was happy to retell *The Thieves Who Ran Away*, as she loved to keep track of what Ilika's bracelet could do. Then she told the others about the newest addition to her list, the blue light that had held the fire at bay in the stable.

Misa, seated between Ilika and Buna, looked at the bracelet, but didn't dare touch it.

Mati told *Tera and the Invisible Dragon*, and even though she loved her donkey dearly, admitted that Tera wasn't the most intelligent creature in the kingdom.

Sata had a story to tell, and couldn't think of a better name than *Sata and the Ocean*. All her friends had seen her sitting at the edge of the water, but now she shared what was going through her mind as she tried to work out her relationship with the powerful forces of the universe.

Rini attempted *The Fox and the Wolf*, but had a hard time putting his own part into words. Eventually he accepted suggestions such as "brave" and "determined."

"I wonder if I'll have stories someday . . ." Misa pondered out loud.

"You already do!" Miko assured her. "Someday, you'll be able to tell the story of the fire."

Misa cringed and closed her eyes.

"Sometimes they're a little painful at first," Kibi admitted, "but as time passes, they get easier to tell. Stories are like that."

Buna put her arm around the girl. "And if you stick with us, you'll collect stories very quickly, I promise!"

✳

The following morning, Misa was completely confused when Ilika got out paper and pencils.

"I've mentioned the distributive property before, but now all my students need to get comfortable with it, as you'll need it very soon. It works with division, but *only* a divisor can be distributed. Addition, as usual, can also be subtraction. Let's practice."

$$(A + B + C + ...) \times M =$$
$$(A \times M) + (B \times M) + (C \times M) + ...$$

$$(A + B + C + ...) / N =$$
$$(A / N) + (B / N) + (C / N) + ...$$

He gave them each an expression to distribute, and another to do the reverse. Rini, Toli, and Sata had it from the general formulas. The rest had to work.

Once all his students had mastered the process, Ilika turned to Misa. "What do you think?"

She frowned with worry for a moment, staring at the mysterious formulas. Then she glanced around and saw smiles and grins on all the faces around her, including Ilika's, and relaxed. "Looks like magic to me!"

After a simple lunch of bread, cheese, and berries, they packed and continued up the road. Toli offered Misa a ride.

They hadn't gone far when Toli came to a sudden halt. "Ouch! Stop it!" he said with a deep frown, looking up at his passenger.

Everyone gathered around and looked up at Misa, her expression a cross between a grin and a pout.

"I thought they were mosquito bites," Toli whined, "but they were pinches."

"I won't let you hurt my students," Ilika said firmly to Misa. "Let her walk, Toli."

Misa pretended to be happy, for about the first hundred yards. Then the whimpering began.

Ilika and Toli talked quietly, and agreed a half mile would be good for her. After they covered that distance, with Misa picking her way behind as if walking on something hot, Ilika called a short rest stop.

Misa disappeared into the bushes, and a few minutes later knelt before Toli with two little outstretched hands full of berries.

Toli was deeply touched, almost moved to tears. After sharing the berries with the seven-year-old, he lifted her up to his shoulders.

Chapter 43: Proposal

About mid-afternoon, they came over a rise and suddenly left the trees behind. In front of them, a huge mountain meadow stretched for miles, with the rutted dirt road slicing northward almost straight as an arrow. Dark green forested slopes surrounded the meadow. Above the forest, the entire northern and eastern horizons were jagged with gleaming snowcapped peaks.

Several log buildings clustered at the side of the road not far ahead. Many goats grazed nearby, as well as a few horses.

"As we go up in elevation," Ilika explained, putting on his sun hat, "the ultraviolet radiation will get stronger."

"That's another thing we need for Misa," Buna declared.

As they approached the buildings, a tall, muscular man came striding out to meet them, his grass-cutting scythe held high. All the students froze, and Misa hid behind Buna.

"If you're homeless refugees looking for a handout, you just head right on back! There's nothing here for you! If you're goat thieves, I'll *chase* you back!"

Ilika could feel Kibi at his side bristling with anger. He put a hand on her shoulder before she could say anything.

"What if we're honorable travelers who can pay for supplies with good copper and silver?"

The farmer lowered his scythe and softened his tone. "Well, that's more like it. I'm Koto. Did you say silver? What might you be needing that would make you part with silver?"

Ilika and the group gathered around. "Buna?"

Buna took a deep breath to collect herself. "Um . . . shoes for this little girl, a couple of good blankets, and a sun hat of some kind. Oh, and a rucksack if you have one, hopefully small."

"Well, now, I ain't no cobbler, but I bet the wife could make up some moccasins for her — we've certainly got enough leather around here. And it being summer, we could sell you a couple of blankets. Come on over to the house."

"Thank you," Ilika said. "Also, we'd pay a silver and a copper for a hearty meal for all eleven of us, more if there's dessert."

"Well, my friend, in that case there certainly will be dessert!"

✳

They entered the sturdy log structure with its steep thatched roof. A large hearth, currently without fire, dominated the main room. Nearby, the well-stocked kitchen had its own small hearth, and could easily feed dozens. Work tables held goat skins and cheese presses, vegetables being cleaned and sewing projects. Above them, under the thatched roof, two or three more floors were accessible only by ladder.

Koto's wife and eldest daughter, a quiet girl of about sixteen, cleared off a work table and set to work making moccasins and a sun hat for Misa, who sat proudly as she was measured. Buna stayed near to oversee.

One of Koto's teenage sons climbed a ladder and brought down two good wool blankets.

Ilika got out his map and sat with the farmer, making notes about the roads and the trails as the local man spoke. Koto told of two herders who lived farther up the meadow, and was sure one of them would have a rucksack. He also described the only place in the mountains where supplies could be purchased.

When Misa received her moccasins, the newly-tanned goatskin felt so soft and cool against her sore feet that she danced around the room with happiness. The farmwife brought out several pairs of knitted socks, and Buna nodded.

Soon the eldest daughter finished the simple sun hat, and Misa insisted on wearing it, even inside.

Buna smiled, remembering herself not so long before.

✳

Two other youth came in with herbs and roots from the garden, and Koto's wife busied herself making goat stew, fresh bread with soft goat cheese, and fresh mint tea sweetened with honey.

With plenty of tables in the house, the travelers and the entire large family ate together. A lively chatter broke out, especially among the youngest daughter, the middle son, Kibi, Neti, and Miko. The middle daughter, about fourteen and very mature, didn't say much during dinner, but looked at all the travelers with keen eyes — especially the males.

As they ate, they could smell plum and berry pies in the oven. Ilika continued to chat with the farmer about the mountain trails that lay ahead of them, and the farmer was proud to share his lifetime of knowledge. Some of the students listened carefully, as the mountains still looked a bit frightening to them.

Mati and Sata sat with the farmer's wife, paper and pencil in hand, to agree on a list of foods they could buy from the family. The woman looked at the written words with wonder and suspicion, as if gazing at a magical incantation instead of a simple shopping list.

Toward the end of the meal, the middle daughter fastened her admiring eyes upon Boro. When she caught him looking back at her, she smiled. It wasn't long before everyone at the table was aware of her interest. Sata swallowed several times and tried to focus on the shopping list.

*

After dinner, the family had evening chores, so the travelers got their beds ready in the soft meadow grass. Mati and Sata went around checking to see how much packing space each person had.

Soon the eldest son, newly-returned from herding, kindled a fire in the outdoor pit beside the house, and the eleven travelers and eight family members gathered around for pie and stories. The middle daughter found her courage and asked to sit with Boro. He agreed.

Sata, arriving at the fire after packing some supplies, suddenly wore a very distant expression.

To the delight of the family, the travelers had many stories ready to tell. Ilika announced at the beginning that this was not a good place for bracelet stories, and his students grinned with understanding. The family members shrugged.

The travelers and the family alternated the telling of tales. Ilika and his students learned many things about dealing with deep winter snow, unprepared travelers, and mischievous goats.

"Is keeping goats about the same as shepherding?" Buna asked.

"Goats are smarter," the youngest daughter spoke from experience, "and have minds of their own. Sheep wander off. Goats *sneak* off!"

Buna looked thoughtful, and everyone else laughed.

When another story was requested, and they were running out of those that did not include the bracelet, Boro took a deep breath and asked Ilika for their book. By the light of the fire, he slowly read the first chapter of *The Adventures of Godi and Tima* to the spellbound family.

After he handed the book to Kibi, the fourteen-year-old girl sitting close beside him whispered in his ear, "Will you walk with me in the moonlight?"

They both stood up and strolled into the meadow together.

Sata made mistakes constantly when she was asked to read a chapter. The family assumed it was just because she was the youngest of those who could read.

*

An hour later, Koto announced it was time for chores and sleep. As soon as no one else was around, Sata plopped down beside Ilika. In a choked voice she barely managed to say, "What do you think they're talking about?"

Ilika took a slow, deep breath. "Way out here, far from any town, it's very hard for young people to find partners. I imagine Boro is getting a marriage proposal."

Sata was silent for a long time. Finally, in a tiny, broken voice she said, "It's not fair. Me and him were getting close."

Ilika put his arms around her. "It's actually one of the very best things that could happen, Sata. If he stays with her, you'll know Boro is the kind of boy who would give up his education, give up his place on my ship, and give up the relationship he's developing with you, just because a goat girl takes a fancy to him. Would you want a partner who's that weak and fickle?"

"Um ... I don't know ... maybe not."

"Or, if he turns her down, you'll probably learn some new things about his feelings for you."

"I ... I think I see what you mean. But it hurts."

"Tests like this are good for relationships. And yes, they hurt. Kibi and I are closer after being apart for a while and realizing how much we care about each other."

"I saw you kissing."

Ilika chuckled. "Try to think of this as a blessing. If he can be enticed away so easily, then the sooner you are rid of him, the sooner you can get close to a boy who likes you enough to stick with you."

Sata was silent for a long moment. "I'll ... try to think about it like that."

✳

Ilika and Sata joined the others who were crawling under their blankets to gaze up at the moon and stars.

Sata lay in her bed thinking about the things Ilika had said when suddenly Boro appeared, carrying his bedroll. "Can I sleep beside you?"

"If you want to."

He got comfortable under his blankets. "Josa asked me to stay here with her."

"I know."

"I knew you'd figure it out. I listened to everything she had to say, just ... to be kind, I guess. But I finally had to tell her ... I have a road in front of me, and a girl I like already."

Sata's hand crept out from under her blankets, and found Boro's hand waiting for her.

✳ ✳ ✳

Chapter 44: Trigonometry

After a hearty breakfast of porridge and custard with Farmer Koto and his family, Mati and Sata bought everything they could squeeze into the rucksacks, from carrots to hard crackers, dried onions to porridge oats.

Ilika sat down with the farmer and made a list, and the total came to nearly eight small silver pieces. Since the list didn't include all the valuable information the farmer had given, Ilika felt good about handing the man a great silver piece.

The farmer and the teacher shook hands, and Ilika went out to see if his students were ready.

After making sure the provisions were all packed, and tying Misa's blankets into a neat bundle with rope, Buna stood up and looked around. She saw Boro and Sata helping each other shoulder their heavy packs, and smiled.

When everyone was ready, with sun hats on their heads, all eleven travelers waved farewell to the family and made their way out to the road.

Ilika stopped and opened his shoulder bag. "This will do nicely."

"But Ilika!" Kibi challenged with a puzzled look, "we're still right in front of the farmhouse where we ate breakfast!"

"Today we have a wonderful opportunity that would be hard to find anywhere else. Are you all ready to do some serious trigonometry?"

Toli spoke with slight exasperation. "We've already measured about a hundred trees using tangent!"

"You told us about sine and cosine," Rini added calmly, "but we haven't tried them."

"Trees are easy," Ilika responded. "You can walk right up to them, and they form a convenient right angle with the ground. Today we'll get more serious. See that snow-covered mountain, the pointy one that looks tallest?"

Mati turned in the saddle and shaded her eyes from the morning sun.

"Yeah."

Everyone else gazed toward the northeast. The jagged white peak, wreathed in thin clouds, stood out starkly against a deep blue sky.

"I want to know how tall it is, and how far away," Ilika continued.

Miko spread his arms. "Very tall, and very far!"

"I want to know *exactly*, in feet."

Several students shrugged.

Toli frowned with worry. "I bet this'll take more than the tangent of forty-five degrees."

"Yeah, a bit more," Ilika admitted with a smile. "First we need a note-taker. Um . . . Rini." He handed paper and pencil to the quiet lad, then pulled the little hand-held device out of his bag and flipped open the cover. "The best name for this tool, in your language, is *knowledge processor*."

Buna quickly got close so she could see.

Ilika pressed some tiny buttons. "Compasses in your kingdom are too big to carry with us, so we'll make do with a simulation."

"Is that magic, like your bracelet?" Buna asked, grinning as she looked at the screen.

"Same kind of . . . magic."

Everyone gathered around. The little screen appeared to contain a compass rose and needle.

"Buna, this road runs fairly straight across the meadow. Take a bearing, please."

Buna received the knowledge processor with trembling hands. She had never touched Ilika's bracelet, nor imagined she ever would. Now she was holding, and was supposed to use, an even larger magical item, one with a constantly changing magical picture. "I'm . . . not sure . . . how."

"Face the direction the road goes, hold it out in front of you so you can move your eyes up and down to see the road and the compass. The thick lines are five degrees, the thin lines are one degree."

"Um . . . seven . . . eight . . . ten . . . no, nine . . . eight! . . . no, seven . . . damn!"

"That's okay. Just take some time with it, look way up the road, and see where the needle is most of the time."

"Most of the time . . . where are you little needle? Eight!" Buna declared.

"Got that, Rini?" Ilika asked.

"Got it!"

Ilika stepped close to Tera. "Mati, compass bearing to the mountain, please."

Mati received the little device, then nudged Tera slightly so they faced the mountain. "Um . . . let me see . . . no . . . yes . . . no . . . most of the time . . . thirty-one."

"Neti, the angle between the road and the mountain?"

Neti stared at the two numbers on Rini's paper.

Toli was about to explode with the answer, but Ilika, Boro, Miko, and Rini all flashed him stern looks.

"Twenty . . . three?" Neti dared to say with a very worried expression.

"Right!" Toli burst out.

"I did it!" Neti almost screamed, bouncing up and down. "For the first time, I did it in my head!"

Ilika smiled. "You sure did! Now, Rini, draw a right triangle. We are at one of the acute angles, call it A1. The right angle is ahead of us, up the road somewhere. The mountain is at the other acute angle. Yes, that looks good."

Everyone gathered around to see what Rini had drawn.

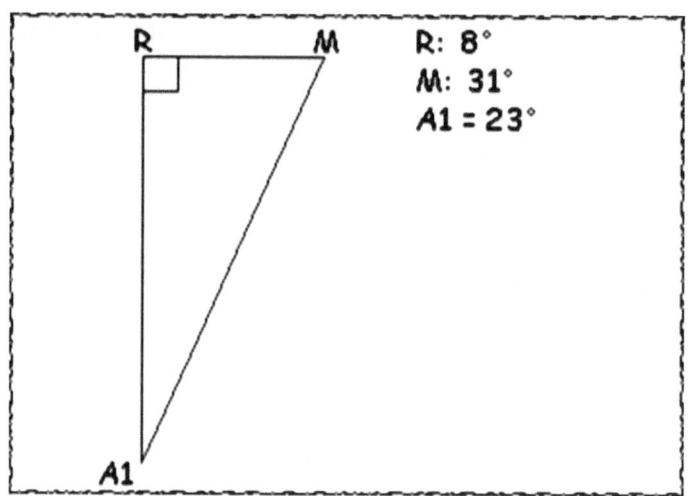

"Now it's time to move on. Toli, I want you to use that nice, even stride of yours and measure the distance from here to . . . somewhere up the road, we don't know where yet. If you forget your count, you'll have to walk all the way back here and start over."

"I won't forget!" he squeaked.

"Sata, your turn to take the compass. You need to find the place up the road where the mountain has changed its angle by one degree. It will be about half a mile, I think."

Sata received the device from Mati and started walking up the road.

Misa grabbed her bundle of blankets. It had been cold last night, and just looking at the white mountains made her shiver.

✳

Farmer Koto stood up from pretending to weed the front garden when the travelers finally took to the road. He had heard the rumors of sorcerers who could cast spells to put whole towns to sleep, and start or put out fires at will. These were strange folks who spoke of unnatural things like trigomancy and tangometry, but they didn't seem to be doing any harm.

As an afterthought, just to be sure it was still solid and real, he tossed the great silver piece up and caught it. Then he turned his mind to how to get his precocious middle daughter married off before she ran away.

✳

Sata stopped about every hundred yards, pointed the compass at the mountain, then shook her head.

Toli strode along behind, counting out loud.

After several more stops, Sata announced that her reading was getting close, but she wasn't quite happy with it yet. She marched on.

The others walked behind. Misa came last, dancing or hopping over clumps of grass with her new moccasins.

Sata stopped and took one more compass bearing. "That mountain is at thirty-two degrees, or I'm a billy goat."

Boro grinned. "You're much cuter than a billy goat."

Sata blushed.

Ilika took off his rucksack. "We'll be here awhile, so get comfortable. Toli, how far?"

Toli brought his strides right up to Sata's position. "One thousand and four!"

"I have determined," Ilika announced, "that a Toli-stride is about three point two feet long. Kibi, how many feet between the two points, rounded to the nearest foot?"

She received paper and pencil and went to work. Everyone else sat near Rini to look at his drawing, or near Kibi to watch her do the multiplication. After a few minutes, she handed the answer to Rini.

"We are at A2, Rini, and the line segment we just measured is B. From here to the right angle is C, and the far side of the triangle is D. Neti, how many degrees in angle A2?"

Neti grinned with happiness as she picked out the important numbers and worked out the difference in her head. "Twenty-four!"

Ilika looked in his shoulder bag and found a sheet with many numbers arranged in neat columns. "Miko, we need the tangents of twenty-three and twenty-four degrees."

Rini made notes as Miko found the numbers. Neti watched, then smiled at the boy she loved.

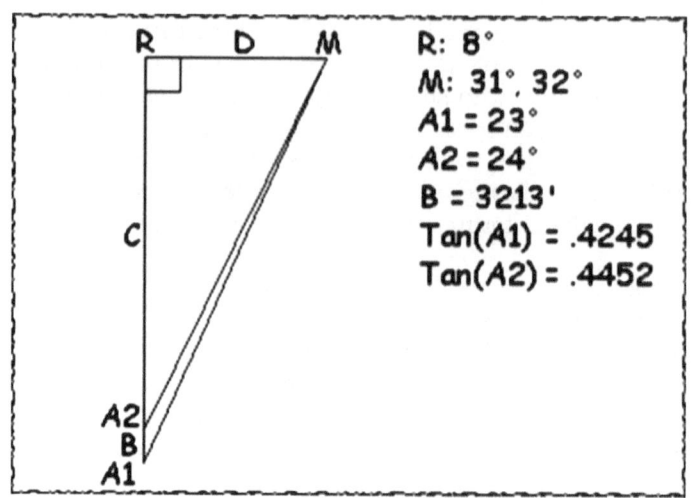

R: 8°
M: 31°, 32°
A1 = 23°
A2 = 24°
B = 3213'
Tan(A1) = .4245
Tan(A2) = .4452

"Boro, what is the relationship of the tangent function to the sides of a right triangle?"

"Wow ... err ... um ..." Boro began as he lay back in the grass, scrunched his face and searched his memory, "the tangent of the ... um ... angle is equal to the ... far side ... divided by the ... um ... near side."

"Perfect," Ilika complimented.

"Whew!"

"Toli, the tangent of angle A2 equals ..."

"D over C."

Ilika nodded. "Rini, the tangent of angle A1?"

Rini looked at his drawing, then got another piece of paper and wrote down Toli's answer and his own.

"Okay," Ilika announced, looking around. "Everyone take a good look at these two equations. We need to solve them."

Sata frowned. "I see a huge problem. Both have two unknown variables. No matter which one we solve for, there will always be another one, so we can never do a calculation!"

All the others looked at Ilika with blank faces. Misa chewed on a blade of grass.

"If we had only one equation," Ilika went on, "that would indeed make it unsolvable. But since we have two equations ..."

Rini's mouth suddenly opened.

"Do you see it, Rini?"

"I'm not sure, but when you look at something from two different directions, you can sometimes see a lot more about it."

"Yes. Since we have two equations, we can solve both for the same variable, then drop out that variable and put them together."

"I think we should solve for D," Rini suggested. "It looks easier."

Toli agreed, and did his work first. Then Rini did his part and combined the results.

Toli	Rini
$.4452 = \dfrac{D}{C}$	$.4245 = \dfrac{D}{3213 + C}$
$.4452 \times C = \dfrac{D}{C} \times C$	$.4245 \times (3213 + C) = \dfrac{D}{3213 + C} \times (3213 + C)$
$.4452 \times C = D$	$.4245 \times (3213 + C) = D$

$$.4452 \times C = .4245 \times (3213 + C)$$

"Hurray!" Buna cheered. "Only one variable!"

"Now we have to solve for C," Ilika continued, "and it's going to take some work. Everyone ready?"

They nodded.

"Buna, would you please distribute the right side?"

"Me?"

"I think you could use the practice."

Buna sat down with paper and pencil. After several scratch-outs, she started turning red. "I don't remember how," she whimpered in a broken voice.

"You just ..." Toli started to say, but Boro stuck an elbow in his ribs so hard he doubled over with pain.

Buna stared at the paper for several more minutes. Suddenly she screamed, "I CAN'T!" then jumped to her feet and stomped off into the grass, sobbing deeply.

Everyone remained silent, and Toli looked at the ground. Kibi and Misa went to sit with their friend. The rest stretched out in the grass to take a break.

After wiping her tears on her sleeves, Buna glanced back toward her teacher every minute or two. Other students also looked at Ilika off and on, expecting him to give Buna a hint or ask someone else.

Kibi knew him better than that, so she stretched out in the grass to watch the clouds go by.

✳

About a quarter hour later, Buna wandered back with Kibi and Misa at her side. "I guess . . . I'm ready to, you know, try it again, if that's okay," she said in a timid voice.

"It sure is," Ilika said softly. "Maybe . . . there's something you need to ask for that will help."

Everyone gathered near. The other girls gave their friend reassuring words and touches.

Buna thought for a long moment. "Would you . . . show me the formula again?"

Buna took the paper after Ilika wrote the formula, then looked at the problem. Toli handed her a pencil without daring to open his mouth. Buna carefully worked out the distribution, digit by digit, symbol by symbol, while everyone watched in silence.

$$M \times (A + B + C + ...) =$$
$$(M \times A) + (M \times B) + (M \times C) + ...$$

Buna

$$.4452 \times C = .4245 \times (3213 + C)$$
$$.4452 \times C = (.4245 \times 3213) + (.4245 \times C)$$

A shepherd on a hillside about a mile away heard the cheering and clapping, and looked toward the meadow, but had no idea what the happy occasion might be. He glanced around at his sheep, then went back to whittling designs into his walking stick.

*

Ilika could see a sparkle in Buna's eyes that hadn't been there earlier. "Now we can do that multiplication. Who needs to practice? Mati!"

With help from Sata, Mati lowered herself to the ground. Buna handed her paper and pencil, and stayed close to watch.

Mati was slow and careful at arithmetic, but always remembered the steps. She worked her way through the difficult multiplication as Buna watched with wide eyes. At the very end, with a nod from Ilika, Mati rounded the answer.

Ilika smiled. "Now we need to divide both sides by C. Would you take care of that, Kibi?"

"Sure," she agreed, got another sheet, and quickly finished.

"You can keep going," Ilika prompted, "distribute that C on the right side, please."

After a deep breath and a glance at the formula, Kibi went to work. Again Buna watched closely.

"And you have some simplifying you can do," Ilika nudged.

Kibi frowned. "I . . . don't see it," she said with a hint of irritation in her voice that Ilika heard clearly.

"You have two places were you are multiplying by one."

Kibi closed her eyes for a long moment, took a deep breath, then opened them. C divided by C nearly jumped out at her, twice.

$$\textbf{Mati}$$

$$.4452 \times C = (.4245 \times 3213) + (.4245 \times C)$$

$$.4452 \times C = 1364 + (.4245 \times C)$$

$$\textbf{Kibi}$$

$$\frac{.4452 \times C}{C} = \frac{1364 + (.4245 \times C)}{C}$$

$$\frac{.4452 \times C}{C} = \frac{1364}{C} + \frac{.4245 \times C}{C}$$

$$.4452 = \frac{1364}{C} + .4245$$

Everyone clapped.

"Now I think . . . Neti should subtract that tangent of twenty-three degrees from both sides."

Neti grinned. "I'm the subtraction queen today!" She looked at the numbers for a long moment as her smile slowly faded. "Ilika . . . is it okay if I don't do this one in my head?"

"Yes, Neti," he said, chuckling. "I don't think I could!"

Neti breathed a sigh of relief, took the sheet of paper Miko handed her, and began to work through the difficult arithmetic problem.

Buna was right beside Neti for the entire process, watching every step, sometimes holding her breath for a moment, sometimes smiling.

$$\text{Neti}$$

$$.4452 = \frac{1364}{C} + .4245$$

$$.4452 - .4245 = \frac{1364}{C} + .4245 - .4245$$

$$.0207 = \frac{1364}{C}$$

"Here's a challenging step for Rini. Get rid of that number on the right side."

Rini made quick work of his teacher's request.

"You fell into a trap," Ilika pointed out.

Rini looked hard at his work, then laughed. "Oh, donkey turds!"

"What?" Mati probed with obvious interest.

"I accidentally inverted C." Rini corrected his mistake. "Now I should invert both sides, right Ilika?"

Ilika nodded. Everyone watched Rini do the division.

Rini read the answer, the largest number he had ever used, then flopped backwards into the grass.

$$\text{Rini}$$

$$.0207 = \frac{1364}{C}$$

$$\frac{.0207}{1364} = \frac{1364}{C \times 1364}$$

$$\frac{.0207}{1364} = C$$

$$\frac{.0207}{1364} = \frac{1}{C}$$

$$\frac{1364}{.0207} = C$$

$$65894 = C$$

After running around in the meadow for a few minutes to unwind, everyone settled down to a snack of bread, goat cheese, and plums. Boro sat silently with his brow furrowed. Ilika waited until he found his voice.

"I was just wondering . . ." Boro finally began, "what good is figuring out things like this?"

"On a ship, if that mountain's in our way, our lives might depend on knowing how far away it is."

"But it takes so long to figure it out!"

"We're doing it by hand. On my ship, you would have instruments and tools to do the work for you, giving you the answer in seconds. But to intelligently guide your tools, you have to understand the process. If you don't, then the numbers become the masters, and you become the slaves."

Boro looked very thoughtful as he ate his plum.

Toli looked at Rini's drawing. "The road would have to go straight for ten miles to get to the right angle."

"Which it doesn't," Buna pointed out sharply.

Ilika stepped in. "The right angle is somewhere far up in the mountains, somewhere we probably couldn't find. That's why we had to work with two different angles."

"Can we figure out the slanty line now?" Rini asked with sparkling eyes.

Ilika smiled. "Yes, we've done the hard part, now finding the hypotenuse will be easy. Since we know the near side, we'll use the cosine function. I'll go through the steps while all of you watch."

They quickly closed the food sacks and crowded around.

"I look up the cosine of twenty-four degrees, and put in the value of C, the near side. H is unknown. Next I divide both sides, eliminate the identity, invert, and I've solved for H. Everyone with me?"

Some of them took a moment to catch up.

Ilika looked around. "I think . . . Sata needs some division practice."

She got pencil and paper and worked through the problem. "Wow. That's big."

$$\text{Ilika}$$

$$\text{Cos(A2)} = C / H$$

$$.9135 = 65894 / H$$

$$\frac{.9135}{65894} = \frac{65894 / H}{65894}$$

$$\frac{.9135}{65894} = 1 / H$$

$$\frac{65894}{.9135} = H$$

$$\text{Sata}$$

$$72134 = H$$

"That's the answer to my first question," Ilika announced. "Since a mile in your kingdom is about six thousand feet, that mountain is twelve miles away, plus a stone's throw."

*

After everyone took a break to throw rocks toward the mountain, none of which made it. Ilika sat down with Rini's drawing again. All the students gathered around. Misa continued picking little flowers.

"Now we need another angle measurement, angle A3. It's a vertical angle, so we use an instrument called an inclinometer. It's simpler than a compass, and just compares the angle to the gravity of the planet." He touched some keys on his knowledge processor and the display changed. "Miko and Neti, would you take a reading to the mountain top?"

Miko received the knowledge processor, which now had a circular scale and a line going from the center to the outside. He quickly discovered that the line always pointed downward. "So . . . I should use it sideways?"

"Yes," Ilika answered. "Sight along one edge while Neti reads it. Then switch and see if you get the same number."

While Miko sighted to the top of the mountain, holding the little device as still as he could, Neti peered at the screen. "Seven . . . no, eight degrees."

Miko read eight or nine degrees, so they settled on eight.

"Kibi," Ilika said with a smile, "you're in charge of finding the elevation. You don't have to do all the work yourself, but you're in charge."

After showing her teeth and snarling slightly at Ilika, Kibi sat down by Rini and his sheet of numbers. Rini soon finished drawing another triangle to represent the elevation problem.

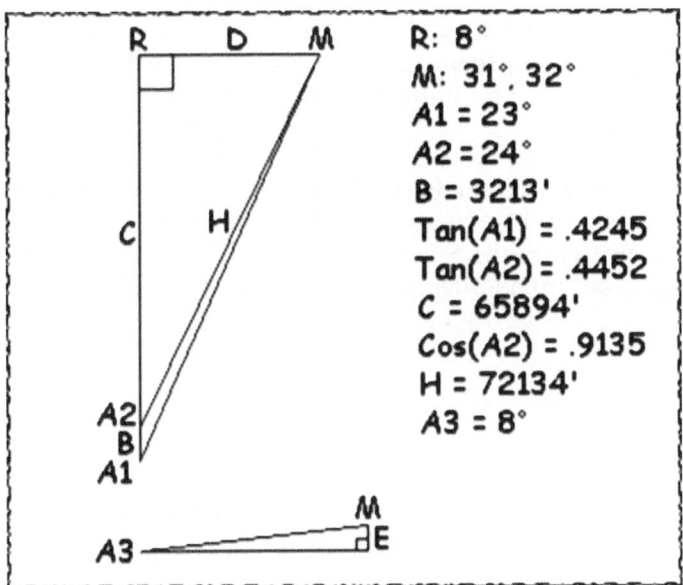

R: 8°
M: 31°, 32°
A1 = 23°
A2 = 24°
B = 3213'
Tan(A1) = .4245
Tan(A2) = .4452
C = 65894'
Cos(A2) = .9135
H = 72134'
A3 = 8°

"Rini, we're at A3, right?" Kibi asked.

"Yep."

"That makes the bottom line of this triangle the same as H, right Toli?"

"Exactly."

"Sata, review for me the tangent function."

"The far side divided by the near side."

Kibi got a piece of paper and started writing a formula. "Boro, check me."

"Looks right."

"Buna, tangent of eight degrees, please."

She shuffled through the papers, then read the number to Kibi.

Kibi looked at her equation in which the unknown was still part of a division problem, and took a leap. "Toli, Sata, Rini, check this step for me."

They all nodded.

Kibi

$$Tan(A3) = \frac{E}{H}$$

$$.1405 = \frac{E}{72134}$$

$$.1405 \times 72134 = E$$

"Whew. Any volunteers for the big bad multiplication?"

"I'll do it!" Toli blurted out.

No one else made a sound. He worked his way through the four partial answers, finally summing them and inserting the decimal point.

"Thank you, Toli. I'll round that to ten thousand one hundred and thirty-five . . . feet."

The next ten minutes were filled with dancing, whooping and hollering, hand shakes, and pats on the back. Ilika was very proud of all his students. Each had, in his or her own way, wrestled dragons to help solve their first serious trigonometry problem.

Misa peeked out from under her new sun hat. "Can we go now?"

✳   ✳   ✳

Chapter 45: Precious Freedom

Before the troop of happy students reached the end of the meadow, they came to the track to the goat herder's cabin, just where Farmer Koto said it would be, winding it's way into the dense, dark forest on the eastern side of the meadow. After following the narrow track for several minutes, walking single-file with Mati and Tera in the lead, they came upon a huge old stump nestled in the trees beside a little stream.

As Mati rounded the massive tree stump, she first saw an irregular mossy roof, then little windows. Eventually a door came into sight, and on the far side she glimpsed a rock chimney. "It's a house! It's the most beautiful, magical house I've ever seen!"

Miko and Neti walked up to the house that was, to their eyes, very crude and cramped, little more than an animal burrow. They found a rope tied through the door handle. "No one's home," Miko announced.

As Boro arrived, he looked over the empty goat pen and shed in the yard, and other signs that they had, indeed, found the dwelling of a goatherd.

Everyone got comfortable on some fallen logs not far down the stream, and Buna handed out ripe plums.

"So, Ilika," Boro began, resting his heavy rucksack on a log and slipping out of the straps, "the crew of your ship will have hard problems to solve, like the one we just did, but instruments and things will make it easier?"

"Much easier. But we'll sometimes pretend something is broken, just for practice."

"What if . . ." Miko pondered out loud with a soul-searching look on his face, "there's a *real* emergency . . . and someone makes a *big* mistake, a *dangerous* mistake?"

"Just like with anything in life, Miko, we scramble to fix it if we can. If we can't, well . . ."

There was a long moment of silence as others nodded, even though Ilika hadn't finished his sentence. Miko continued to quietly wrestle with some very personal feelings.

"I've heard that . . . lots of ship hands . . . die on long voyages," Toli said with a shaking voice.

"Not where I come from!" Ilika assured them. "The ships in your harbor can sink very easily. The crews have miserable living conditions, bad food, no medical care, and terrible leadership. Misa would make a better captain than some . . ."

The girl grinned proudly.

"But in the Transport Service, the death of a crew member is very rare. Also, long voyages are rare. My ship is fast, so most trips will take just a few hours, at most a few days."

Miko and Toli both looked happier.

A thoughtful look came to Neti. "I think we should pick a new emergency meeting place."

"Good idea," Ilika said and pulled out the map as everyone gathered around. "We are here, at the north end of the big meadow, this area on the map with no trees. Before we cross the first mountain pass, here, our meeting place will be Koto's farm. After the pass . . . it will be the village in the middle of the mountains."

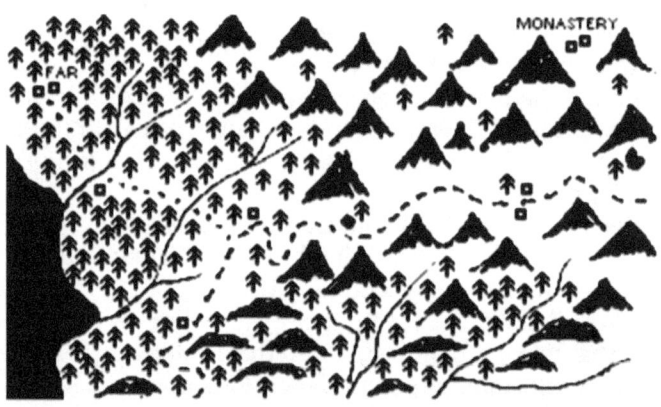

"Is that a monastery of a religious order?" Buna questioned with a frown.

"It's not the same order that gave us trouble. From what little I've heard, it's a very secretive order that doesn't get mixed up in politics."

Buna sighed with relief. "That's good."

Soon they began to hear the sounds of goats coming through the trees from the meadow, a herding dog nipping at their heels. The sounds continued and grew louder as the animals approached their home.

Eventually the dog sensed the strangers and broke off his work. He placed himself between the house and the group, snarling.

Finally a young man about Ilika's age came into view, a worried look on his face. With each step, he let his long walking stick take most of his weight on one side. Arriving at the far bank of the stream, he stood beside his faithful dog and looked down at the strangers with cautious eyes peering out from under wild, tangled hair. After a few moments, he relaxed. "It's alright, Sam, they look harmless."

"We are," Ilika said, still seated.

The young goatherd, with the help of his dog, coaxed the fifty or more goats into their pen. After hobbling by his house to glance at the knot securing his door, he returned to the stream. "What brings you to my home, strangers?"

"We stayed with Farmer Koto last night and bought some supplies. Now we're looking for a rucksack for this young lady to carry her blankets . . ."

Misa waved shyly.

"Koto said you might have one you could sell us."

"Hmm. I might."

"Also, maybe some hard cheese if you've got too much."

The goatherd looked at each member of the group, then limped back to his house, untied the knot, and disappeared inside. He returned a few minutes later with a rucksack. "It's small, so I don't use it much, but it might be okay for the girl."

Ilika examined the sack — old but sturdy. He handed it to Misa, who looked it over, then stuck her head inside. When she came back out, she was smiling.

Kibi noticed the goatherd looking at Mati the entire time.

"What will you sell it for?" Ilika asked.

The young man pulled his attention from Mati with an effort. "You tell me what it would cost in town."

"You mean the town that burned up?" Buna asked with a twisted smirk.

"I heard about that. It's gonna be a long trip for supplies until they rebuild."

"At Port Town," Ilika began, "I'd pay seven coppers for it. But since we're way up here in the woods, I'll give you a silver."

"Done!" the goatherd said quickly to seal the deal.

Ilika dug the coin out of his pouch.

The young handicapped man looked at Mati again while he spoke. "I think I've got three or four fully-cured cheeses in my cellar . . ."

"Your magical house has a cellar too?" Mati asked with wide eyes, looking directly at him for the first time.

Their eyes met and time stood still for both of them.

"Um . . . yes," the goatherd managed to say, finally remembering the question but not taking his eyes from Mati. "Way up here in the woods we smoke meat, press cheese, dry fruit, and gather whatever we can from the forest, so a cellar is important. It's already late," he went on, reluctantly looking at the others, "so you're welcome to camp here and make a fresh start in the morning."

Ilika nodded. "Thank you. Tomorrow we head for the mountain pass."

With an effort of will, the goatherd turned and hobbled toward his house.

✳

As the group made camp among the fallen logs, the other students quickly noticed that Mati's head was elsewhere. She spent most of her time looking at the little house in the old tree stump, and very little time caring for Tera, or helping with the camp. Rini made sure Tera had everything she needed.

Soon Boro had a fire going, and Neti started soup. Miko brought in armloads of wood, and Sata assembled their bags of dried herbs and spices on a log for Neti.

When they were about to eat, the goatherd appeared with a big wedge of cheese on a board. As the twelve of them began passing around bowls of steaming soup, chunks of bread, and sticks of cheese, the setting sun sent farewell shafts of orange light into the clearing for a few minutes.

"I found four small wheels of well-aged cheese," the goatherd said as he finished his soup, some of which had gotten into his wild hair. "But one thing that's in very short supply up here in the mountains is . . . young ladies who will even look at a man who . . . doesn't walk too well. If you'd let me talk to the beauty here who has the same problem I do, I'd sure appreciate it."

A tense silence came over the group.

Ilika had to swallow before he could speak. "She's not mine to say what she can or can't do. She belongs to herself."

"Would you like to talk, pretty lady? Maybe . . . check on the goats with me?"

To the surprise and frustration of all her friends, Mati sat grinning from ear to ear, and a moment later nodded.

The handsome brown-eyed goatherd rose, took a moment to steady himself with his walking stick, then held his hand out for Mati. With his help, she got her crutch under her and they slowly hobbled together toward the goat pen.

"You and me could be happy out here, me tending the goats, you keeping the house. You could ride your donkey when we go to town. Koto lets me borrow one of his horses . . ."

"Ilika!" Neti whispered loudly once the handicapped pair was gone. "You have to stop him!"

Ilika looked back at Neti and frowned. "You have all questioned me, again and again, to be sure you are free. Are you, or are you not, willing to respect Mati's freedom now that she might choose her own way?"

They all looked at the ground.

"We're sorry," Boro mumbled. "It's just . . . hard to imagine heading up the trail and doing lessons without . . . Mati and Tera."

"I know," Ilika agreed softly.

Kibi gazed thoughtfully into the flames of the campfire while the others whispered their frustrations to each other and slowly got ready for bed.

About an hour later, the goatherd delivered Mati back to the camp. They said good-night tenderly, and Mati crawled into her bedroll quietly, as if already in a dream.

＊

The entire group was thoughtful, almost sullen, the following morning as porridge simmered over the fire. The night had been cold, and most of them still wore their cloaks. Misa sat wrapped in her blankets.

"Ilika, is Tera mine?" Mati asked suddenly. "I mean . . . if I decide to stay here, do I get to keep her? I'd give you back all the money in my pouch . . ."

Ilika hesitated for a second. "Yes, Mati, Tera is yours, completely yours. And if you decide to stay, the coins in your pouch will be a gift from us."

"But Mati, you can't!" Buna burst out with a pleading tone.

Mati locked eyes with Buna and took a deep breath. "You guys have to understand . . . I was a crippled slave. I had no hope of any kind of life. Ilika gave me hope, and many other things. He says I have a chance to be on his crew, but I'm not stupid. I'm a cripple! What am I going to do on a ship, peel potatoes?"

Everyone else was stunned into complete silence by Mati's words.

"I have never, in my entire life," she went on, breathing hard, "had a man tell me he liked me, and wanted to share a home with me. I can't walk away from the only man to ever say that, on the chance that four of you are going to die tomorrow so Ilika will have to pick me."

In the silence that followed, Kibi put down her porridge and moved close to Mati on the log. "We're friends, right?"

"Of course, Kibi."

"Will you take a short walk with me before you make your decision?"

"Okay."

With Kibi's help, Mati stood up, took her crutch, and the two girls walked slowly to the far side of the goat shed.

Ilika looked much older and sadder as he watched Kibi and Mati walk away.

＊

They found some old wooden boxes behind the shed and sat down.

"Mati, I just want to share some things I know are true."

"Thanks, Kibi. You've always been honest with me."

"And I'm going to be honest with you now, because it might be the last chance I get. The absolute truth is, Mati, you have the same chance of being picked as I do."

Mati's eyes opened wide. "But you're . . ."

"That's right. And I know he's going to pick you also, for a real place, not just for peeling potatoes. But he can't tell us yet. It would ruin the group."

"I know. He wants everyone to do their best."

"And there's a boy in our group who is dreaming of sharing a bed with you someday. He's just not the kind of boy who's going to blab about it until the time is right. He wouldn't have faced that wolf for just anyone. He's going to be on that crew too. You stay here, and you'll never hear him say those words to you."

Mati looked troubled.

"And if that isn't enough to convince you," Kibi continued, "then I want you to tell that goatherd all the things you know, all the things you can do, and see what happens."

Kibi stood and walked back to the group alone.

＊

Mati sat for another quarter hour, then made her way slowly back toward the camp, toward her teacher Ilika, toward her friend Kibi . . . and toward Rini. As she rounded the goat pen, the magical tree-stump house came into view. Just at that moment, the handsome young goatherd came out, walking stick in one hand, four small cheese wheels under his other arm. A resolute expression came to Mati and she hurried so she would arrive at the camp before him.

"I appreciate what you tried to do, Kibi, but I'm staying here. I can't give up something real for things other people might do someday in the future if they happen to get around to it."

"Ilika, aren't you going to do something?" Buna spat out with frustration.

"No, Buna, I'm not. I'm not Mati's master. If Mati, or any of you, truly needs my help, I'll be there, to my last breath if necessary. But there's nothing happening here Mati can't handle."

"But Mati, our group wouldn't be the same without you!" Neti pleaded.

Miko, Toli, and Boro all mumbled agreements, but were unsure what else to say. Rini looked sad, but said nothing.

Buna stood up, red-faced, hands clenched into fists. "I won't let him take you away from us!"

"Stop it! All of you!" Mati screamed. "I'm free, and I've decided. I'm staying here, and it's time for you to go!"

The goatherd, hearing the entire argument as he approached, stepped beside Mati wearing a subtle smile.

Ilika slowly rose. "I wish you well, Mati. Like I said, Tera is yours, and the coins in your pouch are a gift from us. We will pack up and leave as soon as I pay for the cheese."

Buna suddenly turned and ran down the path toward the meadow, shaking her fists and crying.

Rini just sat on a log looking at the ground.

＊   ＊   ＊

Chapter 46: Grief

Mati and the handsome young goat herder sat side by side on a log. Each person in the group, with the exception of Buna who had already left, gave lukewarm farewells, then went to pack rucksack and bedroll. With voices hardly louder than a whisper, no laughter brightened the forest clearing where the little tree-stump house stood silently.

Last of all, Rini came forward and mumbled good wishes for Mati's future. She didn't dare look into his sad eyes.

When the remaining travelers were ready to depart, a cold fog began to creep in from the meadow, causing all the leaves and pine needles to drip.

Tera stood looking around with confusion. She saw most of her people take to the trail, and took a step to follow, but then noticed that Mati was not moving, nor even calling her to be saddled.

Mati hugged her donkey with one arm and held hands with the goatherd as she watched Ilika pause before leaving the clearing, turn and wave, then disappear into the trees.

*

Toli reached out his hand to Buna when they found her sitting in the meadow, tearing at the wet grass. She stood and started walking, but her angry pout warned Toli not to bother her. He silently carried her rucksack and bedroll for the next mile.

Ilika carried a different kind of weight, standing up for Mati's freedom even as he dreaded losing her. Everyone else walked with slumped shoulders and downcast eyes as they trudged along through the mist. Kibi could see the pain in Rini's eyes on the rare occasions he looked up from the trail.

The road soon narrowed at the northern end of the meadow. Two trails continued, one into the far northwestern corner of the kingdom where few people lived, and the other into the heart of the mountains. Neither could accommodate wagons or carts. From this point, only feet or hooves could pass. Boro led them onto the right branch toward the mountains.

✳

The trail quickly climbed above the fog and into bright sunshine. A few hundred feet above the meadow, they came to the cabin of the other herder Farmer Koto had mentioned, an older man with many sheep, a few goats, and two dogs. He and Ilika agreed they would camp in his yard and the group would make a hearty stew with smoked mutton and other supplies from his cellar.

"I thought you didn't like to eat meat," Boro asked, just for something to say.

"I don't, but for the next week or two we'll be in a colder climate. The fat in the mutton will help our bodies keep warm, especially at night."

With little joy, the students set up camp around the shepherd's outdoor fire circle. After unrolling her bedroll, Kibi faced Ilika. "We need to stay here for a little while," she said with her firmest voice. "At least . . . three days."

Ilika looked into her eyes and saw complete determination. "Can you tell me . . . what's up?"

"I . . . um . . . planted some seeds . . . and they need a little time to sprout." Ilika nodded.

✳

"Are you sure you didn't get burned out of Lumber Town?" the old shepherd asked as they sat around the campfire drinking tea that evening. "I've rarely seen a group of souls look as sad as you folks."

"We . . . lost a friend," Neti said, "but not in the fire."

"A girl, I'd guess," he went on as he looked around the circle with keen eyes, "and I bet she belonged to . . . the quiet freckled lad there."

Rini looked up with moist eyes.

"Death comes to all of us," the old man said, taking a deep drink of his tea. "I was not always alone up here."

"She didn't die," Rini said softly. "She just . . . chose to live with someone else."

"That's cold. A better one will come along. You just have to wait."

"I will," Rini whispered as a tear rolled down his cheek.

✳

By mid-morning the following day, the shepherd's cabin was bathed in warm sunshine even though the meadow below was still enshrouded in thick, cold fog. With a hearty breakfast of porridge and milk in their bellies, Ilika announced a review of all the mathematics necessary for trigonometry.

For an hour, their teacher gently coaxed them along, but not even Toli or Sata could find any interest in the subject.

After reheated stew for lunch that none of them tasted, Ilika asked them to write about their feelings. Boro succeeded in breaking another pencil. Neti couldn't remember how to spell even the simplest words. The rest fared little better.

By late afternoon, Ilika got the message and let them just sit, or wander in the nearby trees, or talk quietly among themselves. He and Kibi worked with the shepherd's supplies to make mutton soup with dumplings. They all ate dinner in silence.

Misa asked for someone to tell a story as they sat around the fire in the evening, but no one offered.

*

"I think we need a week for everyone to get over it," Kibi said late the following morning as she and Ilika sat on a nearby hillside. Below they could see Boro and Neti working on something for lunch. In the background spread the large meadow, now full of painful memories.

"I'm . . . not willing to wait that long."

Kibi looked at him with questioning eyes.

"On my ship, things will sometimes happen to make us sad. That doesn't mean we can completely cease to do our jobs. I'll give you those three days. Tomorrow I'm leaving, with those who are ready to continue learning, while they grieve if necessary."

Kibi was silent for a minute. "Count me in. And . . . as strange as it sounds . . . I'm sure Rini will be with us."

*

After lunch, the shepherd prepared to take his flock to a meadow several miles to the north. Once he and his animals were gone, the camp became deathly quiet. The warm afternoon air was very still, and Misa thought she could hear Farmer Koto's sheep at the south end of the meadow.

For a few moments, no one responded to the sound of hooves on the trail below. Suddenly everyone jumped up and ran down the path.

Tera gave her two-toned call when she saw her people. She seemed to be carrying a large sack, which slid off into Boro's arms as soon as the donkey came to a halt.

Mati, barely conscious, eyes swollen and caked with dirt, looked out from the mud-covered rag that had once been her cloak. "Never . . . again . . ." she mumbled.

* * *

Chapter 47: Mati's Story

Everyone wanted to help. So many volunteers crowded around that Ilika was able to slip away, leaving Kibi in charge.

Sata, making a pot of soup, had people offering their services constantly. The pile of firewood was rapidly growing and threatening to topple over. Tera had her every need fulfilled by Rini, with extra helpers when they were shooed away from the cooking fire.

Neti and Buna tended their stricken friend, cleaning and applying ointment to bruises and scratches, while Miko and Toli bumped into each other bringing water, cloth, or anything else the girls needed.

Soon Sata was feeding Mati warm soup, a spoonful at a time, while Misa tucked blankets around her and Kibi rubbed her feet.

It occurred to Mati that she may have just gone through Hell, but now she was in Heaven.

✳

Although Mati looked terrible when she first arrived, none of her injuries were serious. Her worst problems were hunger and thirst, and Sata's delicious soup quickly remedied both. Mati slept for a few hours, and when she awoke, the sun had set, the fire was built up against the evening chill, and Neti was passing out mugs of tea.

After sipping her tea for a few minutes, Mati's story began with a very unexpected statement. "He really is a good man."

Mouths fell open all around the fire circle as everyone, including Ilika, struggled to understand how Mati could have been in the condition she was, and then made such a statement.

"He just wanted a good wife, a companion to cook and clean for him, a girl to warm his bed and bear him children. There's nothing wrong with that. The only problem was . . . by the end of the first day, I felt like I was back in slavery. It felt so bad . . . I knew I couldn't be a simple, obedient wife to him

. . . or anyone else."

"But he didn't have to beat you!" Buna burst out, seething with anger.

Mati looked at Buna with understanding. "He didn't beat me. In fact, he offered to help several times, but I wouldn't let him. All the scratches and bruises and mud . . . were all my fault."

Disbelieving looks met Mati's glance all around the circle.

"I'd better start over from the beginning."

Boro nodded slowly.

"During the first afternoon, he showed me his house and told me all the things I could do to help him. I loved the little house, and I was completely willing to cook, and clean, and warm his bed."

Mati glanced at Kibi before continuing. "But I also wanted to do something I could do well, so I told him I could read and write. It could earn us money — scribes aren't cheap!"

Everyone nodded or laughed.

"He brushed it off and said I had to learn to milk goats. I was willing to milk goats, but I didn't want to feel like a slave, so I told him I knew arithmetic, even a little trigonometry. Lumber Town's going to need an accountant, maybe a surveyor, when they rebuild. He laughed and said I had to clean the house."

"Creep," Misa mumbled under her breath.

Mati smiled. "After that I didn't hold anything back. I told him I knew the rules of logical inference, and the fallacies, and I could help him solve problems. He said he didn't need that kind of help, and I had to learn my place. That made me mad."

Miko nodded and grinned. "Good for you!"

"I told him I knew the atomic numbers of the common elements, and could figure out their electron levels."

Kibi tried to keep from grinning, but wasn't doing a very good job.

"Then we just stopped, right there in the middle of the house, and glared at each other without saying a word. At that moment I knew in my heart I couldn't be a simple wife to a simple goatherd. It's all your fault, Ilika."

Ilika smiled.

"What do you mean?" Toli challenged.

"I know what she means," Boro said. "I felt the same thing back at Farmer Koto's house. We can never go back to being simple people, can we, Ilika?"

There was a long moment of silence.

"Probably not. Mati found out what it's like to have all her knowledge belittled. You, Boro, were recently offered a life without trigonometry or chemistry or the deep trust you've developed with your fellow students. The fact is, none of you are simple people. Most people make life choices by basic emotions and simple needs. I picked all of you because I thought you could go beyond that."

Boro pondered his teacher's words for a moment. "I thought so. Thanks."

"Thank you for choosing the harder road, Boro. And you also, Mati."

Mati smiled at the black-haired girl beside Ilika. "Kibi helped. She told me things . . . I already knew, but just didn't quite believe yet. But . . ." Mati paused and sighed. "I had to find out for myself."

Kibi glanced up from her mug of tea.

"The next two days were a living Hell worse than anything I ever experienced as a slave. But every bit of it was my own doing.

"I wouldn't let him help. I had gotten myself into that mess, and I wanted to get myself out. It took me hours to get my saddlebags and bedroll to the back of the shed where Tera was tied. By then it was dark. I cried and talked to Tera, then curled up in the dirt beside her and slept."

"I wish we had known . . ." Neti said with sympathy.

Mati smiled for a moment. "Then yesterday it was cold and foggy all day. I woke up shivering and I don't think I ever stopped. About noon I tried getting Tera saddled. I stacked up old boxes, but most of them were rotten and wouldn't hold me. I got it on once, but it slipped off and fell right on top of me."

Boro growled. "I feel so guilty for not being there to help!"

"No!" Mati shouted. "I needed to do it myself. Ilika understands."

Teacher and handicapped student made eye contact.

"Then, just before dark, I was whimpering and close to giving up when suddenly Tera looked at me and lay down. I laughed and cried at the same time because I had been doing everything the hard way."

Several of her friends chuckled.

Mati smiled. "I easily got the saddle on and Tera stood up when I asked her. In the twilight I got it cinched a little, but then I was exhausted. I curled up in the dirt again and cried myself to sleep. Poor Tera had to sleep all night with the stupid thing on her back, but she lay down next to me and kept me warm on one side."

Sata and Buna smiled.

"This morning I cried again when I realized I had put on the saddle without the saddlebags."

Moans of sympathy came from all around the fire.

"But I refused to leave them, still packed with supplies from Farmer Koto, my clothes, and the ointment. So after feeling sorry for myself for an hour or two, I got over it and just put them on top of the saddle."

Rini, who had unsaddled Tera, grinned knowingly.

"Even with Tera down, it took another hour to get the bedroll tied on. I was so weak and tired, I looked to see if it was getting dark so I could sleep again."

Buna started laughing. "It was probably about noon!"

Mati grinned. "Next came the hardest thing I've ever done. I never actually sat in the saddle. With the saddlebags sticking out, all I could do was hold on while Tera stood up. Then I just hoped and prayed she knew which way to go."

Neti smiled. "She did."

"She's a good donkey, and I love her with all my heart," Mati declared. Suddenly her eyes snapped open wide. "Oh, no! I forgot my crutch!"

Rini snickered.

Ilika reached behind him and brought the precious item into view. "This one?"

Mati sighed deeply.

"So *that's* where you went after Mati arrived!" Miko said with gleaming eyes, looking at Ilika.

Buna grinned. "Did you have to use your bracelet on the dog?"

Ilika nodded.

* * *

Chapter 48: Perspective

After a good night's sleep and plenty of hot porridge for breakfast, Mati quickly regained her strength, and a new light of confidence showed in her eyes. She and Boro had much to talk about that day. They had both been offered relationships that would include all the pleasures and rewards of marriage and family. A few months before, neither of them could have imagined better fortune.

The old shepherd and his flock returned in the late afternoon just as Neti cut vegetables and Sata added spices to the pot. After tending his animals, he was glad to sit down to a bowl of tasty stew, with plenty of goat cheese on the side.

With the missing traveler back in the circle and spirits lifted, the old man asked for a story. A new tale, called *Three Birthdays*, was told for the first time, with Buna's permission — and embarrassment.

The shepherd told of a time when a goat helped him find a lost sheep, and another time when a goat butted a sheep over the edge of a cliff to its death. Different goat, he explained.

Buna snorted. "Now I'm *sure* I prefer sheep!

As evening light faded from the sky, the temperature dropped and cloaks came out. The shepherd said good-night and went about checking on his flock and talking to his dogs.

Toli put another branch on the fire. "Does the trail through the mountains go near that ten thousand foot peak we measured?"

"I don't know, Toli. By the way, that peak is ten thousand feet *higher* than the meadow, which is three thousand feet above sea level."

"So it's thirteen thousand feet high!"

Ilika nodded. "That reminds me ... I haven't taught you negative numbers yet, have I?"

The crackling of the fire was loud in the silence that followed.

"They're easy. For many things, we count not just in one direction from zero, but in two directions. For example, sea level is zero, land elevations are positive, and depths in the ocean are negative. The only time they're a little tricky is when you cross over the zero. Say I am standing on a rock ten feet above the ocean, and I jump down fifteen feet. Where am I?"

Rini chuckled.

Toli's hand shot into the air.

Sata grinned.

"Yeah, I know you three have it nailed already. Miko?"

"Um ... ten feet above, go down fifteen ... you are now *drowning* five feet underwater."

"Good. Mati, a fish is eight feet underwater, and swims up ten feet."

"It ... jumps out of the water two feet ... and lands in the fisherman's boat!"

"Right. Kibi, three minus five."

She took another sip of her tea as she visualized the situation. "Negative two," she said in a distant voice.

"Yes. Buna, negative two plus four."

"Oh shit."

"Deep breath, picture the situation. You are two feet under water, now jump up four feet."

"Um ... I can do it ... um ... I'm a little birdie flapping my wings ... um ... two feet up!"

"Perfect!"

Buna wiggled and glowed with happiness. Ilika ended the lesson there, seeing that most of his students were getting sleepy.

After tucking her blankets into her bedroll cover, Mati decided to check on Tera, who was tied to a tree not far away where she had some grass to eat. Looking in that direction, she saw Rini already brushing and talking to her precious donkey. Mati smiled and crawled into her blankets.

＊

As a pot of porridge simmered the following morning, the sun rose behind a snowcapped peak, appearing to emerge right out of the top of the mountain. Ilika overheard chatter as they reminded each other that the two were actually eighty million miles apart.

The old shepherd came out of his goat shed with fresh milk to add to the meal, and a small pot of molasses. "A little something to help celebrate the return of your friend."

They all glowed with youthful happiness as he added a spoonful of the sweet substance to each of their bowls.

With a warm breakfast under their belts, they made ready to depart, as they knew it would take all day to get over the first mountain pass. Boro bought a sack of smoked mutton from the herder and tied it to the outside of his rucksack, as no one could find any more room in their bags.

They waved good-bye as they took to the trail and the shepherd turned his attention to his flock.

✳

At about three thousand seven hundred feet, the troop paused on the rocky trail. Below them spread the huge meadow where they had worked through their first hard trigonometry project together.

Buna recalled the embarrassing moment when she couldn't remember how to distribute multiplication, and had to go off by herself to struggle with feelings of failure.

Some of them thought they could see Farmer Koto's place at the far south end of the meadow, where Misa had acquired her moccasins and sun hat. Boro remembered the sweetness of the hour he spent with Josa, listening as she revealed her heart's desire and inviting him to stay and share life with her. Sata remembered different feelings.

They couldn't see the goat herder's house, but knew about where it nestled in the trees beside the little stream, and thought they could make out a flock in the meadow. Mati swallowed, realizing how close she came to making that her new home, and hoping she wouldn't someday be kicking herself for her decision.

Almost straight below them down the slope, the old shepherd's cabin was visible. They all liked him, but knew he was now heading northwest with his sheep and goats.

✳

The path angled up a long ridge to the south, and then changed direction at about four thousand five hundred feet. The trees became smaller and fewer as they climbed. Finding a good place to rest, they brought out bread, goat cheese, and plums.

Miko looked to the west where he could see a sliver of the ocean. Somewhat against his will, the memory of the bluff returned, and his attempt to convince Kibi that Ilika would not be at the emergency meeting place. He was beginning to accept the fact that he was good at certain kinds of leadership, like finding the best way to get from one place to another, but not other kinds. Those other kinds of leadership took something he didn't yet understand. He kept trying to put his finger on what it was about Kibi and Boro that made Ilika pick them for tough leadership jobs . . . but hadn't found it yet.

Misa stared southward. The burned area that started a little west of her town, and went for many miles east, could be clearly seen. She hoped with all her heart that her mother and father had run fast enough. But she was ready to accept that even if they had, she couldn't find them right now. She was with some nice people, she was having adventures and hearing stories, and even thinking about her own story. Maybe someday she would find them.

Maybe she wouldn't, and would stick with her friend Buna. Or if Buna went on the ship, there would still be four who were staying. She decided, at that moment, to make friends with everyone so she would have someone to stick with no matter who went and who stayed.

Toli was looking in the same direction, reliving the moment the wolf had appeared in front of him. He never consciously decided to run away and leave Mati alone. It was just something his body did, and the next thing he knew, he was cowering behind a log and wondering what had happened. Even though he was fairly sure his chances of being on Ilika's crew had ended in that moment of panic, he still wondered if there was any way he could do better next time.

He filled his lungs with the cold mountain air. "I think I should give you a lift, Misa. These sharp rocks are going to slice up your moccasins."

"That would be fun, Toli. And I'm really sorry I pinched you. That was Misa the Scared Little Kid. This is Misa the Adventurer, and she doesn't hurt her friends."

Toli smiled, shouldered his rucksack, and hoisted the seven-year-old onto his shoulders to tackle the next part of the trail, which climbed the rocky slope northward.

*

At about five thousand three hundred feet, the trail turned directly east toward the pass, but a rock outcropping gave them a better view just a few hundred feet west. The wind was stronger and colder, and the ocean now clearly visible, all the way down to the bay they had visited twice.

For Sata, that bay held special meaning, the place where she finally realized the world could be completely friendly, even though it contained many ways to hurt or kill her. She had struggled with the notion at the steam vent, at the cave near Port Town, and all during their passage north along the coast. She found the courage to put the idea into action when they huddled inside their tiny refuge at high tide and Boro needed help with Tera. When she stepped back onto the beach and walked with her fellow students into that bay, something about her had changed, she was somehow stronger, and all the things out there that could kill her suddenly seemed . . . okay.

She could remember herself before she had gone through that transition. From where she stood now, the Sata who had once washed tables and delighted in earning a copper piece seemed very small.

That same refuge at high tide taught Neti something different, and she remembered those thoughts and feelings as she gazed southwest toward the bay. Before that day, she had worshipped Miko. He had promised her they would find a way out of slavery and someday have a home and a family, and two months later Ilika selected them and they were free. Her admiration for her true love had not been tarnished at the steam vent. Accidents happen to everyone. But when he panicked in the waterfall bowl at high tide, she realized he could make serious mistakes, and that she was going to have to stay sharp and make good decisions when he could not. He was just a boy, and even though she loved him, she would have to protect herself . . . and her children.

It was mid-afternoon, and the pass called to them. It looked close now, perhaps just a mile or two away. They shouldered their burdens once more and returned to the trail.

*

The two priests, wearing satisfied expressions, stepped out of Farmer Koto's house.

"It's amazing how little silver it takes to loosen the tongues of peasants," one said, staying a half-step behind his superior.

The other was silent and thoughtful as he mounted his horse. Finally, a hundred yards up the road, he spoke. "They're two days ahead of us, and could easily be deep in the mountains by now ... or to that blasted monastery. We'll have to ride hard."

They pushed their horses to a trot, knowing such speed would not be possible once they started up the mountain path.

*

After the eleven travelers walked about five miles from their last stop, they all knew they had greatly misjudged the distance. It was true that the highest point on the trail they could see from their last stop was about two miles away. Then an alpine meadow stretched for half a mile, the long climb up to the saddle between two peaks took another hour, and finally the slow zigzag through the broken rocks of the pass itself wore them out completely.

When they finally approached the real pass, the wind was threatening to freeze them solid and push them, willing or not, right through the narrow gap. Ilika's bracelet informed him they were at seven thousand one hundred feet above sea level.

They braved the wind to look back for the last time, and could see the line of hills that marched eastward from Port Town, but could not see the capital city itself.

Rini was amazed at the beauty and grandeur of everything he could see. He had no idea if Ilika was going to accept him, or if he was ever going to have a home and a family with any girl. The present moment, in which his spirit could soar from ocean to mountains, hills to forests, was enough to make him happy. Even if he became a slave again, they could never take away his ability to be filled with the wonder and majesty of everything he saw, everything he touched, even everything he imagined.

Kibi gazed at the scene before her, and at the same time remembered the globe, and how small a part of the world this was. She knew, more than ever before, that she was born to travel to far-away places, see strange things, speak other languages, and befriend people everywhere she went. She couldn't yet see how she would get there, as every time she imagined herself on Ilika's ship, sails billowing in the wind, she somehow knew it wasn't going to be like that. But she knew for an absolute fact that she was going to spend the rest of her life traveling, even if she had to walk.

Ilika was silently amazed at what this assignment — and this kingdom — had done to him. Just three months before, he thought he could walk into a medieval city, hire five crew members, return to his ship, and leave. It would all take a week at the most. He laughed out loud at himself.

Instead, he was being transformed and remade, like metal in a blacksmith's forge, and was now part of a flow of people and events that went far beyond himself and his little assignment. He would take with him a crew to which he was deeply bonded, and he would leave behind four people, five if he counted young Misa, who had been changed forever by their time with him, and who would probably go on to change their world.

"I'm freezing!" Misa screamed.

"Let's get through the gap and down out of the wind!" Kibi yelled.

After one more glance at the western half of the kingdom spread out below them, they turned and filed through the pass, not knowing what awaited them in the mountains, or whether they would ever see the lowlands again.

✳   ✳   ✳   ✳   ✳

About the Author

Born in the Mojave Desert, J. Z. Colby now lives and writes deep in a forest of the Pacific Northwest.

He has studied many subjects, formally and informally, including psychology, philosophy, education, and performing arts, but remains a generalist. His primary profession as a mental health counselor, specializing with families and young adults, gives him many stories of personal growth, and the motivation to develop his team of young critiquers and readers.

All his life, he has been drawn toward a broad understanding of human nature, especially those physical, emotional, mental, and spiritual situations in which our capacity to function seems to reach its limits. He finds fascinating those few individuals who can transcend the limits of our common human nature and the dictates of our cultures.

In his spare time, he flies helicopters and airplanes.

He may be contacted at the email address listed on the internet site www.nebador.com.

www.ingramcontent.com/pod-product-compliance
Lightning Source LLC
Chambersburg PA
CBHW031335170626
46807CB00002B/713